INTRODUCTION

A Length of Silk by Tracey Victoria Bateman
Always the obedient daughter, Zhao Hanshi has defied her parents by accepting Christianity. Now she must leave her homeland or be forced into a godless marriage. Stowing away on a merchant ship carrying Chinese silk and other treasures, she quickly realizes the danger she has put herself into. Can a friendship with the ship's captain lead to love, or only deliver her back into her father's arms?

The Golden Cord by Judith McCoy Miller
Suey Qui Jin has been sold like livestock and taken across the Pacific Ocean to California. But mercifully, she is befriended by an American-born Chinaman who promises to help her. Can a symbolic ribbon from a Bible be the key to getting her out of slavery of body and soul?

The Crimson Brocade by Susan Downs
From the day Han Shiren first learns of her arranged marriage to Shin Dewan, she dreams of the time when her betrothed will return to China and take her for his bride. Yet she fears her father's desire to see her wed to a Christian man may come to naught in light of the present battles raging both inside and outside Shiren's home. Will Shiren's non-Christian mother follow through on her decision to travel to Nanking and withdraw her approval for the Shins' son to wed Shiren? With the catastrophic urgencies of war pressing in around them, will God still hear and answer Shiren's prayers for a Christian mate?

Bindings of the Heart by Jennifer Peterson
Lisa Perdue may have some Chinese heritage in her blood, but she is an all-American girl. She is unprepared for the harsh realities of a mission trip to China. And in the midst of eye-opening lessons, she m—————— ————ce between two men in her l—— ———————d when it is time to go home——

CHINA TAPESTRY

*Four Romantic Novellas Woven Together
by Asian Traditions*

Tracey Victoria Bateman
Judith McCoy Miller
Susan Downs
Jennifer Peterson

BARBOUR BOOKS
An Imprint of Barbour Publishing, Inc.

A Length of Silk ©2002 by Tracey Victoria Bateman.
The Golden Cord ©2002 by Judith McCoy Miller.
The Crimson Brocade ©2002 by Susan Downs.
Bindings of the Heart ©2002 by Jennifer Peterson.

Cover Photo © PhotoDisc, Inc.

Illustrations by Mari Goering.

ISBN 1-58660-397-3

All Scripture quotations, except in *Bindings of the Heart,* are taken from the King James Version of the Bible.

Scripture quotations in *Bindings of the Heart* are taken from the HOLY BIBLE, NEW INTERNATIONAL VERSION ®. NIV ®. Copyright © 1973, 1978, 1984 by International Bible Society. Used by permission of Zondervan Publishing House. All rights reserved.

Published by Barbour Books, an imprint of Barbour Publishing, Inc.,
P.O. Box 719, Uhrichsville, Ohio 44683, www.barbourbooks.com

 Member of the
Evangelical Christian
Publishers Association

Printed in the United States of America.
5 4 3 2

CHINA TAPESTRY

A Length of Silk

by Tracey Victoria Bateman

Dedication

To Mom
for a million different reasons.
I love you.

Prologue

Canton, China, 1768

The fishy odor wafting from booths in the noisy marketplace assailed Chun Yi's senses, nearly over-whelming his stomach. Vendors called out to him as he passed the open-fronted shops filled with books, cloth, jade, and assorted foods.

Above the calls of the pushy sellers, he heard peals of children's laughter. His ears perked up at the delightful sound. After six months at sea, he felt anxious to return to his father's house. But curiosity got the better of him.

Following the sound of the laughter, he pushed through the crowd and rounded the corner of a candy booth until he found what he searched for. He smiled. A young woman sat on a low bench at the edge of the road, away from the bustling crowd. At least a dozen children encircled her, each vying for her attention.

Yi's stomach tightened as he watched the sun dance across her long, dark braid. He stood motionless, scarcely remembering to breathe.

With a slender, delicate hand, she reached forward and caressed a little boy's shoulder. The child leaned into her palm, an expression of rapture shining from his black eyes.

Her lips curved into a tender smile. She spoke in tones too soft for him to make out many of her words from his vantage point a few yards away. He took a step forward, then stopped short. One discernible word seemed to reach out and draw him.

Yesu. Jesus.

His heart hammered against his chest. Perhaps he had misunderstood. He edged closer still, aware he now stood only feet behind the children.

Shangdi in heaven, he prayed, *is she the one?*

The young woman lifted her head sharply as his shadow fell across the center of the group. Yi felt his fingertips tingle with a desire to test the softness of her flawless cheek. Almond-shaped eyes stared back at him from under silky, delicate brows. Yi swallowed hard. His feet refused to move, though his mind screamed for him to say something. . .anything.

The young woman seemed to shake herself from the hypnotic effect of their locked gazes and scrambled to her feet. Yi's heart sank. Though her chin lifted with royal dignity, her robe was made of light summer cotton, and woven straw shoes encased her tiny feet—peasant's clothing. He'd been so enchanted, he hadn't noticed her status.

The law would never allow a match between them. He gave her a polite smile and bowed. Her face registered her own disappointment. She returned his gestures and turned away to the children clamoring for her attention.

Chapter 1

Two years later

Following her father to the pavilion at the end of a wooden zigzag bridge, Zhao Hanshi struggled to find pleasure in the mist rising from the water or the mandarin ducks swimming across the pond. But a sense of urgency engulfed her, taking away all the joy she usually experienced in the garden. She had to find a way to make her father see reason before it was too late.

Giving him the respect he deserved, she held her tongue and waited for him to initiate the conversation she could recite by heart—the same discussion they had repeated time and again over the past two years.

His shoulders rose and fell as he stared across the misty water. A sense of guilt pricked Hanshi. She didn't want to be a difficult woman or a bad daughter, but Father had to see she simply could not do as he asked.

He turned to face her. The troubled frown clouding his beloved features sent a stab of pain through Hanshi's heart. If only she could close the gap between them by acquiescing to his demands—but she couldn't.

When he finally spoke, his voice sounded weary, as though he, too, knew the conversation by heart and would rather not go through it again. "Chun So pays you a great honor by requesting your hand in marriage for his son. You should be more grateful."

Hanshi glanced out at the lilies floating on the pond. According to ancient culture, water lilies represented truth. Even if speaking honestly cost her everything, Hanshi knew she must not back down now. To do so would be to condemn herself and her future children to life in a godless home.

She gathered a breath for courage and turned to face her father. "I am aware of the honor he bestows, but I cannot marry the merchant's son." Knowing what was at stake, Hanshi drew herself up with as much dignity as she could muster. "Father, I will not allow my children to learn the ways of a man who worships Buddha. I will marry a man who worships the true God of my mother, or I will marry no one at all!"

Waving his arms furiously, her father paced before her. "You dare to show me such disrespect?" He stopped and wagged a bony finger inches from her face. "Would you have your father ridiculed among honorable men?"

Hanshi tossed her long braid across her shoulder so it hung like a rope down her back. She met his gaze head-on. "Ridiculed for what? For refusing to give your daughter in marriage to a simpleton who worships a fat statue?"

His hand shot out and landed with a ringing smack across her cheek.

Shrinking from her father's wrath, Hanshi clapped her fingers to her face. Never in her sixteen years had he raised his hand to her, but the sting of her cheek confirmed that she had gone too far this time. She opened her mouth to beg forgiveness, but he silenced her with a stern glance and an upraised hand.

"Through my weakness, I allowed your mother to follow her ridiculous God. Now my only child holds such contempt for the religion of our ancestors that she puts the honor of her family at stake?"

"Father," she said, tears thick in her voice, "please forgive my disrespect. I meant no dishonor."

His face softened. He stretched out his thin, wrinkled hand, beckoning her.

"This marriage must take place, Daughter," he said softly, gathering her into his arms. "The betrothal gifts have been exchanged, and I have given my word to Chun So."

"Oh, Father," she groaned. "How can I?"

He held her at arm's length and brushed his hand over her cheek to dry her tears. "You are a good daughter, but I have raised you too much as though you were a son." With a weary shake of his head, he moved away from her, turning to stare into the water once again. "I have done you a great disservice by encouraging your independent ways since your mother's death."

Tears choked Hanshi at the sight of how his thin shoulders slumped. She shuffled slowly to her father's side and reached out to touch his arm. "You have always been a wonderful father. I consider myself fortunate that you raised me with such kindness." She pressed his arm slightly, and he turned to face her.

Encouraged by his silent, questioning gaze, Hanshi continued. "But don't you see, my father? I want my children to be as fortunate. I know of no other man who would allow his child to serve a God in whom he, himself, does not believe."

Father's head jerked back, his expression as stone. "My folly."

"No, you have given me the freedom to serve the true and living God." She drew a swift breath and forged ahead before she lost her nerve. "Will you not allow me to tell you of His great love?"

His face twisted in anger. "I will hear nothing of a God who encourages rebellion against a father's wishes. The matter is settled. When Chun Yi returns from his voyage, you will be wed."

⚭

Hanshi tiptoed to where her maid, Yongmei, slept on a mat in the corner of her room. Moving with caution so as not to waken her, Hanshi bent and gathered her young maid's clothing that lay folded in a neat pile at the foot of her mat.

She wanted to awaken her friend and say good-bye, but she dared not. If she took the clothing and left, no one could accuse Yongmei of helping her escape.

She dressed quickly in the borrowed clothing and slipped on the pair of straw shoes.

14

Swiftly and silently, she made her way through the large family dwelling and left the only home she had ever known.

Outside, in the moonlit night, Hanshi allowed herself one last look at her home. Tears stung her eyes at the heartbreak she knew she would cause her father, and she almost changed her mind. She'd never once disobeyed, but now she had no choice. How could she marry the merchant's son? The merchant, a renowned Buddhist, would teach her children lies against the one true and living God.

The last thought strengthened her resolve. Tearing her gaze away, she straightened her shoulders and hurried through the darkened streets. She didn't know where to go, but it didn't matter.

As she walked, the smell of the sea beckoned, and an idea formed in her mind. If she stayed in Canton, she'd soon be discovered and sent back to her father's house.

Lawfully, her father could kill her for her disobedience. Though Hanshi knew his love for her would prevent such a horrible fate, he'd see to it she had no other opportunity to escape before the wedding. Summoning all of her courage, she set her course for the port.

Yi stepped from his cabin onto the deck of his junk, *China Dream*, and gathered a deep, cool breath of sea air. This would be his last voyage as a single man. When he returned from Portugal, he would marry Hanshi.

He smiled at the thought of his betrothed, the young woman he'd observed two years ago in the marketplace.

Unable to remove her image from his mind, he had made some inquiries and found she was the daughter of Zhao Guoliang, a landowner with many tenants. Upon discovering the girl was no peasant and therefore a suitable match according to law, Yi immediately went to his father requesting a betrothal to Hanshi. Gifts had been exchanged, and the betrothal period would soon end in a wedding.

He felt the vessel shudder in the stiff southern wind. Shangdi had provided a good day to begin the journey. Excitement nearly overwhelmed him, sending a sense of anticipation through his midsection.

The ornate house located at the edge of Canton might be his home, but his father claimed ownership to that monstrosity. The sea belonged to Yi.

Half a dozen crew members roamed the deck, checking sails and loading supplies. Yi nodded to each of his subordinates and made his way across the deck. Resting his forearms on the rail of the ship, he watched the moon glimmer on the rippling water.

As he did before each journey, he bowed his head to commit the voyage to Shangdi. "Honorable Father in heaven," he prayed. "I humbly ask Your protection over my ship and crew as we sail the magnificent waters You created. Please give me wisdom to accept the best prices for our goods, and keep my crew from evil at foreign ports. If it be Your will, provide opportunities for me to share Your great love during our journey."

A rustling noise behind him gave him a start, and he left his prayer. Turning, he saw nothing. He scanned the ship. A few more crew members had arrived on deck, but nothing seemed amiss. As Yi twisted back around, he caught movement beneath a cloth sail which had come loose from its confines and hung down like a tent.

He smiled. A dog had most likely wandered aboard. He'd need to coax the animal out of its hiding place and off the ship before Cook decided to serve it to the crew.

Crouching, he spoke in a soft voice. "Come out, little one. I will not harm you."

Yi's brow furrowed as he heard a soft gasp come from beneath the sail. The intruder was no animal. Stowaway!

He grabbed the errant sail and snatched it back, bent on flinging the intruder overboard. His anger melted as he stared into dark, fear-filled eyes. Hanshi.

Faint recognition flickered in her expression but vanished as quickly as it had appeared. Yi knew she didn't know him as her betrothed, because they had never been formally introduced. Though Yi would have liked the opportunity to know her before the wedding, her father had discouraged a meeting.

"What are you doing here?" He tried to keep the emotion from his voice.

She ducked her head as befitting a young woman speaking to a man and whispered, "Please, I–I must get away from Canton."

The desperation in her voice sent a ripple of concern through Yi. If someone was out to harm her, he'd deal with them personally—swiftly and without mercy.

"Are you in danger?"

She shook her head. "No, but I must leave."

Bewildered, Yi reached forward and cupped her chin,

raising her head so he could see into her eyes. "If you are not in danger, why must you leave your father's house?"

Hesitation clouded her eyes.

"I will only help you if you are honest with me," Yi said sternly.

She dropped her gaze. Yi gently pressed her chin. "Allow me to see the truth in your eyes."

She jerked her chin away. The small act of defiance amused Yi. He should have known she would have a stubborn streak. Any young woman who would dress in peasants' clothing to share the Christian message in the marketplace was no ordinary lady. Carefully, he guarded his amusement and took her chin once more, gently forcing her gaze upward. "Why are you running away if you are in no danger?"

A sigh escaped her slightly parted lips, sending Yi's heart racing.

"My father is forcing me to marry a man I can never take as my husband."

If she had struck him, Yi couldn't have felt the shock any more than he did at her revelation. He cleared his throat, searching for the right words. "You are in love with another, perhaps?" Yi tensed as he awaited her answer.

She glanced up in surprise. "No, I am in love with no man."

Yi would have pressed for a satisfactory answer, but the sound of laughter ringing from a group of crewman only yards away reminded him of Hanshi's precarious position. He needed to get her off the ship and safely home before she was discovered.

"Come," he said, extending his arm. "I will see you to your father's house."

She shrank back, her eyes wide with pleading. "Please, allow me to stay aboard. I will be no trouble and will leave as soon as we dock in another port. I must not be forced to marry this man."

Again, Yi was taken aback by the force of her aversion to marrying him. Suddenly, a determination to find out why shot through him and he nodded. "All right, I will help you. But we will have to disguise you as a boy if you are to be kept safe on a sea voyage. Come with me."

This time, she placed her tiny hand in his. At Hanshi's touch, a desire to protect her surged through Yi. He had taken this young woman into his heart that day in the marketplace. He didn't believe in coincidence or fate, only in God and His divine intervention. God had led Hanshi to his vessel for a purpose. Of that, Yi was certain. Somehow, he must discover her reason for not wanting to marry him. . .and if he couldn't change her mind, he would have to summon the strength to let her go.

Chapter 2

Hanshi tossed on her mat, longing for a reprieve from Cook's loud snoring, which seemed to echo off the cabin walls. She propped up onto her elbow and glared at his shadowy form, wishing she had the nerve to toss a shoe across the room to hush him.

In a fit of sleep-deprived temper, she flung herself back onto the mat, then immediately regretted the impulsive action as pain shot through her shoulders.

After two days aboard *China Dream,* Hanshi's muscles ached from her strenuous duties in the galley. Worse still, the aging cook had no qualms about letting her know when she wasn't moving fast enough to suit him. After a lifetime of kindness and respect from her father, the sharp insults were difficult to bear. She knew her back was safe from a lashing, only because Captain had warned the short-tempered cook she was not to be harmed. For that, Hanshi was grateful.

If only she could explain to Cook why she was forced to drag the cumbersome bags of rice and soybeans, when any boy her size should have been able to sling them across his shoulder with relative ease. But Captain strictly forbade her to reveal her identity to anyone. He had instructed her in arranging her hair into a topknot, like a young man's, and gave her a set of clothing from his cabin boy, Tang He—of necessity, the only member of the crew who knew her true identity.

The captain had introduced her to the cook as Xing. Often, Hanshi failed to respond to the unfamiliar name, earning her further insults. Not only did Cook consider her incompetent and lazy but dim-witted as well. Even now, in the dark, his low opinion of her sent flames of humiliation to Hanshi's cheeks.

She rolled onto her stomach and rested her cheek against her forearms. Still, sleep eluded her. When she could no longer bear the persistent grating of Cook's snores, Hanshi rose from her mat and tiptoed to the door.

Grateful to be out of the stuffy confines of the cabin, she stepped onto the deserted deck and gathered a full breath of the salty air. The still waters of the South China Sea glimmered beneath a glorious display of lights in the night sky. The moon shone down brightly without even the hint of a cloud to hide its illumination, and stars dotted the vast expanse.

As she leaned against the side of the ship, the contrasting light and dark filled Hanshi with a sense of wonder, and her mind drifted to the story of creation, a favorite among her mother's bedtime stories.

She closed her eyes and, in the stillness of the night, could almost hear her mother's soft voice. "God commanded the light and it appeared in a dark world. Never doubt His power to create, my beautiful daughter. Even in your life, He can cause light to break through your blackest moments."

Tears stung Hanshi's eyes at the memory. *My heavenly Father, everything appears so hopeless. But You have only to command light to appear, and all will be well. Must I never see my beloved father again if I am to serve You?*

"What are you doing on deck?"

Hanshi jumped and spun around as the captain's stern voice broke through her silent prayer. She dashed the tears from her cheeks with her fingertips. "I–I—" Her voice faltered at the intensity of his dark gaze upon her, a combination of concern and irritation.

"You mustn't be on deck." He grasped her upper arm, the feel of his fingers burning through the thin, summer cloth.

Hanshi puzzled at the ardor spreading through her belly at his touch. Heat crept to her cheeks, and she puzzled at that as well. She had always despised foolish, giggling girls who spoke of the wonders of love. But since her only encounter with this man in the marketplace two years earlier, she had been unable to push him from her thoughts for more than a day. At night, his image invaded her dreams.

"What if someone realizes you are not a boy?" His voice held not an ounce of the gentleness she had come to expect from him. Instead, he spoke with an edge of reproach that sent Hanshi's defenses soaring.

"I cannot stay in my cabin every minute of the voyage, Captain," she insisted, keeping her voice low and her gaze fixed on the deck, lest she increase his anger. "I would go insane." The last words were barely above a whisper.

The captain released her arm. "Nor would it be healthy, I suppose."

Keeping her head down, Hanshi shifted her eyes upward very slightly so she could see his face.

"Lift your head and look at me." His words, though soft, held an edge of command Hanshi couldn't refuse. "You are supposed to be a boy, remember, Xing?"

Hanshi raised her chin. Her knees nearly buckled at the smile creasing his handsome face. Unbidden, her own lips curved into a smile.

He drew a sharp breath. "Maybe you should stay in your cabin after all."

Alarm shot through Hanshi. "But—"

The captain stepped closer until the heat from his body cut through the chill of the salty night air. Transfixed by his intense gaze, Hanshi remained immobile, her pulse racing.

"You are much too beautiful for anyone to believe you are a boy," he whispered.

Streaks of excitement blazed a trail up Hanshi's spine. He thought her beautiful? Suddenly her childhood friends and their whispers of love didn't seem quite as foreign as they had before.

In her dreams, Captain was strong, but gentle. . .able to command without ruling her. Was he truly such a man, or only a figment of her imagination?

No one had ever looked at her the way he did now.

She could not discern the look but instinctively knew what he thought as his gaze flitted to her mouth. Surely he had too much honor to try to kiss a woman who was not his wife!

In an instant, the captain's face grew serious. He stepped back suddenly, clearing his throat. "Yes, I believe it might be best for you to stay hidden."

Yi struggled to gain control over his emotions as he watched the disappointment flicker across Hanshi's face. Clearly, she dreaded the thought of being forced to remain in her cabin.

If only she were plain, there would be no difficulty in her masquerading as a boy. Her body was slender, and the baggy clothing she had borrowed from Tang He hid her womanly figure; but nothing could hide her beautiful face.

Thus far, her only contact with the crew had been at mealtimes when she served the hungry sailors. During those times, the men were too intent upon filling their bellies to take notice of the cook's new helper. But Yi feared it was only a matter of time before someone noticed.

Suddenly aware of her tense gaze upon him, Yi smiled. "I won't confine you to your quarters, but only come on deck when I am with you. Like now."

Relief flooded her face. "I am grateful."

Lost in her liquid brown eyes that shone up at him in the moonlight, Yi longed to take her into his arms, reveal himself as her betrothed, and promise her anything if only she would return to her father's house and carry through with the wedding. But reason prevailed. If Hanshi's affections did not belong to another, he could win her heart before the voyage ended. Then he would be free to disclose his identity without fear of pushing her away.

"When I approached, your eyes were closed," he said in an effort to divert his mind from further thoughts of kissing her. "What were you doing?"

"Praying."

Yi's brow lifted. "With no altar?"

"My heart is my altar," she replied softly, dropping her gaze once more.

"Look at me and tell me which god you serve." He knew she served Yesu, as did he, but something inside of him longed to hear her say the words.

She squared her shoulders and faced him. "Shangdi, as did my mother and her mother and father before her. I serve the only true and living God who sent His Son, Yesu, to die for me."

Joy raced through Yi's heart at the simple gospel message Hanshi had just spoken. "As do I."

Her lips curved into a smile. "You know of Yesu?"

"Yes, I learned of Him five years ago during a voyage to Portugal."

"I have known of Him since my childhood," she replied. "My mother told me many stories."

"Your father, he is a Christian, as well?"

Hanshi's face clouded, and a sigh pushed through her slightly parted lips. She shook her head sadly. "He will not even allow me to speak of it. He worships Buddha."

"It is the same with my father, though I pray one day he will come to know the truth."

"I will pray for my father as long as I live," Hanshi said, turning to stare across the vast sea. She rested her hand on the side of the junk. "It is all I can do, for I know I will never see him again."

Yi's throat constricted at the tears in her voice. Reaching out, he covered her hand. "I will take you home when the voyage is over."

"I have dishonored the family name by running away."

The sadness reflected in her face tore at Yi's heart.

"Your father will forgive you."

She shook her head. "Nothing has changed. I cannot go home."

Yi gathered his courage to ask the question begging to be released. "Is your betrothed a cruel man or, perhaps, too hideous for you to bear the thought of marriage to him?"

A shrug lifted her slim shoulders. "We have never met."

At least she was truthful. "Then why do you run away from your father's house just to escape this marriage?"

She remained silent for so long, Yi thought she might not answer at all. Then she turned a thoughtful gaze upon him. "The man who was chosen for me is not the kind of father I would choose for my future children."

Perplexed, Yi felt compelled to press for a satisfactory answer. "How do you know this, if you have never met?"

"I know," she said, placing her fist against her chest. "In my heart, I know. During my time in the marketplace, I have heard rumors of his father's ruthless dealings."

"You would betray your betrothed because of his father?"

She glanced at him sharply, her silky brows narrowing.

"I would betray Shangdi if I were to marry such a man, knowing his father would rule the house in which my children are raised." Eyes blazing, she pursed her lips and lifted her chin. "You cannot possibly understand. As a man, you are free to teach your children about Yesu. Chun So would rule my family, teaching the message of Buddha to my children as soon as they were old enough to be instructed. That is even worse than teaching them to conduct business in an unscrupulous manner."

Yi wanted to laugh. Although his father claimed Buddhism and conspicuously worshipped at the temple, at home things were much different. He rarely spoke of his religion at all, let alone instructed anyone in how they were to believe. If his father worshipped anything with devotion, it was his business and the riches his hard work brought.

Still, relief washed over him. If her only objection to the marriage was that she would not be allowed to raise her children with the knowledge of Yesu, he could set her mind at ease this moment.

"Would you marry your betrothed if you could be assured of the freedom to teach your children about Yesu?"

"It isn't possible. I have heard many rumors of Chun Yi as well. He is as ruthless as his father."

Taken aback, Yi frowned. "Ruthless? How?"

"Yi commands his father's merchant ship. Tales abound about the way his men are horribly abused. One false move sends him into a rage. I have even heard he threw one poor man to the sharks simply for asking for more rice."

Yi couldn't help the smile flitting to his lips. Men vied for the opportunity to serve aboard *China Dream*, mainly because his men were well fed, treated fairly, and paid more than fair wages for their labor. "I can certainly understand why you would be reluctant to marry such a man."

She nodded decisively. "So, you see, a man that cruel would never allow his wife to teach his children about Yesu."

"But surely your father knew about your betrothed before he consented to the marriage."

Hanshi waved her hand toward the sea. "My father says I should not believe anything Zhang Cho, the fish seller, says. He does not believe there is any truth to the stories, but I believe most gossip begins with a seed of truth."

Yi fought the impulse to enlighten her. Even if he were able to dispel the rumors she so steadfastly believed, she would feel awkward in his presence and obligated to honor the terms of the betrothal. Yi did not want her to come to him out of obligation. Now that he had spoken to her, observed her spirit, and discerned her passionate heart, he wanted her to come to him because of love. He had prayed, and Shangdi had given him an extraordinary woman. He could be patient awhile longer.

Chapter 3

You are much too beautiful for anyone to believe you are a boy.

Releasing a dreamy sigh, Hanshi stared into a haze of steam curling from the cooking box and gloried at the memory of those wonderful, heart-stopping words. There had been no more such words spoken in the two weeks since that night. And no more frighteningly near kisses. But she relived the memory over and over, her stomach swirling like a typhoon with each recollection.

They met secretly each night so Hanshi could breathe the fresh sea air while the captain protectively watched over her. Daily, she counted the minutes until she could tiptoe away from Cook's snoring and escape the stuffy confines of the cabin.

Hanshi thrilled at the stories Captain shared with her. Stories from Shangdi's Holy Book told to him by a priest in Portugal.

During their nightly rendezvous on deck, the captain and Hanshi talked of other things as well. He listened with interest while she spoke of her escapades in the marketplace and laughed at her stories of the children's antics—applauding when she told of the converts.

His attention to the details she gave mystified her, and his interest in her ideas—even those in conflict with his own—shocked her. It was almost as though he considered her an equal. A silly thought, she knew. Even her father, a rare man for his willingness to listen to her ideas, had instructed her to keep her place in the presence of a man—a lesson she'd learned with much difficulty. Was the captain so forward-thinking as to count a woman's ideas as important as his own?

While she pondered this last thought, a pungent odor wafting from the cooking box drew Hanshi sharply from her dreams. She shot to her feet, staring in horror at the black smoke curling above the pot of rice she should have been watching.

Cook would have her head for this!

She grabbed for the handle, then jerked back with a cry as pain seared her palm. The pot crashed to the wooden galley floor, spilling the scorched, half-cooked rice.

"Look what you have done, you stupid, lazy boy," Cook railed, shaking a fist inches from her face. "Now the crew will have to wait an extra hour for their midday meal while I prepare more rice."

"I–I'm sorry." Hanshi winced in pain from her blistering hand. Oh, if only she could pay more attention to her duties rather than being carried away by dreams of the captain's handsome face! This was the second meal she'd burned in a week. "I–I will go get more rice."

Cook's hand curled around her upper arm, his fingers

digging in cruelly. "I will get it myself. You are such a weak boy, it will take too long for you to bring another bag." He flung her to the ground. "Clean it up! And do so with haste."

Tears stung Hanshi's eyes. "I—I'm sorry."

His face grew red with rage, and a vein popped out on his forehead. "Do not speak to me, or I will be forced to ignore the captain's orders and give you the beating you deserve. I have never met such a stupid, lazy boy."

"What is going on in here?"

Hanshi's stomach tightened as the captain entered the galley, his face dark with anger. As if in a horrible nightmare, she watched him step down on the slippery mess. His feet flew out from beneath him, sending him hurling to the floor.

Before she could scramble to his side, Hanshi felt her arm captured in a painful grip once more.

"Do you see what you have done?" Cook shrieked.

She glanced up in time to see the back of his hand coming down fast. Instinctively, her arm went up in defense, but not in time to prevent the cook from meeting his objective. Pain exploded in her cheek as his hand made contact, clouding her senses as she fell. She heard her own cry of pain mingled with the captain's roar.

"What do you think you are doing?" Captain jumped to his feet. He slipped again, nearly losing his footing, but righted himself just in time to gain control.

"I am sorry, Captain." She sat up slowly, every movement agony, and tried to blink away the tears threatening to become a torrent.

"I am speaking to Cook," he snapped, then his expression softened and he reached out to her. "Let me help you up from there."

"Thank you," she murmured as he helped her to a nearby stool. Trying to shake off the burning pain in her hand and the ringing in her ears, Hanshi stared at the two men. Cook's eyes held defiance, while the captain's anger nearly radiated from his body. His fists clenched and unclenched, and Hanshi feared he might strike the irate cook.

"What have I instructed you concerning your treatment of her?"

Her? Hanshi gasped at his slip of the tongue. She cut her gaze to the cook to see if he had noticed, but he flung his hands toward her and glared back at the captain.

"This boy is a good-for-nothing, lazy girl-boy. He cannot even carry a bag of soybeans. He dreams incessantly and ruins the food. He is a fool. We would be better off to throw him to the sharks and be rid of him."

Captain's hand shot forward and grabbed the front of the cook's dirty shirt. Menacingly, he pulled him close until it looked to Hanshi as though their noses almost touched. "If you had not been with me for so many years, I would be tempted to throw you to the sharks. As it is, perhaps a few days locked away from others will teach you some patience."

Hanshi noticed fear creep into Cook's face. His eyes grew wide. Unbidden sympathy arose inside of her, and she slowly stood.

"Please, Captain," she spoke, closing her eyes against

the burning pain on her hand and her throbbing head. "I provoked him terribly. He is right. I was daydreaming when I should have been watching the rice." She stepped toward the two men. Reaching forward, she placed slight pressure on Captain's arm to encourage him to turn the cook loose.

He complied, and Cook stumbled backward. Hanshi gave the captain a trembling smile. "If anyone should be punished, it is I. I have ruined a pot of food for which Cook is responsible. He was only trying to prepare a pleasurable meal for you and your crew. I–I beg of you not to punish him."

Slowly the anger left Captain's face, and his lips curved into a tender smile. He covered her hand with his own. "All right. I will not punish him." He turned his gaze to the cook. "This time."

The cook's gaze flew to the captain's hand, which still covered Hanshi's.

Heat rushed to her cheeks, and she snatched her hand away.

"Captain, I have known you for five years and would never have believed—" Cook's voice faltered and his lips twisted as though he might be ill. "This girl-boy and you. . . This is why he sneaks out at night. He is coming to you."

Hanshi gasped at the implication.

Captain's face reddened and his brows knit together dangerously. "Don't be a fool," he snapped. Glancing from the cook to Hanshi then back to the cook, he lowered his voice. "I suppose I will have to tell the truth now, but if you say a word to anyone, I will throw you overboard."

Fear clutched at Hanshi's belly. The cook hated her

enough when he believed her to be a boy. Once he discovered the deception, life would be unbearable.

She chanced a peek at the cook while Captain enlightened him. A sickened scowl twisted his lined face.

"A woman? You have brought a woman aboard *China Dream?*"

Again, heat rushed to Hanshi's cheeks as his confused frown became a knowing grin. "So this is why she sneaks out every night. She is your concubine."

"No, she is not," Captain declared with an exasperated sigh.

The cook opened his mouth, but Captain held up a silencing hand. "Her reason for being aboard does not concern you."

Cook's curious gaze flitted to Hanshi, his eyes narrowing, but he nodded. "Yes, Captain. I will not reveal your secret."

"You would do well to remember your promise." The captain's voice held unmistakable warning.

The cook cleared his throat nervously. "I will cook more rice." He glanced pointedly at Hanshi. "But first this must be cleaned up."

Relieved the encounter had ended, Hanshi knelt carefully and began to scoop the slimy mess from the floor with her uninjured hand.

The salty scent which always clung to the captain filled her senses as he crouched beside her and took her injured hand. His nearness sent her pulse racing. Gently, he turned her palm up. Something akin to a growl escaped his throat as he examined the burn.

He gripped her arm and stood suddenly, pulling her with him. "Hanshi will not work for the rest of the day," he informed the cook. "I will send Tang He to assist you with the meal. I suggest you get this cleaned up and cook more rice before the crew starts grumbling about their hunger."

Resentment hardened the cook's face, but he inclined his head.

Captain turned to Hanshi. "Come. Let's get you cleaned up and dress your burn. Then you must rest."

Hanshi allowed herself the luxury of being led from the hot galley. Despite her pain, she couldn't help enjoying the heady feeling of being cared for by the captain. Only when they reached his cabin did she experience alarm. She hung back as he opened the door and stepped aside for her to precede him into the room.

"I–I cannot."

"Come, no one will think anything of it. To the rest of the crew, you are Xing, Cook's helper."

"But Cook will think. . ." Her cheeks warmed.

"He is much too busy to think anything. Should he have such vile thoughts, he will not voice them, for if he does, I will put him off the ship at the next port and find someone else to cook for the crew."

Hanshi's knees nearly buckled as he placed his hand against her back and pressed slightly with his fingertips. She hesitated only a moment, trying to slow her racing heart, then stepped inside.

Surveying the cabin, she felt nervous at being inside this decidedly masculine room. When her gaze rested on his sleeping mat in one corner, she glanced away. She scanned the rest of the room and drew an awed breath at the sight of a wondrous table on the opposite side of the room.

"How beautiful."

Captain's face lit. "This is a desk," he explained proudly. "I traded a load of dyed silk to a Spanish trader for it. There are compartments for my maps and documents." He held out his hand to her. "Come."

Hanshi stepped forward slowly. She drew a sharp breath as he grabbed her around the waist and lifted. Before she could voice her objection, he gently seated her atop the desk. "What are you doing?"

"I'm going to dress your hand. This way you may rest while I do so." He arched a brow and a smile flitted across his lips. "Unless you would rather sit on my mat while I take care of you."

"This—this is fine."

Closing her eyes against the throbbing pain in her head, Hanshi wondered at the captain's skill as he applied herbs to the burn and wrapped strips of cloth around her hand.

"I'm finished," he finally said. Hanshi opened her eyes to find him studying her face.

He reached forward and touched her cheek with such aching gentleness, she wanted to weep. "Your face is bruised," he whispered, sending a shiver down her spine. "I should have locked Cook up for this."

Shaking her head, Hanshi covered his hand with hers. "No, you must forgive him. As must I. He does not know Yesu as we do. He is to be pitied."

He removed his hand, but his gaze roamed her face. "You are right. I have prayed for an opportunity to share the love of Yesu with Cook and the rest of my crew." He gently lifted her from the desk. "But you have shown much more love and mercy toward him, despite his cruel treatment, than I have from my position as captain of this vessel. I can learn much from you."

Hanshi ducked her head. "I am only a woman," she mumbled. "It is not my place to teach you."

With a short laugh, he placed a finger under her chin and pressed slightly until she met his gaze. "And yet you have already taught me much."

Flustered, Hanshi ducked her head again and scurried toward the door. "I will go back to the galley now. Thank you for dressing my wound, Captain."

His brows knit together and he regarded her sternly. "You will go nowhere. You will stay here and rest."

He strode across the room and pulled a silk robe from a hook on the wall. "Put this on. Your clothing is covered with rice."

Hanshi drew herself up with as much dignity as she possessed at that moment. "I cannot put on your robe!"

"Yes, you will." He pressed the garment into her hands. "I will return in a few moments, and I expect to find you wearing what I have given you, or I will be forced to dress you myself."

Eyes widening at his scandalous statement, Hanshi pressed the robe tightly against her chest. "I–I will do as you say."

"See that you do." He strode toward the door. After a

final glance, he shut the cabin door behind him.

By the time the captain returned, Hanshi nearly swam in the ridiculously large robe. Its long sleeves hid her hands, but the silk against her skin felt heavenly after weeks of wearing rough cotton garments.

At the sight of her, an amused grin curved his lips. "Good." He handed her a porcelain cup.

She eyed the contents skeptically. "What is this?"

"It contains *sheng ma,*" he replied, inclining his head for her to drink. "It will take away the pain in your head."

Hanshi tipped the cup and drank the bitter tea, then shuddered.

Captain gave a nod of approval and held out his hand. "Come and lie down now."

"I will not."

He sent her a scowl and walked across the room to a door. "This is where Tang He sleeps. There is even a lock."

"Your cabin boy has his own room?"

"I like my privacy," he said with a nod. "You will sleep here until the voyage is over. Tang He will help Cook from now on."

"How will this be explained?"

He shrugged and opened the door for her. "You are so inept in the kitchen, I am forced to replace you with Tang He. That is all the crew will think."

"It is true," she replied, her voice growing thick.

The captain led her to Tang He's mat and stood as she lowered herself, grateful to lie down. She closed her eyes. "Thank you, Captain," she mumbled. "You are such a kind man."

From far away, Hanshi heard his footsteps move across the room. He shut the door firmly behind him. As she felt herself drift, she whispered a prayer. "Captain is a good man, Shangdi. Please keep him in Your mercy." A sigh escaped her lips. "And never let him know he holds my heart in his gentle hands."

Chapter 4

Yi cast a furtive glance toward his cabin door. Hanshi was later than usual this evening. Perhaps she had fallen asleep while waiting for the deck to clear.

During the past three weeks, there had been no hint from the rest of the crew that Cook had revealed her identity. This relieved Yi immeasurably. He didn't want to dismiss Cook from his duties and put him off the ship, but he would do so if the need arose. Hanshi could not be put in danger. He would not stand for it.

He abhorred deception, but in this instance, Hanshi's life and virtue were at stake. He couldn't watch her every moment to ensure her safety. Yi rested a little more easily at night, knowing only a wall separated them; but in his absence, he worried about the delicate woman with whom he had fallen so deeply in love.

His glance flitted once more to the closed door. Still no sign of Hanshi. A wave of disappointment washed over him. He had grown used to the nightly meetings and found pleasure in his betrothed's presence.

During his many travels, he had observed with interest the relationships between men and women of different lands. He enjoyed the thought of a union established upon love between a husband and wife. For the most part, the women of every culture deferred to their husbands, but most were cherished in return.

He knew of too many women in his own country who were abused by their husbands, set aside for not bearing sons, and treated little better than the household slaves. Even his own mother feared his father.

Yi had always been troubled by the all-powerful-father image in a family. While he believed strongly in disciplining a child, he despised the fact that a father could kill a child for disobedience. Though he knew these traditions were unlikely to change, he determined to run his own household differently.

Hanshi was the woman Shangdi had chosen for Yi. Her strength of character and independent nature were proof of Shangdi's approval of Yi's decision to treat her with respect and teach his children to do so as well. . .if only he could convince her to return to her father's house so their marriage might take place.

Yi released a sigh and leaned his forearms against the railing. *China Dream* rolled with the waves, and the rising wind brought with it the scent of the sea, filling Yi with a great sense of contentment. He watched the waves crash against the side of the ship. The time had come to tell Hanshi the truth. If only he had been honest from the moment she appeared from beneath the sail. His only excuse was that he feared she would run elsewhere and become forever lost to him.

Deep in thought, he jumped when a gentle hand touched his arm. He turned to find Hanshi's lovely face looking up at him.

"I am sorry for my delay," she said breathlessly. "I drifted to sleep while reading the pages you allowed me to borrow."

"Think nothing of it. You are under no obligation to meet me each night." He smiled. "Remember, I am only here for your protection. It is your desire for fresh air that brings us on deck."

She ducked her head and turned to look out over the sea. Drawing a deep breath, she smiled and closed her eyes. "I will miss the beauty of the moon shining down upon the water, when we reach our destination."

Yi nodded. "It is a wondrous sight to behold."

Turning, Hanshi regarded Yi with a questioning gaze. "I have read the words of your Portuguese priest." Her otherwise flawless skin wrinkled between her brows. "Do you agree with his ideas?"

"Which ideas? He has many that are rather unorthodox for a man of the church."

Hanshi's lashes fluttered downward. "Perhaps it is not my place to question."

Yi resisted the urge to cup her chin and raise her head. He had determined not to touch her wondrously soft skin. It was too tempting. And he would not put them in the position of acting in a way which they would both be ashamed of or doing something Shangdi would frown upon. "Of course you may question anything you like," he urged. "I do not expect you to agree with everything I believe. Look at me, and tell me what troubles you."

She lifted her gaze to meet his. "Father Manuel writes that all who are in the truth should be allowed to know God personally and search the Scriptures for themselves. Do you believe this?"

Yi nodded. "I am beginning to. There are no priests in our country to hear our confessions and read to us from the Scriptures. Would Shangdi punish us for this?"

"I–I do not know. I would like to believe He would not. I know so few prayers approved by the church. Sometimes I worry I have offended Him with my floundering."

"I cannot imagine you capable of offending Shangdi."

Her lips curved into a tender smile. "You are kind. You remind me a great deal of my father."

Yi's heart clenched at the sadness crossing her features. He quickly continued the previous line of thought.

"Have you read where Father Manuel wrote the believer should be able to form his own prayers—that the words should come from an individual's heart rather than relying upon prayers prescribed by man?"

She inclined her head. "It is a difficult concept to believe."

"Father Manuel shared a Scripture with me that I believe supports his theory. Would you like to hear it?"

Her eyes widened. "Please tell me."

"Very well. I have memorized this Scripture because it gives me peace. I hope it will do the same for you. 'For we have not an high priest which cannot be touched with the feeling of our infirmities; but was in all points tempted like as we are, yet without sin. Let us therefore come boldly unto the throne of grace, that we may obtain mercy, and find grace to help in time of need.' "

Casting a glance at Hanshi, Yi smiled to note the tears shining in her eyes, her delicate lips curving upward.

"Thank you, Captain. Though I have felt Shangdi's closeness during my times of prayer, I falter so much while trying to voice the concerns of my heart. I was certain He must think me a very foolish woman for approaching Him without benefit of a priest."

"I do not believe so. In England there are those who call themselves Protestants and believe in this approach to Shangdi. Many have even left England in order to follow their own hearts in this regard."

"It is difficult to change the beliefs of one's childhood," Hanshi said, her eyes distant as she gazed over the water. "But in my heart, I think I have always suspected there was another way."

Silence fell between them, and Yi felt the time for truth had come. He only prayed she knew him well enough by now that she wouldn't believe him capable of the terrible rumors spoken about him. He cleared his throat, but Hanshi's gasp removed the words from his mind.

"Look at the sky," she said, lifting a hand and pointing to the west.

Yi followed her fearful gaze. On the horizon, flashes of lightning spread across the sky, revealing ominous, black clouds. "A storm is heading this way."

"Will it be a bad one?" Her voice trembled.

Knowing storms terrified her, Yi took her elbow and

nudged her toward the cabin. "I do not know, but it will not be upon us for awhile. You should get inside and try to rest. Perhaps you will sleep through it."

She bit her lip and nodded.

Tenderness swelled Yi's chest. "Remember," he said gently, "Yesu promised to give us peace in the midst of the storm. Do not worry."

"I will try not to," she murmured before disappearing inside the cabin.

Yi watched until she closed the door to her small cabin, then turned to alert the deck crew.

Hanshi jerked awake and let out a startled yelp as her head hit the cabin wall. She sat up, trying to get her bearings.

The cabin rocked, adding to her confusion, until she realized it wasn't just the room moving. The entire ship swayed, first one way, then back again, sliding her across the floor as it did so.

The sleep-induced confusion receded, and suddenly she realized they must be in the midst of the storm. That was the only explanation to make any sense.

She could hear shouting from the men, and fear seized her. In the five weeks since *China Dream* had left port, Hanshi had endured two storms, but neither had rocked the ship so intensely as this one.

Placing her hands flat against the wall, she used the rough surface as a support and stood with difficulty. She cast a furtive glance about the tidy cabin, hoping to locate her shoes. After a futile search, she headed, barefoot, toward the door.

Just as she entered the captain's room, the ship swayed suddenly in the opposite direction. Pain shot through Hanshi's knee as she lost her balance and landed on the wooden deck. Unable to regain her footing, she crawled until, mercifully, she reached the door. The ship steadied enough for her to stand, and she flung the door open.

Water sloshed over her feet and ankles, filling Hanshi with alarm. She stood frozen just outside the cabin door, watching the crew fight to scoop water from the ship.

"Move out of the way, Girl." Cook's shout resonated above the roar of the wind as he came up behind her and roughly shoved her aside. Tang He followed, carrying pots in each hand.

"You better get back inside," Tang He called. "Captain will be angry if you are harmed."

Hanshi nodded as he passed, but her feet refused to move. She watched as Cook and Tang He dipped their pots into the foot-deep water, trying to keep the deck from becoming engulfed.

"Get that sail down!"

Hanshi jerked her head about and stared in horror as one of the huge bamboo posts holding the middle sail split in two, sending a crewman careening into the sea. Four men scrambled into action and immediately threw out a lifeline. Hanshi moved closer, grabbed the mast holding one of the smaller sails, and watched. With bated breath, Hanshi waited for him to be pulled back in. Her heart dropped as the four crewmen gathered the empty rope back into the ship, shaking their heads sadly.

Hanshi turned away, tightening her grip on the mast

as a blast of wind shook *China Dream*. Tears pooled in her eyes at the loss of life.

She looked out at the raging sea, which only hours before had been so calm and beautiful. Suddenly, her eyes widened in horror as a gargantuan wave arose and headed straight for the ship and right where Cook, Tang He, and a dozen others fought to scoop out the water.

"Cook!" she screamed, her voice barely audible even to her own ears over the roar of the storm. Before she could call again or make her way to the cook and Tang He to warn them, the wave descended, tipping the ship onto its side. Hanshi felt herself being pulled downward, and she clung desperately to the mast. "Shangdi," she cried. "Have mercy!"

Barrels burst from their lashings, rolled past her, and crashed against the side of the ship. Screaming men, groping for anything to hang onto, slid down the upright deck. Hanshi squeezed her eyes shut, unwilling to watch anyone else die.

Gradually, *China Dream* righted itself. Hanshi drew a thankful, shaky breath. Rain still poured from the sky, and though the wind receded, the ship still rocked precariously, causing Hanshi to keep her tight grip on the mast lest she be plunged overboard.

She scanned the deck, searching for Cook and Tang He. Tang He was nowhere to be found. She breathed a prayer for his safety and continued her search. A gasp escaped her lips as she spied Cook on the deck, pressed against the bulkhead. He lay facedown in the water, unmoving.

Knowing there was no time to lose, Hanshi released her death grip on the mast and waded through the water. Sharp rain pricked her skin as she struggled against the wind.

A sudden gust overtook the ship, tipping it enough that Hanshi lost her footing and landed on her stomach. She felt herself sliding toward the edge. Panicked, she groped for anything to hang onto, but her hands caught only empty air. She opened her mouth to cry out for help, but the water rushed in, choking back her words.

A vision of her father's sad face flashed through Hanshi's mind as she closed her eyes and waited to be swept overboard. If only she hadn't disobeyed. Death must be her punishment from Shangdi, as it could very well have been at her father's hands. *Forgive me, Shangdi. I accept my punishment.*

Suddenly, the ship righted itself once more. Shaken and relieved beyond words, Hanshi scrambled to her feet. Standing on trembling legs, she glanced around to get her bearings and spied the cook, now lying near the middle of the deck.

Wading through the water, she reached him, breathing a prayer of thanks that the gale had quieted, at least for the moment. She knelt beside his unmoving form and quickly turned him over, cradling his shoulders so he didn't sink back under. "Cook!" Lifting his upper body higher, she pounded his back. "Shangdi, I beg of You to spare his life. He must not die without knowing You."

"Hanshi! What are you doing on deck? Do you not know how dangerous it is? Get inside your cabin and stay there until I come for you."

Captain's voice brought her about, but she was in no mood to explain herself when she still lived and Cook could be at death's door.

"Cook is injured. I cannot wake him up. Water covered his face." The words left her in short bursts.

Captain lifted the aging cook and shook him for several tense moments until, finally, water poured from his mouth and nose. He coughed and sputtered awake. The captain set Cook gently onto the deck, keeping a hand at his back for support.

"Thank you, Captain." A shudder ran through Cook's body, and his teeth chattered violently.

"You should thank Hanshi. If she had not discovered you facedown in the water, you would have drowned."

Cook glanced up at her for a long moment, then he bowed his head. "I thank you, Hanshi. I am an angry old fool and am not worthy of living the life you have spared."

Tears stung Hanshi's eyes. She took his wrinkled hand between hers. "No one is worthy of life, Cook. It is a gift from Shangdi."

The captain's sharp intake of breath drew Hanshi's attention, and she glanced up. Noting the sickened expression on his face, she followed his horrified gaze to the tattered sail. A scream tore at Hanshi's throat. A crewman had become entangled in the torn sail. His feet dangled, his arms pinned against his sides.

Hanshi shot to her feet and grabbed the captain's arm. "Someone must save him!"

"There is nothing we can do," he replied, the muscle in his jaw twitching.

"S—someone must climb up and cut him down before he hangs himself!"

The captain grabbed her arms, his eyes boring a hole through her. "One support is broken—the sail will not bear up under another man's weight."

Hanshi's heart sank at the senseless loss of life. Then, a sudden, fearful thought came to mind. She straightened her spine instinctively, meeting his gaze head-on. "Will it support a woman's?"

He hesitated a moment then shook his head. "No."

Hanshi read the truth in his eyes. "You must allow me to try to save him."

"I will not," he growled. "Go inside your cabin. You do not want to watch a man die in this manner."

"But he does not have to die!"

"I will not allow you to risk your life."

"Is my life worth more than his?" Hanshi's lips trembled, and she bit down in a desperate attempt to keep the tears at bay.

When he set his jaw stubbornly, refusing to answer, Hanshi knew what she had to do. Darting past him, she sprinted toward the sail before he could reach out and grab her. She pushed past a nearby crewman, grabbed the dagger from his sash, and tucked it into her own, never slowing her pace.

"Hanshi, I order you to stop!"

Ignoring the captain's command, Hanshi grabbed hold of the loose sail and began to climb.

Chapter 5

Yi's mouth went dry. His heart hammered against his chest as he watched Hanshi begin her ascent. One misguided step, one cracked batten, and she would plunge into the sea or fall to her death on the deck. He shuddered at the image that sprang to mind of her twisted and lifeless body.

A collective gasp went up from the crew as a blast of wind rocked the sail. Yi watched helplessly while Hanshi swung forward, then back again. It seemed an eternity passed before the wind died and the bamboo battens holding the sail steadied.

Yi released his breath. If Hanshi made it down, he would flog her and confine her to her cabin for the rest of the voyage. He rejected the ridiculous thought immediately. No, he would gather her into his arms and confess his love and reveal himself as her betrothed.

He watched as Hanshi reached Zongwei, the burly crewman caught in the tangle of the torn sail and lines. She grabbed the dagger from her sash and began to slice through his confines.

Protect her, Shangdi, he silently beseeched, never removing his gaze from Hanshi's form high above the deck. *Surely You would not bring this woman into my life and take her from me so suddenly.*

After a few tense moments, Yi noted with relief she had cut Zongwei free. Though he could not hear their words, he knew Hanshi was insisting the man climb down ahead of her. Obviously losing the argument to the stubborn young woman, the crewman began his descent, cautiously finding the right lines on which to place his feet and hands.

When he reached the deck, he fell to his knees, his hands covering his face, and wept like a baby. Yi wanted to strangle him, though he knew it wasn't the man's fault. Why should Zongwei be safe when Hanshi's life still hung in the balance?

All eyes stayed fixed on the sail, waiting for Hanshi to climb down. Alarm clenched Yi's stomach. She appeared to be frozen. He couldn't make out her features but knew she was looking down at him for support. Slowly, he raised his arms to encourage her, wishing for all he was worth that the sail was strong enough to hold his weight so he could climb up and carry her down. He put the thought from his mind. To climb up after her would put her life in even more danger. She would have to do this alone.

Releasing a breath, he watched as she slowly began to move from batten to batten. Pale and shaken, she reached the deck amid shouts of victory from the crew.

Yi strode forward, and with one look at her white face, gathered her into his arms. She crumpled against him, and he could feel her body tremble as she sobbed and clung to him. Yi's heart swelled with love. Relieved she was safe in his arms, he felt he could weep along with her. Yi laid his cheek against her rain-soaked hair and spoke soothing words of comfort.

Suddenly aware of a deafening silence from the crew, Yi pulled back. His eyes scanned Hanshi once more to assure himself that she had no injuries. He drew a sharp breath. No wonder the crew stared, some in bewilderment, some in open hostility, and some leered in a way that made Yi want to throw them to the sharks. Hanshi's sodden clothes hugged her body, outlining every feminine curve. There was no way to disguise her now. He could only do whatever it took to keep her safe. Drawing her protectively to his side, Yi eyed the crew sternly.

"This brave young woman is Zhao Hanshi," he said, his gaze roving over the men. "Today, she saved the lives of two men aboard *China Dream* with no thought given to her own safety. She is not to be harmed or molested in any way. Is that understood?"

"We understand, Captain. She belongs to you."

Beside him, Hanshi gasped as a rumble of laughter shook the air.

Anger boiled Yi's blood. He swung his gaze to the crewman who had spoken. "You are obviously too stupid to understand anything, so allow me to enlighten you."

The man's suggestive grin left his face in an instant, and he became subdued under Yi's stern gaze.

"Hanshi is a woman of virtue and, as she has proven this day, valor. I want it understood that she is under my protection. She sleeps in the cabin next to mine, but there is nothing improper between us. Any man among you who insinuates otherwise will be flogged."

"And she is under my protection," a voice called from behind Yi. All eyes turned to the cook as he made his way through the crowd of men and took a position on Hanshi's other side. "This brave young woman saved my life today, when I have been nothing but cruel to her during the voyage thus far. I am her servant for the rest of my miserable life, and I will kill any man who dares to so much as insult her."

"As will I." The crew turned as Zongwei parted the crowd with his burly presence and stood next to Cook. Bare-chested, Zongwei made an imposing figure, the muscles in his arms and chest flexing with the clenching and unclenching of his fists. No one would dare cross him unless they were ready to die.

"And I," a small voice called.

Yi released a breath of relief as Tang He moved through the crowd of bewildered crewman. He had feared the boy's demise when he couldn't locate him after the storm.

One by one, the men pledged their protection of Hanshi until only a handful of dissenters remained on the other side of the ship.

"All right. Those of you who object to Hanshi's presence aboard *China Dream*, I warn you to take a look at what you will be up against should you decide to voice those objections to her in an insulting manner. One dishonorable word or look, and you will be locked away until we reach the next port—at which time, you will be removed from the ship. Is that clear?"

The dissenters mumbled amongst themselves, clearly disgruntled by the threat. Yi knew they were in a dangerous position. Women were held in such low esteem, these men would never understand Hanshi's worth—let alone why over half the crew would risk their lives to protect her. But it took only one man to cause an uproar, which could lead to mutiny. Many of the crewman were new to *China Dream* and had no loyalty to Yi.

Yi prayed for wisdom as he addressed his men. "Today we have lost at least five men to the sea. Each of you whose life was spared by Shangdi is valuable to the success of our voyage, and I would not want to lose even one more of you. As you have observed, many of your mates have pledged to protect Hanshi not only from harm but from insult as well. If you cannot pledge your protection, can you not at least vow to show her the respect such a brave woman is due?"

Tucked safely in the crook of Captain's arm, Hanshi watched the hostile faces of the crewmen who objected to her presence. Her cheeks burned. She wished she could hide inside her cabin and never come out again. Though grateful for the men who supported her, she knew they were in a dangerous position. If the other men refused to accept her presence aboard *China Dream,* the opposing groups could very well come to blows. Hanshi loathed the thought of being the cause of an altercation.

The glittering eyes of her champions spoke silent challenges, which the rest of the crew returned without flinching.

"May I speak?" she asked the captain in a soft tone for his ears alone.

He glanced down at her, brow furrowed. Hesitancy flickered in his wonderful eyes, and he scowled.

"Please?" she pressed.

He nodded slowly, then turned back to the crew. "I have given Hanshi permission to speak. You will listen without interruption until she finishes what she has to say."

Hanshi pulled slightly away from the captain's protective arm. He tightened his hold. Glancing up into his eyes, she silently pleaded with him to allow her the dignity of appealing to the men without his reminder to them that she was a frail woman under his watchful care. Slowly, he released his hold and allowed her to step forward. She turned to speak first to the men who had pledged their protection.

"Please accept my humble gratitude," she said, bowing. "I will pray every night that Shangdi rewards each of you with tender mercies and wondrous grace."

Embarrassed smiles flitted to each face, endearing each of the men to Hanshi's heart.

She turned to face the other men, who stared back at her, a combination of curiosity and hostility written on each face.

"I bear you no ill will for your opinions," she said, aware her voice trembled but powerless to make it stop. "I am a woman of China. I have no desire to be a man. I am aware that I am not your equal in strength and bravery, and I am also aware that any one of you would have put yourself in harm's way to save this man." She motioned toward the crewman she had freed from the sail. "Only my size and strength from Shangdi, whom I worship, allowed me to cut him loose."

Fearfully, she watched as one by one faces of stone seemed to crumble into expressions of grudging respect.

She gathered her courage and continued, "I have no desire to see fellow crewmen pitted against each other because of my presence. It—it is not the captain's fault I am here. I sneaked aboard and hid because I ran away from my father's house." At this admission, many of the faces hardened once again.

Hanshi felt the captain's hand on her arm, but she shook him off gently and went on. "I know this was wrong of me, and I am willing to accept my punishment when I return to my father's house. Rather than see you jeopardize the success of *China Dream's* voyage, I will depart at the next port and try to book passage home aboard another vessel."

"She will not."

Hanshi spun around at the captain's voice, which rang with challenge. He stared past her to the men, daring any one of them to suggest she leave the ship.

Suddenly, from the group of dissenters stepped a middle-aged man. The captain took a threatening step forward to stand at Hanshi's side. The crewman ignored him and kept his fierce gaze riveted on Hanshi. A jagged scar lined one cheek, giving him such a fierce appearance, she had to fight the urge to step back into the captain's protective embrace.

His gaze flitted to the dagger tucked inside her sash,

and suddenly Hanshi recognized him as the man whom she had pushed aside. The dagger belonged to him.

Slowly, she lifted the knife from her sash and held it out to him. "Th–thank you," she said, bowing.

Wordlessly, he took the dagger and turned to his comrades. "I have sailed most of my life and have seen few men show as much bravery as this woman. If I had been caught in the sail in Zongwei's place, I would be grateful for her presence of mind and swift action in saving my life. For the rest of the voyage, I will not consider that she is female but will treat her as a fellow crewman. She earned my respect and deserves such an honor." He turned to face Hanshi. Placing the dagger across both palms, he extended it to her and bowed his head. "This is my gift to you, along with my pledge of protection."

Tears burned Hanshi's eyes and throat. "Thank you," she choked, as with trembling hands she accepted the gift and tucked it back into her sash.

"All right, let's get to work." The captain broke the spell of silence that had descended over the crew. He ordered groups of men to different tasks and waited as they set about doing their assignments, then he turned to Hanshi. "You should go to your cabin and rest after your ordeal."

Though she would have liked nothing more, Hanshi lifted her head stubbornly. "You just told these men I deserve their respect. How will I earn it if I run to my cabin and hide away as though I do not believe they will honor their word? Please assign me a duty and allow me to work alongside the crew."

He scowled and drew an exasperated breath. "Help

Cook and Tang He scoop the water from the deck."

"Yes, Captain." Triumph surged through her being that the deception was over, and she felt as though God Himself smiled upon her.

Squaring her shoulders, she grabbed a pot from the deck and began dipping it into the water, which was already receding in the aftermath of the storm.

A sudden, troubling thought invaded her mind, making her happiness seep away. With the crew aware and accepting of who she truly was, there would be no reason for her to meet Captain on the deck each night.

Disappointment sifted through her, but she knew this was for the best. After all, she had promised Shangdi she would return home and obey her father's wishes. She would try to put the captain from her mind and trust Shangdi with her heart.

Chapter 6

Chun Yi drew a relieved breath at the sight of Hanshi leaning against the side of *China Dream,* her forearms resting on the railing, eyes staring out at the calm sea.

He strode across the deck. "I grew concerned when I did not find you in your cabin."

"I could not stay away from this place." She tilted her head and smiled up at him. "There is no longer any reason for you to watch over me, Captain."

The tender curve of Hanshi's neck drew Yi, beckoning a kiss he knew he could not give. Swallowing with difficulty around the sudden lump in his throat, he averted his gaze to her eyes. He wanted to declare that he would watch over her for as long as she lived if she would allow him to do so, but he merely smiled and matched her position against the railing. "It has become a habit." He glanced at her from the corner of his eye and gathered a deep breath. "You decided to return home after all?"

She sighed and nodded. "I must. I was wrong to disobey my father. During our last conversation, he said he would never believe in a God who encouraged rebellion against a father. I believe Shangdi was trying to tell me then not to go, but I allowed my fear and stubbornness to rule my thinking. I neither honored nor obeyed my father, and as the Scriptures declare, all has not been well with me since I left his house."

Yi's heart sang with the knowledge that she would be his forever. He only hoped when she discovered he was to be her husband she wouldn't feel betrayed. "What of your fear that your husband will not allow you to teach your children about Yesu?"

Slowly, she turned to face him. The moon cast a soft glow over her features, sending Yi's heart racing. Her shoulders rose and fell with a deep breath. "I must trust Shangdi with my life. The writings of Father Manuel say if I will commit my way to the Lord, my thoughts will be established. I have done that, and my thoughts are sending me home. Therefore, I know Shangdi must have a plan for me. He would not leave me hopeless."

Her simple faith touched Yi, only deepening his love for her. There remained only one matter between them that he knew he had to set right.

Clearing his throat, he sent up a silent plea for help. He opened his mouth, but his confession stalled as Hanshi spoke before he could utter a word.

"I would like to ask a favor of you, Captain." She lowered her gaze. "Though perhaps it isn't proper."

He could deny her nothing. If only she could feel how his heart hammered at her nearness. How he longed to gather her into his arms as he had when she climbed from the sail after saving Zongwei's life. Even now, the memory of her slender arms clinging to him while she sobbed filled his senses. Reaching toward Hanshi, he cupped her face, marveling at the softness of her skin.

"Look at me and tell me what I can do for you," he commanded softly.

A shudder rippled through her slight frame as she lifted her gaze to his. In her eyes, he saw confusion, hesitation.

"Go ahead," he urged.

"I–I only request that you assign me duties to perform. I do not want the men to think I require special treatment. I must carry my share of the workload."

Yi's heart sank. His own thoughts drifted away on beams of moonlight and a fresh sea breeze. He'd hoped the woman he loved, loved him in return. But all she wanted was to work and keep the respect of his crew.

He gave a short laugh, mocking his own foolishness, and dropped his hand to his side. "What do you have in mind? There isn't much for you to do other than help Cook in the galley, and if memory serves me correctly, your talents don't lie in that direction."

"Perhaps not, but—"

"However, I am in need of a cabin boy since I assigned Tang He to your duties. You sleep in his cabin. Would you like to take care of your captain's daily needs, as well?"

At the mortified expression on her face, Yi inwardly cringed, wishing he could snatch back his bitter attempt to repay her for not loving him as he loved her.

"I am sorry," he said tenderly. "Forgive me for speaking

to you in such a manner."

"I—I forgive you," she replied, her eyes searching his for understanding. "I am sorry I was so clumsy in the galley. Perhaps now that Cook knows I am a woman, I can go back and try to do better." Her lips trembled with self-reproach.

With a soft moan, he gathered her into his arms. Her lips parted as a gasp escaped. She raised her chin, her eyes flitting to his mouth then back to his eyes.

"Hanshi," he whispered and covered her mouth with his own. His heart soared as she relaxed against him, soft and unresisting. Her tiny arms slid upward until her hands clasped behind his neck. He kissed her willing, eager lips again and again.

Shaken and fearful of losing his fragile, remaining shreds of control, Yi pulled away. He crushed her to his chest, sure she could feel his racing heart. He rested his cheek against her silky hair, marveling at what had just occurred between them but knowing it must not happen again until she was rightfully his.

He gripped her shoulders and held her at arm's length. Tears shimmered in her beautiful eyes, filling Yi with remorse for his actions. He released his hold upon her. "I can give no excuse for my dishonorable treatment of you. I must beg your forgiveness once more, my Hanshi."

"You acted no more dishonorably than did I, Captain," she whispered. "I have done my betrothed a disservice in giving my heart to another." She raised on her toes and placed another soft kiss on Yi's lips. "I will carry this memory in my heart as long as I live."

Before he could react, she slipped past Yi and left him

to watch her walk away.

As she disappeared through the cabin door, Yi's mind replayed her parting words, his heart leaping. Hanshi loved him.

※

Hanshi closed her cabin door quickly and leaned back against it. Her hands flew to her hot cheeks as she relived the captain's kiss over and over in her mind, relishing the memory of his touch.

Her heart thrilled with the knowledge the captain loved her. She hadn't merely imagined the longing in his eyes over the past few weeks. His tenderness didn't simply show a desire to protect her from the crew. He loved her.

A sob rose to her throat, snuffing out her short-lived triumph, as she remembered her resolve to return home. Tears burned her eyes at the hopelessness of her love for the captain. . .the hopelessness of his love for her. Why had they only now discovered this feeling after she had surrendered to Shangdi's will for her to go home and marry her betrothed?

With a disheartened cry, she flung herself to her mat. How could she face Yi again after her brazen display on deck? What must he think of her? She had invited his kisses—practically begged for them. Without her obvious invitation, Yi never would have acted in such a manner, knowing she was soon to marry another. He possessed too much honor.

Stirring on the mat, Hanshi felt something soft and unfamiliar beneath her cheek. She raised up on her elbows. Drawing a breath, she gazed in wonder at the most beautiful length of red silk she had ever seen. She gathered the cloth carefully into her hands and pressed it against her cheek. Her pulse quickened as she realized who had bestowed the gift. Only the captain had access to her cabin. She allowed the smooth silk to caress her tearstained face, accepting the comfort it afforded her raging emotions.

She sat up cross-legged and removed her dagger, then untied the cotton sash. Carefully, she folded the silk three times, lengthwise, then tied it around her waist. She lowered herself once more to the mat.

Lying on her side, she pulled her knees to her chest. She gathered the end of the sash into her arms and allowed its softness to caress her cheeks. All she would ever have of the captain was the memory of his kisses and his gift of a length of silk. She knew she must not allow herself to be alone with him again. The risk was too great.

Chapter 7

Hanshi dipped a soiled tunic in the large pot filled with soapy seawater. She rubbed the cotton folds together as vigorously as she could to remove weeks of accumulated dirt from the garment.

Hanshi scowled as another crewman stripped off his tunic and dropped it into the rising pile on the deck beside her. She would be here all day. Keeping her gaze averted from the bare-to-the-waist men swarming the deck going about their duties, Hanshi resumed her scrubbing.

"What do you think you are doing?"

She rubbed the tunic harder at the sound of the captain's voice, and she kept her attention focused on her task. She had been expecting this moment. . .had been dreading it, and her response was well crafted. "Since you would not assign me a duty, I created one for myself."

"I forbid you to be a laundress for all of these men."

Expelling an exasperated breath, Hanshi ventured a peek at the captain. His scowl did nothing to deter her from her mission. "I must do something to occupy my time, and I will not lie on my mat reading while the crew works. Besides, these men needed their tunics clean. Please allow me this one duty."

She allowed her gaze to peruse the state of his clothing but refrained from mentioning that his tunic wouldn't suffer from a good scrubbing either.

His face reddened, his scowl deepening as he observed her gaze. "I order you to stop this immediately. It is not proper for you to wash the men's clothing."

She waved in a dismissive manner, flinging droplets of water onto his tunic. "There is nothing proper about my being on the ship at all, but that cannot be helped now," she said firmly. "Please allow me to do my share until we return to Canton."

Letting out a low, frustrated growl, the captain twisted his body and turned his gaze away from Hanshi. She shook her head and focused her attention back to her washing.

"Hanshi, go to your cabin immediately," he ordered, his voice tense and stern.

"Please, Captain. At the very least, allow me to finish my task. If it displeases you so, I will not do it again."

"Do not argue with me. Go now." The captain grabbed her painfully by her arm. Hanshi gasped, tears stinging her eyes from the shock of his treatment. He steered her toward the cabin door.

"Please," Hanshi said, choking back her tears. "You are hurting me."

Instantly, his grip loosened, but rather than let her go, he turned her to face him. With his lips set in a grim line, he stared into her eyes and gave her a little shake. "You must obey me this time. Do not come back to the deck, no matter what you hear."

A panicked cry rose from one of the men on deck. "Sulus!"

Hanshi's stomach clenched, her heart racing furiously at the dreaded word. Sulu pirates roamed the South China Sea, looking for weapons and goods to steal, and they sometimes took slaves. Now she understood the reason behind the captain's sudden change of demeanor.

"Now you see why you must stay hidden." His voice held near-panic, and he was more shaken than Hanshi had ever observed.

"We cannot outrun the Sulu ship," he said. "There are still those among the crew who are angry at your presence. A woman with your beauty would bring a high price as a slave. Hanshi, I am not certain who would betray you to spare their own lives, and I do not want you on deck when the pirates overtake *China Dream.*"

Her heart hammered wildly against her chest at the vivid images his words produced in her mind. Mutely, she nodded.

Taking her dagger from her sash, Captain stared, his eyes glittering and dangerous. "Know this, my love," he said, placing the weapon in her hand, "I will fight to the death to protect you."

"No, do not say—"

He ignored her protest. "But if I am killed, you must not allow the Sulus to capture you."

Hanshi gasped as she realized what he inferred. "I will never take my own life!"

He gripped her arms once more. "You must not be taken captive," he repeated, his voice deathly calm. "I will kill you myself before I allow it."

Reaching out, she pressed her palm to his cheek. "My life is in Shangdi's hands. He will protect me. But I will never take my life out of His hands. Whatever happens, I will trust Him. So must you, Beloved."

Wrapping his hand around hers, he closed his eyes. He pressed a firm kiss to her palm. "Pray, Hanshi. Pray that Shangdi will fight with us."

She nodded as the tears burned her eyes and a lump formed in her throat, choking her words.

"Now go."

Hanshi fled across the deck, not slowing her pace until she reached her cabin. She closed the door, locking it behind her.

After sinking to the floor, she leaned against the door and hugged her legs tightly to her chest. "Shangdi," she whispered, pressing her forehead into her knees. Her mind, muddled with fear, could not form the words her heart desperately sought to pray. Helpless tears flowed down her cheeks.

The ship jerked as though something had rammed against it. Hanshi's eyes flew open. Outside on deck, wild cries rose up, and she could hear the scuffling of what she presumed to be a battle raging on the deck.

Hanshi's pounding heart sent up desperate, silent pleas to Shangdi, knowing only He could keep them safe.

An eternity of time passed, then suddenly silence fell. Hanshi drew a breath, straining to hear something, anything to assure her the battle had gone favorably for her beloved captain and the crew of *China Dream*.

Finally unable to bear the silence a moment longer, she stood on quivering legs and unlocked the door. Her hand froze as she heard a voice speaking in a commanding tone, but she could not discern to whom it belonged. Was it the captain? Had they overcome the Sulus?

She cracked the door slightly, her heart lodged in her throat, her body trembling in fear and dread as she peered through. Her heart sank as she observed the deck, cluttered with dead and wounded, most of whom she recognized.

Frantically, she scanned the deck, searching for the captain. She clapped her hand over her mouth to squelch the scream rising in her throat as she spied him lying, unmoving, in a pool of red. Cook knelt over him, pressing a cloth to his chest, trying to stanch the flow of blood. She shook her head to escape the horror threatening to overwhelm her. With a sense of unspeakable dread, she kept her gaze fixed on her beloved as a man began to speak only a few feet from her hiding place.

"This vessel and its crew now belong to me." He spoke with confidence, but Hanshi could detect no triumph in his voice. "The cargo will be taken aboard my ship, but we have no need of prisoners." His gaze swept the deck. "Any man among you who wishes to pledge his allegiance to me may join my crew. Those who do not will be killed and thrown overboard. Now is the time to decide."

Three of *China Dream*'s crew stepped immediately forward. Fury boiled Hanshi's blood at their readiness to betray the captain. She stifled a gasp as Zongwei stepped forward, his murderous gaze fixed upon the pirate captain's face. She had saved the traitor's life!

"Is this all?" the Sulu captain asked. "Surely, the rest of you are not ready to die for a captain who will, himself, be dead soon, if he is not already."

Tears stung Hanshi's eyes. She glanced to where Cook still fought to save Captain's life. A relieved breath left her as she saw the slow rise and fall of his chest. *Please, Shangdi,* she beseeched, *do not let him die.*

"This crew is loyal to its captain," Zongwei spoke up. "You will find no more traitors such as these three."

The pirate captain gave a short humorless laugh. "And you? You have stepped forward as well."

In a flash, Zongwei sprang forward, grabbing the pirate captain before any of his men could react. Hanshi blinked in surprise as he quickly pressed a knife against the startled pirate's throat.

"I, too, am loyal to my captain," he growled. "We shall see if your crew is so devoted." He glanced at the pirate crew, who stood ready for another skirmish. "Drop your weapons, or your captain will die before your eyes."

Hanshi held her breath for a tense moment until, one by one, the Sulus dropped their swords, daggers, and guns to the deck. The remaining members of *China Dream*'s crew quickly gathered the weapons.

"Prepare to die." Zongwei's menacing growl nearly stopped Hanshi's heart.

Without thought, she flung open the door and shot from her hiding place. "Zongwei, no!" Breathing heavily, she reached the dumbfounded crewman and his captive in a few quick strides.

"Hanshi, you should not be on deck," Zongwei admonished, his voice hard-edged. "This does not concern you."

"Any life concerns me—even this man's. You said you would not kill him if the crew relinquished their weapons. They have done so. You must honor your word."

"Look around. He and his crew have killed over half of our mates. They will all die."

"You cannot kill unarmed men," Hanshi insisted. "It would be murder."

"They would have killed our entire crew without thought, Woman. Now get to your cabin if you do not wish to witness their deaths."

"Please, Zongwei. Show mercy. Killing these men will accomplish nothing. Will it return our shipmates to us? Will the captain suddenly be restored to health?" Her voice shook, and hot tears spilled down her cheeks. "It will not," she answered for him.

She glanced desperately around the deck at the rest of the crew, who appeared more than ready to slaughter the pirates where they stood. "Such actions will only transform you into murderers. I cannot believe you, who have shown such kindness to me, would now take the lives of defenseless men. Please, allow them to leave and take their wounded with them. Keep their weapons so they cannot attack us again. But I beg of you, let them go."

"Hanshi," Zongwei said, "their ship is gunned. If we allow them to leave, they will turn about and fire upon us."

Sending up a prayer for wisdom, Hanshi turned to

the Sulu captain. He stared back at her, his eyes studying her with a glint of admiration she neither wished for nor welcomed. Steadily, she met his gaze. "If you are spared, will you give these men your word you will not attack us again, Captain?"

"You have my word."

Zongwei growled and pressed the knife tighter against his throat. "The word of a blackguard is worthless, Hanshi. He has no honor."

"Where is the honor in slaughtering unarmed men?"

"Zongwei is right." From the group of men, Hanshi recognized Xang, the scar-faced man who had given her his dagger. "We cannot accept this pirate's word that he will not attack." Scanning the deck, he walked toward a young man from the Sulu crew. "But we have no need to kill him or his crew. There is another way. This is the captain's son. We will keep him aboard to ensure his father does not change his mind."

"Xang," the pirate captain bellowed, "you are a traitor to your family. You are no longer my brother."

Xang nodded. "So be it. But I know you well enough to know that you would not have kept your word. When we return to Canton, your son will be set free. If you attempt to overtake *China Dream* before we return to port, your son will be killed."

The captain muttered an oath and nodded with agreement.

The Sulu pirates were escorted under heavy guard to their vessel. Hanshi breathed a sigh of relief and flew to her captain. She knelt beside him. "How is he, Cook?"

Her heart raced in fear at her beloved's pale face. A deep gash stretched across his chest.

"I do not know, Hanshi. He has lost so much blood."

"We must get him to his cabin where we can tend his wound," Hanshi said.

Four crewmen carried the captain to his quarters. Hanshi followed closely behind. The cook cleaned the wound, and to Hanshi's relief, the blood finally stopped flowing from the gash.

After administering a poultice of herbs to stave off infection and help with the pain, Cook glanced around the room. "I need something with which to bind the wound."

Hanshi removed her silk sash, her gift from the man she loved, and handed it to the cook. He tied it tightly around the captain's chest, then sat back and stared frankly at Hanshi. "There is nothing to be done now, except to wait."

"I will stay with him while you go attend to the rest of the wounded," Hanshi offered.

The cook nodded and rose. His shoulders slumped as he left the room.

Turning back to the captain's still form, Hanshi settled onto her knees beside him and sent up a silent prayer for mercy.

Chapter 8

"Hanshi?"

The captain's weak, strained voice woke her from a restless sleep. She quickly went to his side and knelt, nearly weeping in relief to find him looking up at her, his eyes filled with questions.

"The ship?"

"We are safe."

Relief washed over his pale face. "Thank You, Shangdi," he whispered. He started to rise, then fell back on the mat with a grunt, his hand moving to his chest.

Hanshi gently touched his shoulder. "Do not try to get up, Captain. You were severely wounded."

"How long have I been here?"

"Almost a week." For five agonizing days, he had hung between life and death, with Hanshi refusing to leave his side even for a moment. She had placed her mat across the room from his, uncaring of the lack of propriety, and slept lightly in snatches, beseeching Shangdi with every waking breath.

"How did we escape the Sulus? They outnumbered us

two to one. There was no hope."

Hanshi took his hand between hers. "There is always hope when we trust Shangdi, Captain."

His face softened, and the look of love shining from his eyes nearly snatched the breath from Hanshi's body.

His lips curved into a smile. "Then how did Shangdi save us?"

With as little detail as possible, Hanshi recounted the tale of how Zongwei pretended to be a traitor and finished with Xang's surprising family connection to the pirate captain and his son.

"Only Shangdi could have accomplished such a thing."

"Yes."

"We are headed back to Canton?"

Hanshi nodded. "Xang is acting as captain in your absence. The men agree with him that we should not try to make the rest of the journey to Portugal with only half the crew left alive."

Wearily, he inclined his head. "They are wise." He glanced at his chest and fingered the red silk, darkened with spots of his blood and ripped in several places. "Your sash is spoiled."

Hanshi nodded. Words of love pressed against her lips—words she dared not utter. How she wished she could tell him that as precious as the gift was to her, his life was even more so.

His eyes closed, but he squeezed her hand gently. "When I am able, I will get you the silk to make another."

In seconds, the steady rise and fall of his chest indicated he had drifted to sleep.

Hanshi leaned forward and pressed a kiss to his forehead. She would not accept another length of silk—a reminder of the love she would always hide in her heart for this man. Now that she felt sure he would live, she knew she must return to her cabin and allow Cook and Tang He to care for him.

Yi glared at the cook. "I am ready to resume my duties as captain of this vessel."

"No, you are not," Cook said firmly. He pressed a wet cloth to the gash on Yi's chest. "Your wound still seeps at times. If you try to move too much, you will tear it open, and all of our efforts will have been for nothing."

"Why did you not stitch it up to begin with?" Yi growled.

"You know I had nothing with which to sew the wound. I had to use herbs and rely on your body's ability to heal itself. You should be grateful you have mended this well. I am beginning to believe this Yesu Hanshi speaks of is indeed aiding your healing."

"Where is Hanshi? I have not seen her in two weeks."

"She is working alongside the rest of the crew."

Yi drew an exasperated breath. "Are my orders to be ignored from now on? I do not want Hanshi working with the crew."

The cook scowled as he placed a new poultice on the wound. "We need every pair of available hands—including Hanshi's. She works as hard and as efficiently as any of the men on board."

"Tell her I wish to speak with her."

The cook eyed him evenly. "Hanshi would come to you if she desired to do so, Captain. I am tending you at her request, as I have told you more than once."

Yi's heart sank and suddenly, he felt ashamed of himself. The cook was right. Hanshi would be at his side if she wished to be. Instinctively, he knew she stayed away to protect them both. He wanted to reassure her that their love was not hopeless. But he did not want to tell her the truth until he could stand on his own two feet, fold her into his arms again, and declare his love—not like this, when he was weak and pale and only half a man.

"I am behaving like an infant." He sent Cook a sheepish grin. "I am sorry. You have cared for me well. I thank you."

"I do not blame you for preferring to be nursed by a beautiful young woman, but I am afraid you will have to settle for me until you are able to resume your duties."

Cook tied the sash firmly back into place and pushed a bowl of rice into Yi's hands. "Eat. I must attend to other duties."

Yi watched Cook gather his supplies and leave the room. Without appetite, Yi set the bowl of rice down and clasped his hands behind his head, staring at the ceiling.

In two weeks, they would arrive in Canton and he would begin preparations to marry Hanshi. Before then, he would reveal his identity and alleviate her dread of marrying a pagan man. She would come to him willingly.

Smiling, he closed his eyes. He drifted to sleep amid images of his beautiful bride dressed in a gown of silk.

Hanshi held her breath and opened her cabin door only far enough to allow her to peek through. Assuring herself the captain slept, she tiptoed through his room and stopped at the door. Turning, she allowed herself one last glance at her beloved. The ship would dock in Canton in just a few hours, and she intended to disembark as quickly and quietly as when she first came aboard.

Though still weakened, the captain had gone on deck several times this week for a few minutes each time. He had spoken to her briefly, his eyes holding a longing which mirrored her own heart's yearning.

With great effort, she had avoided any chance to be alone with him, although he requested that very thing more than once. He never protested her excuses, though she detected his annoyance with each thwarted attempt to speak to her in private. Over the past few weeks, she took great care not to leave or enter the cabin until the cook assured her he slept. The temptation to return to his arms tore at her.

Tears stung her eyes now as she imagined life without the love she had experienced aboard *China Dream.*

With a brush of her fingertips, she dashed away her tears and slipped from the room. Squaring her shoulders, she made her way across the deck and settled into a corner. She watched the lights of Canton in the far distance. Pain seized her heart as she realized the closer she drew to those lights, the sooner she would leave the captain, never to see him again.

He would be hurt when he discovered she'd left

without a word of farewell, but she knew it must be this way. Tears burned her eyes, and she fought to squelch the onslaught.

Please, Yesu, she silently prayed, *protect him always. Somehow give me the strength to open my heart to my new husband.*

The gray dawn faded into glorious pinks and lavender, and the sun lightened the sky by the time Hanshi stood in her father's garden, watching his slight form in the pavilion at the center of the pond. Her heart pounded as she stepped onto the zigzag bridge and slowly walked forward.

He turned and met her gaze. She drew a sharp breath and halted. He regarded her for a moment, then opened his arms. With a cry, Hanshi rushed forward and fell into his embrace.

"I thought I would never see you again, Daughter," he said, his voice choked with tears.

"Shangdi sent me home, Father." Tears flowed unchecked down her cheeks.

He held her out at arms' length and studied her face for a moment. She knelt before him and bowed her head. "I beg your forgiveness for my disobedience, my father. I will marry Chun Yi. I only pray I did not cause you too much embarrassment."

"Chun Yi still has not returned from his voyage, so he was never aware you ran away," her father said softly. "In my hopes that you would return, I avoided speaking to his father. No one is the wiser."

Relief washed over Hanshi that her father had suffered no humiliation because of her actions.

He extended his hand. "Come, your grandmother will be anxious to know you have returned unharmed."

Chapter 9

Yi chuckled as he watched his nieces and nephews scrambling for the red dates, oranges, peanuts, and pomegranates spread over the bridal bed. The children were part of the ritual to bring good luck and fertility to Yi and Hanshi.

To mollify his mother, Yi had agreed to this one ceremony, though he knew luck had nothing to do with the children Shangdi would undoubtedly bring to his union with Hanshi.

Other than the moving of the bridal bed, he staunchly refused any of the pagan traditions for staving off demons and other forms of bad luck. He and his bride were in the hands of Shangdi, who had brought them together and created the love between them. Their life together would be directed by the Creator. When they knelt before the family altar tomorrow, he and Hanshi would pay homage to only one God.

So far, since returning home, Yi had not been able to see or speak with Hanshi as he wished to do before the wedding.

After sending news of his arrival in Canton, he had requested a meeting, but Hanshi's father refused. With the marriage to take place so soon, he said, they needed time to ready Hanshi for the wedding ceremony.

According to tradition, Yi knew Hanshi had spent several days in a loft, secluded from all but her closest female friends and family members. She would emerge in the morning and prepare to make the short journey to his home where the ceremony would take place.

Yi smiled at his nieces and nephews as they giggled and ate the fruit and nuts, thus ending the ceremony.

Fingering the frayed piece of silk tucked inside his sash, he strode from the chamber with a smile. In moments, he stood next to the bridal sedan chair. He pulled back the heavy veils to reveal the chair, which was completely covered in red satin and fresh, sweet-smelling lotus flowers. Yi removed the length of silk from his sash and laid it on the seat. He smiled as he dropped the veils back into place. Tomorrow he would arrive in a procession to claim his bride and bring her back to his home for the ceremony. Tomorrow, Hanshi would be his.

Hanshi lay in the predawn darkness, listening to the light snores of the other women sleeping in the loft. For the past month, since receiving the word her betrothed had returned from his voyage and was anxious for the marriage to commence, she had prayed for another way and cried out her love for the captain—the man who shared her faith and fulfilled her heart's desire.

Despair, a constant companion, gripped her heart.

She felt as though she had been offered a beautiful gift only to have it snatched away just as she was about to receive it.

Today she would be forced to put away all dreams of her beloved. She would become another man's wife and bear his children.

Hanshi flopped onto her stomach. She rested on her elbows and hid her face in her hands.

"Commit thy works unto the Lord, and thy thoughts shall be established."

The Scripture writings from Father Manuel came back to her in a rush, and suddenly Hanshi saw the hardness of her heart. *Oh, Shangdi,* she prayed, *forgive me. I have been so angry. Help me commit this to You. You know better than anyone how I yearn to belong to the captain. It feels as though I cannot live without him, but my heart knows that Yours is the only love I cannot live without. I surrender him to You, Shangdi, and I pledge to be faithful to my new husband in thought and deed.*

As she ended her prayer, Hanshi felt a weight lift from her heart, replaced with a great sense of peace.

Kneeling before the family altar, Yi breathed a silent prayer to Shangdi as his father placed a cap decorated with cypress leaves upon his head. Following the ceremony, his father removed the silk ball from Yi's sash and placed it on the bridal sedan chair.

Silently, Yi rose and climbed into the blue and yellow teak sedan chair which would carry him to Hanshi's home.

His racing heart kept rhythm to the *rat-a-tat-tat* of firecrackers accompanied by drums and the loud gongs that started the procession to the bride's home.

Hanshi would be his this day and forever.

Behind the groom's chair, many attendants carried banners and musicians played loudly enough to announce to all that a wedding was in progress.

Once they arrived at Hanshi's home, Hanshi's attendants met Yi's. Yi's lips curved into an amused smile at the sight of the haggling taking place.

His attendants offered only one of the red silk bags of coins they had brought in order to "buy" the bride. He knew, as did all concerned, that in the end, every bag would be offered and accepted, then Hanshi would appear.

His throat tightened in anticipation. They would not stand face-to-face until the procession, including the bride, arrived back at his home and he lifted her veil from her beautiful face.

Would she know he was her betrothed when she discovered the length of silk in her chair? His lips curved at the thought.

Determined not to allow the heaviness to engulf her once again, Hanshi closed her eyes behind her red silk veil and sent another silent surrender to Shangdi.

With her attendants' assistance, she climbed into the sedan chair, wishing she could catch a glimpse of her betrothed. *Soon*, she reminded herself, trying to still her racing heart. One look into his eyes, and she would know what sort of man with whom she would share her life.

Please let him be kind, Shangdi. If only the rumors she had heard about Chun Yi were false. . . .

She trailed her fingers along the satin seat as the sweet fragrance of lotus flowers filled her senses. Feeling a lump on the seat, she frowned and curled her fingers around it. She raised her veil slightly and caught her breath as she glimpsed the tattered silk in her hand.

Her heart raced furiously, and hope rose up to torment her.

It was not possible! How had the captain obtained access to her bridal chair? Would he be at the ceremony? The captain could very possibly know her betrothed. After all, they both captained merchant vessels. Must she feel his presence even as she married another? Surely Shangdi would not test her in this manner.

Hanshi gasped suddenly as a thought more absurd than anything she had ever dreamed came to mind. Could it be? Instantly she rejected the foolish notion. She pressed the silk tightly to her chest. Fighting back the hot tears threatening to spill from her eyes, Hanshi allowed the sash to slip from her fingers. Her honor and her family's honor were at stake. She would not break her promise to Shangdi by allowing herself to dream of the captain when she was moments away from marrying her betrothed.

The popping of firecrackers announced the wedding party's arrival at Chun Yi's home. Hanshi gathered a deep breath and readied herself for the next few ceremonial moments before she would look into the eyes of the man to whom she would pledge her life.

Servants pushed aside the veils covering the bridal chair, and Hanshi stepped onto a red mat placed on the ground so her feet did not touch the earth.

Keeping her gaze fixed on the ground, she saw through her veil that her groom approached wearing the traditional, red silk shoes.

"Welcome home, my Hanshi." The familiar voice sent a tremor down her spine. Hanshi's throat closed with shock. Trembling, she drew a sharp breath and raised her chin. He lifted her veil from her face.

Hanshi's heart nearly shouted for joy. Her dear captain stared down at her, his eyes shining with love. "Come," he whispered.

She reached out and felt the familiar warmth of his touch. She closed her eyes while her mind tried to wrap around the fantastic turn of events. Could this be real? Slowly, she opened her eyes again and met the gaze of her beloved.

A lump lodged in her throat as he led her to his family altar. Together, they knelt. Hanshi closed her eyes, her mind reeling as Yi threw off centuries of tradition and prayed, not to a false god, but to the One whom they both worshipped.

"Shangdi," he said, his voice filled with tender emotion. "Today, you give me the dream of my heart and allow me to take as my bride the woman I love. I pledge our lives to You now."

Taking her cue from his silence, Hanshi clasped her hands together. "I, too, pledge to honor You as a wife to the man You have given me as my husband."

Yi rose and assisted Hanshi to her feet. Facing each other, they bowed, thus ending the ceremony.

Hanshi stared in wonder at the man she loved, now her husband. So many questions plagued her mind.

He gave her a reassuring nod as everyone escorted them to the bridal chamber. They sat side by side on the bed, and Hanshi ducked her head, her cheeks hot, while friends and family heckled and wished them well.

With a combination of relief and anxiety, Hanshi watched the last person leave the room, some time later.

Yi slid the door closed and turned to her. He extended his hand, a tender smile playing at the corners of his lips. Trembling, Hanshi rose and went to him.

Gathering a shaky breath, Hanshi waited, unsure what to say to her husband.

Yi searched her face, his eyes suddenly filled with anxious questions. "Are you angry?"

How could he doubt her love for him? Reaching forward, she placed a palm to his cheek and smiled. "Never."

Yi covered her hand, then clutched it to his chest. "I tried more than once to tell you the truth, but the time never seemed right."

"Do you know what a welcome gift from Shangdi I received when yours were the hands that lifted my veil?"

His features relaxed into a warm smile, taking Hanshi's breath away. He wrapped his arms about her waist and drew her close. A teasing glint appeared in his eyes. "Do you still believe I would throw a man to the sharks simply for requesting more rice?"

Laughter bubbled from her lips. "It would appear

Zhang Cho, the fish seller, is not entirely reliable with his information."

Her pulse quickened as his gaze flitted to her lips. He dipped his head closer and drew her tighter into his embrace. "I am glad to hear you no longer believe your husband to be a ruthless barbarian," he said against her ear, his breath sending a shiver through her.

"Never," she whispered.

Hanshi closed her eyes as Yi trailed kisses along her cheek, whispering words of love against her tingling skin. She sent up a silent prayer of thanksgiving.

Yi's lips found hers, sealing their union. When he pulled away, he lifted her gently into his arms.

No words passed between them as he gazed deeply into her eyes for a long moment. Indeed, none were necessary. Her beloved's eyes held a silent promise, and Hanshi knew that just as Shangdi had guided them thus far, He would forever guide their steps.

TRACEY VICTORIA BATEMAN

Tracey lives in Missouri with her husband, who is a prison guard, one daughter, three sons, a loveable Husky dog, who is more brawn than brains, and an aging stray dog, who wandered into the Batemans' lives one day and took the whole family under her wing. When not focusing on the enjoyable role of wife and mother, Tracey loves to read, cook, play piano, and send and receive E-mail.

Visit her website at: www.traceyvictoriabateman. homestead.com/index.html

The Golden Cord

by Judith McCoy Miller

Dedication

To Mary Greb-Hall,
for her valuable and timely assistance,
her quick smile, and her friendship—
thank you!

Chapter 1

Pearl River Delta, China, 1885

Panting and drenched in perspiration, Suey Hin sank back onto the cot, the birthing finally over. Another girl! For the fifth time, she watched her husband place a pair of shoes outside the window. This was a custom with which she had become all too familiar. Only once had her husband placed shoes facing inward under the bed, signifying the birth of a son. Her heart ached with the knowledge that the birth of this child meant the departure of her eldest daughter, Qui Jin. There were always mouths to feed, but there was never enough food. The sale of Qui Jin would provide additional funds to feed those mouths. It was a way of life, this peddling of females. Sons were the revered children. Suey Hin despised the practice, but she accepted it. She had no choice. Wives of peasants quickly mastered the ability to safeguard their hearts where daughters were concerned. It was less painful when the day of parting arrived.

Qui Jin glanced back one last time, capturing a final look at her family who stood peering from the doorway. *I'll see them again,* she thought, scurrying along behind her father. But deep in the recesses of her heart, she knew she wouldn't. Quickly brushing away a tear that escaped one of her dark, almond-shaped eyes, she momentarily considered inquiring about their destination but censored the idea as quickly as she had brushed away her tear. Such behavior would not be tolerated from a daughter. Silently, she hurried onward toward her father's unknown goal, with fear and sadness her constant companions.

Several hours later, the bedraggled pair arrived at the water's edge near the outskirts of Canton. Qui Jin stood silently behind her father, watching as merchants and sailors swarmed about them while a mixture of noises, smells, and sights assaulted her senses. Spellbound, she listened to the instrumental music of bamboo flutes, zithers, and chimes that floated through the air from the flower boats. Soon the clanging gongs and chattering voices of the boatmen broke the spell. She had never been so far from home, and the flurry of excitement was astonishing. Her attention darted from place to place until her gaze finally rested upon a cluster of factories that appeared to balance in midair.

"I wonder why those buildings don't topple into the water," she murmured.

No answer came, but she expected none. Her father and a strange-looking man with round eyes and pale skin were too busy with their own conversation.

"That's as much as I'll give you," the stranger replied in a determined voice. "Take it or leave it. I don't have time to haggle."

Qui Jin watched her father nod his head in reluctant agreement and take the money being offered. Instinctively, she cowered behind him, but the man reached around her father and pulled her forward.

"Go with this man, and do as he tells you. You now belong to him," her father ordered, shoving her toward the stranger. As soon as he spoke the words, she watched her father turn and scurry away without so much as a backward glance.

Qui Jin cautiously studied the captain's features. Sometimes, late at night after her parents were in bed, she had listened to them talk about the Gold Mountain in America and the round-eyed people who lived there. This sailor's appearance confirmed that he was from *Gam Saan*, the Gold Mountain. A large man with rough-looking hands and dirty clothes, his unshaven face and matted, brown hair attested to his need for soap and water. Beads of perspiration trickled down his forehead until they reached the cotton bandanna tied around his head. Qui Jin looked into his eyes. She thought she saw a glimmer of kindness, but she couldn't be sure. She had never before seen an American, and she was afraid to trust her instincts.

Breaking the silence, the man pointed toward the water. "They're built on piles. When you get around to the other side, you'll see them—long, slender columns of wood hold up the suspended parts of the building."

"What?" Qui Jin asked, staring at him wide-eyed.

"The factories. They don't fall into the water because the part of the building that overhangs the water sits on top of tall, wooden pillars. Isn't that what you asked about earlier?"

"Yes. But I didn't think anyone was listening," she softly replied.

"I hear everything going on around me. It's the only way to survive as a captain the shipping business. Now, come on! We've got to get moving," he ordered as he pulled her along toward a junk at the water's edge. Lifting her with one arm and jumping onto a small junk with a practiced ease that amazed Qui Jin, he shouted orders to the boatman. The brightly colored craft slid quietly through the water, making its way toward one of the large clipper ships anchored several miles offshore.

"What's your name?"

"Qui Jin. Suey Qui Jin," she meekly replied.

"Well, Suey Qui Jin, here's the way things are between us: Your father sold you to me. I guess you already figured that out for yourself. I'm not in the business of buying and selling humans. In fact, I'd much rather haul cargo than people—fewer problems. Sometimes I break my own rules, and I'm usually sorry for it later. Don't make this be one of those times. I don't want any problems on this voyage."

Qui Jin listened intently. He spoke her native language with relative ease, and most of the time, she could make out what he was saying. . .or at least she believed she understood. "I think I am the one with a problem," she murmured, careful to keep her head bowed.

He emitted a deep belly laugh. "You may be right about that, little lady. You'll likely have more problems than you know what to do with when we arrive in California. But don't blame me. Your father was determined to sell you—if not to me, then to someone else."

She met his gaze briefly and nodded. Her young heart ached at his words; she could not deny the truth—but why this decision to sell her to a foreigner? Why couldn't her father have sold her to another Chinese family? She would have preferred to become a servant in a Chinese household rather than this banishment to another country. Becoming a *mui tsai* for a wealthy Chinese family wouldn't have been nearly as dreadful as being forced to leave her family and her homeland. In every way, her father's choice seemed painfully unfair.

Custom forbade her to question a man, yet fear would not allow her to remain silent. "What will become of me?"

The captain leaned back and stared at her for several moments. "I don't know. It's certain that I'll not be keeping you. If I can manage to get you past the immigration officials when we dock in San Francisco, I'm sure you'll fetch a pretty penny."

"You will sell me to someone else? To someone in *Gam Saan?*"

One side of his mouth curled upward into an ugly sneer, and any sign of kindness had disappeared from his eyes. "Most likely. There's lots of Chinamen in San Francisco who would enjoy having a pretty young thing like you working for them."

The thought sent her heart soaring. Perhaps this wouldn't be as difficult as she had anticipated. If she could work as a servant for a Chinese family in Gam Saan, it wouldn't be so bad. "I will be living with Chinese people?"

"You might put it that way," he replied. The junk maneuvered alongside the anchored clipper ship. "Come on—I'll help you up."

"You'll be staying down below," the captain stated when they had finally boarded the vessel. He pointed toward a small, dark stairway. Carefully, Qui Jin walked down the steps and made her way through the narrow passageway, which was flanked by several doors on each side.

"That one," he said, motioning toward a small doorway of rough-hewn timber at the end of the hallway. The captain shoved the door open, permitting a slender shaft of light to fall across the room. Qui Jin moved forward. Squinting as her eyes adjusted to the semidarkness, she focused on a narrow bunk that was bolted to the cabin wall. "Once we've set sail, I'll come back with some food. Do you understand?"

Qui Jin nodded.

"You can wash up if you like," he remarked, pointing toward a washstand across from the bunk.

She was tempted to tell him that his need for soap and water was greater than hers, but she held her tongue. No need to cause undue aggravation and have the captain turn his wrath upon her even before they set sail. Instead, after he left, she paced about the tiny room, back and forth, to and fro, already feeling caged by the walls of her seafaring prison. Fatigued and overwhelmed, she heaved a weary sigh, plopped down on the bunk, and listened as the aged timbers of the groaning ship began to move, steadily taking her farther and farther away from those whom she knew and loved.

Chapter 2

A persistent pounding resonated in the distance. It continued to grow louder until finally Qui Jin awakened and bolted upright from her bunk. Someone was beating on the cabin door. Stumbling, Qui Jin wiped the sleep from her eyes and pulled open the door.

"Thought maybe you was dead. Eat this," the captain bellowed as he thrust a wooden bowl toward her.

Qui Jin stared down at the mixture. "What is it?"

His face was filled with disdain. "It's your supper. What else would it be?"

She cast another glance at the lumpy, congealing concoction and stood motionless. It looked like nothing she had ever eaten before, and although her stomach growled for food, hunger seemed a better option than attempting to eat this strange-looking substance.

"Ain't nothing in there gonna hurt you. In fact, it's a mighty fine stew. Just wait until we've been at sea for a couple of weeks. You'll wish you had something this good. But you suit yourself. If you want to starve, you'll find it's an exceedingly slow death." He gave a mocking laugh as he walked out of the room and pulled the door closed behind him.

She waited—silently listening yet hearing nothing but the creaks and groans of the ship as it cut through the water. She gathered her courage, took a deep, cleansing breath, and tiptoed across the small room. Placing her ear against the door, she stood quietly for a moment. Carefully, she opened the heavy door just wide enough to gain a view and peeked down the dark corridor. Seeing no one, she cautiously made her way to the stairs and stopped, taking note of her surroundings. She could hear the distant voices of the sailors, but it was quiet directly above the steps. Placing a sweaty palm on the wall alongside the stairway, she slowly began her ascent. With her heart pounding wildly, she finally reached the opening and slowly raised her head just high enough to gain a limited view of the deck.

Were her eyes deceiving her? There was a man standing at the railing. A man in a loose, black silk, Chinese jacket with a tightly braided queue of shiny black. Rubbing her eyes, she took another peek. He was still there. She hissed between her teeth as loudly as she dared. Why didn't he look? "Psst! Psst!"

"Over here!" she commanded when he finally glanced in her direction. Lifting her arm above the stairway, she waved him toward her. "I'm over here. I need to talk to you." She watched him scan the deck, then move slowly toward her. Reaching the top of the stairway, he stopped.

"Who are you?" he asked without looking toward her.

She bowed her head. "Suey Qui Jin from Kwantung Province in the Pearl River Delta. Are you going to

America?" She sneaked a glance from beneath her lashes.

He smiled. "I certainly hope we're going to America. If not, I'd better jump overboard. Is that your only concern—if I'm traveling to America?"

Qui Jin shook her head and flashed him an embarrassed smile. "Do you think you could help me? I am being transported to America and. . ."

"You were kidnapped?" he interrupted before she could finish.

"Not really. My father sold me. To the captain," she added.

"And the captain has mistreated you?"

"No, unless you consider that foul dinner he served me to be mistreatment. I'm not sure how I expect you to help—or anyone else, for that matter," she replied, now wondering why she had been so brazen. "It appears my future has already been decided. Do you think I would get in trouble if I came up on deck with you? It's so dark and gloomy down below."

"I don't think there will be a problem. I've sailed with this captain before. He's rough-spoken and permits no nonsense on board his ship, but he's always treated me fairly. Besides, I doubt anyone will notice us. They're all too busy at the moment."

Ever watchful, she stepped up onto the deck and surveyed her new surroundings. The crew was hard at work, and if they noticed her, they appeared indifferent. Carefully, she made her way toward the ship's railing and felt her confidence begin to surge as she leaned forward and watched the sleek bow of the ship slice through the rising swells. A toss of spray shot upward, then showered down upon where she stood. She giggled, the coolness of the water surprising her. Perhaps everything was going to be all right.

The man had moved back, capably avoiding the shower of water. She turned toward him and was met by his grin. "The wind will dry you quickly," he said.

Qui Jin returned his smile while smoothing back the wet strands of hair that had escaped from her braid. "You said you've sailed with this captain before. Have you already been to America?"

He joined her at the railing just as the ship began to plow through a giant swell. The vessel listed and he reached out to grab her hand, but he was a moment too late. She went sprawling across the deck before finally coming to rest a few feet from the stairway.

"You'll become accustomed to the ship's movements after awhile. The Americans say that you must get your sea legs." He offered his hand.

Embarrassed, she kept her eyes lowered while allowing him to assist her. "I hope it doesn't take too long to gain those 'sea legs' you speak of."

"You'll be surprised how quickly you will learn to move with the rocking of the ship." He nodded as she gingerly moved back toward the railing and grabbed hold. "You see? You've already begun to master the technique."

There was no doubt he was merely being kind. She knew she resembled a scrawny duck, wobbling side to side as she maneuvered her way across the deck. "I was asking you about America before I fell down and made a spectacle of myself."

"Yes, I have been to America. In fact, California is my home."

"You live in America?" She was incredulous. "I've heard my parents speak of our countrymen who have gone to live in foreign countries, but I didn't believe it. Why would you want to live in America?"

"I was born in America."

Qui Jin giggled and shook her head. "You are teasing me. You are Chinese. What is your name?"

"Chinese, yes—but born in America. My name is Sam Ying. You will soon learn that living in America is not such a strange thing. Many Chinese live there."

"Sam Ying? That is a funny name."

"It's part American and part Chinese. Names in America are different. In fact, Americans place the family name last rather than first. So, in America, my friends call me Sam."

"How is it that you were born in America?"

"My father left China after his family members got killed in the Punti-Haaka Rebellion. He had heard stories about the gold in California and sold his belongings. He made enough for his passage and the beginning of a new life. He traveled back to China several years later and married my mother. Soon, they returned to California. He's never regretted his decision to live in America."

His explanation sounded reasonable, yet she could not imagine voluntarily leaving one's home. However, before she had time to ponder the idea of such a risky undertaking, her feet began to slip from beneath her. As the ship began pitching downward, Sam's arm came around her waist, holding her fast against the rail in a secure embrace.

She glanced up at him from beneath her lashes. Their eyes met. For a moment she stopped breathing, unable to comprehend the strange stirrings within her. It was oddly wonderful—exciting and exhilarating. She wondered if he felt the same sensation. He smiled down at her, his tempting good looks causing her heart to race at a wildly erratic pace. She could feel a hot flush creeping upward into her cheeks and quickly glanced away, hoping he would not notice her embarrassment.

Almost as quickly as it began, the pitching motion subsided, and the ship resumed its gentle rocking sway across the whitecapped waves. Sam released his grasp from around her waist. For a moment, Qui Jin wished the ship would once again return to its somersaulting antics. His arm about her waist had been breathtaking, and if the truth be told, she longed to have him hold her even more tightly. Ashamed, she quickly forced the thought from her mind.

"If America is your home, why were you in Canton?" She carefully kept her gaze away from his luminous, dark eyes.

"I travel there frequently. When I was young, my parents brought me to visit China. They wanted me to learn of my heritage and be familiar with the country of their birth. Now my visits have more to do with commerce than learning about my ancestors. My father owns several businesses. One of them is a supply house that furnishes merchandise to many of the businesses in Chinatown. He also owns an apothecary and emporium."

"What is—?"

"Say, what's going on here? I told you to stay down below!" The captain loped toward them, his long legs reaching out in angry, giant strides across the wooden deck.

"It was very warm below deck. I merely came up to get some fresh air," Qui Jin stammered, cowering behind Sam.

"You need to get down there and stay out of the way."

"She meant no harm," Sam said to the captain, easily switching to the English language.

"Maybe not, but she's an investment, just like the rest of the cargo I'm hauling. She's better off below deck where the men won't see her and get ideas."

"Your men know better than to disobey your commands, Captain, and what harm is the fresh sea air? She'll be sick and lifeless if you keep her stowed away below deck the entire voyage," Sam replied.

"She's gonna be sick and lifeless anyway if she don't start eating. She's a puny thing. Look at this." The captain reached out and wrapped his thick hands around Qui Jin's waist. "I can latch my fingers around her midsection with room to spare. Who's going to pay a decent price for such a skinny girl?"

Qui Jin shrank away from the captain. His hands felt rough and callous, a far cry from Sam's gentle touch a short time ago.

"She can take her meals with me. I'll convince her to eat," Sam quickly replied.

The captain's lips began to curl into a devious grin. "You got your eye on this one for yourself?"

"No, I just thought I could be of assistance to you."

"All right then, you've got yourself a bargain. She can join you for meals so long as you make sure she eats. You tell her that if she don't eat, she don't get to come up on deck and see you. For now, she needs to get back to her room," the captain ordered.

Qui Jin watched as the two men nodded at each other and the captain strode off. Sam turned toward her and interpreted the conversation, then asked, "Do you understand?"

Qui Jin nodded. She would force herself to eat anything for the privilege of spending a bit of time in the fresh air, especially if she could be with Sam. He was the kindest man she had ever met, and deep inside, she somehow knew he was going to help her. She wasn't sure how or why, but he would help—of that she felt certain. Obviously, he knew about America, and perhaps he would know of a family with whom she could obtain employment. The captain would surely listen to Sam's suggestions.

"Thank you for your aid," she softly said.

"You are most welcome, but I'm not sure how much I've helped. You must go back to your cabin now. I will see you tomorrow for the morning meal. In time, I am certain that the captain will permit you to spend more time on deck."

His smile reassured her. She nodded and made her way toward the stairway before pausing momentarily to look back at him. He leaned against the railing in his black silk tunic, a perfect silhouette against the pink-and-gold sunset. She rushed down the stairway, wondering what he must be thinking of her, dirty and unkempt in her faded, worn, blue tunic and shabby cloth slippers.

Chapter 3

Sam Ying stood by the railing for several minutes, his gaze resting upon the fading sun as it descended into the distant horizon. He wondered what the future held for such a pretty young girl in San Francisco's Chinatown. Since the captain seemed concerned only that she gain weight and stay out of his way, perhaps he would at least permit Sam an opportunity to make the voyage more bearable for her. He attempted to concentrate on Qui Jin's well-being, yet he realized he was thinking of himself as well as the beautiful young woman. A longing or sadness surrounded her—he wasn't sure which, but he knew he must somehow help her.

Sam had chosen to once again sail on the *Falcon*, a smaller and slower ship than many other clippers. The larger vessels sailing out of Canton dwarfed the *Falcon*'s mere 130-foot length and three canvas masts. Unless troubled by storms, the lengthy voyage would provide him with a brief respite from the ever-increasing duties of managing his father's burgeoning business enterprises.

"You thinking about how much you'd like to own that

girl?" the captain asked as he approached the railing.

Sam turned and looked upward, meeting the captain's stare. "I wondered how you happened to have her on board. Never knew you to be a man who traded in human flesh."

"Never have before, but her father wouldn't turn loose; kept up his incessant chatter until I finally agreed to buy her."

Sam shook his head slowly. "I've known you for five years, and I've never seen any man who could force you to do something you didn't want to."

The captain nodded in agreement, his hearty laughter filling the air. "Guess you're right about that! Don't rightly have an answer, but no matter. If I hadn't bought her, there were plenty of others who would—and her voyage would have been much less comfortable."

"That's true. But what are your plans once you get her to California?"

The captain looked away and shifted from the rail. "Haven't had time to give it much thought."

"No? Then why are you trying to fatten her up? Appears to me you have something in mind. I thought perhaps you planned to sell her to one of the Tong members for use in their brothels."

"I will admit I figured she'd fetch a good price—got a pretty face for a Chinese. She's just too scrawny. I don't know if I'll even be able to smuggle her in. You know as well as I do that I'm going to have a problem getting her past the inspectors when we dock."

"I agree. Getting her off the ship will be difficult—perhaps impossible. I think you're going to find that those

Exclusionary Laws the Congress was so anxious to pass may work against your gaining a profit on the girl. Didn't you consider the problem of the inspectors before you bought her?"

" 'Course I did. I'm not stupid," the captain barked. "I'll come up with a plan before we arrive. I might even get some ideas from you," he said with a wink.

Before Sam had an opportunity to reply, the first mate called the captain to the stern for assistance. "We'll talk about this later," the captain called back over his shoulder.

Sam waved in agreement as he watched the captain rush off. "Perhaps I will have an idea for you, Captain Obley," Sam muttered to himself before turning his attention back to the greenish-black waters that swirled and foamed around the hull of the ship.

As the days passed, the captain readily acquiesced to Sam's request that Qui Jin be permitted to spend additional time with him. At first, she had been interested only in hearing about the Gold Mountain of which her parents had spoken. But once Sam convinced her that the streets were not paved with gold and California was a land of poverty as well as opportunity, she became convinced learning the language of her new country would be beneficial. Slowly, painstakingly, he began to teach her. She proved herself a capable student, and daily her skills increased. Her ability to learn continued to amaze Sam—perhaps because he tended to compare her with his sisters. Although their father insisted all of his children receive a formal education,

Sam's sisters had been uninterested students.

"Soon you will understand the language better than I do," he remarked after she quickly interpreted a passing sailor's remark. "It's probably best that you forget most of the words you hear from these sailors, for many are unacceptable."

She nodded and bowed her head. "I know; you have told me so before." Blushing, she lifted her head and graced him with a delightful smile. "Why don't you tell me more about your family? You already know a great deal about my relatives, but you have not spoken of your family since we first met. I would enjoy hearing more— if you would like to tell me," she added quickly.

He laughed and leaned back. "I'm not sure we have sufficient time for me to tell you about my family before we arrive in California."

"There is that much to tell?"

He nodded his head. "Once I get started, it's difficult to stop. Are you sure you want me to begin?"

"Oh, yes, please."

Her enthusiasm touched his heart. "I'll do my best not to bore you. My father is a fine man, highly respected throughout Chinatown and even among some of the American businessmen in San Francisco. He has a good mind for business and enjoys his work. The family business has expanded, creating almost more work than my father and I can manage. That's one of the reasons I chose to return on the *Falcon*. I needed a little time alone to relax. On the other hand, my father never seems to need time to relax. He's up at sunrise each morning, ready to conquer another day. Most days he works fourteen hours, although he does come home for his meals and takes a short rest each afternoon. That's his daily routine except for Sundays, of course. My mother has attempted to get him to slow down for many years, but thus far she has been unsuccessful. I think she's concluded that he will slow down when he's ready."

"And does your mother help with the business?"

"No, Father forbids it, although she sometimes visits the shops. She always offers suggestions about how Father should rearrange the merchandise and immediately begins moving things about. Unfortunately, her actions make Father so anxious, he immediately hastens her departure. It's become a family joke that whenever Mother arrives at the shop, Father will find a reason to send her off to the back rooms to inspect new inventory. Personally, I believe my mother has learned that when she wants a new piece of fabric for a dress, she need only enter the building where he is hard at work."

The family's secret joke caused him to laugh. Qui Jin returned his smile, yet he wasn't sure she understood the humor.

She leaned forward, and the sparkling intensity of her dark chocolate brown eyes captivated him. "You have brothers and sisters?"

"No brothers. Three sisters."

Hesitating for a moment, Qui Jin gave consideration to her next question. It was a brazen thing to ask; yet Sam had given her permission to inquire about his family, so she forged on. "Your father was very sad when he had only one son?"

"I am not certain about that. I suppose he would have been pleased with more sons to help in the business, but my sisters enchant him. I don't think he would have considered trading any of them for a son, if such a thing were possible."

Qui Jin's eyes grew large at the revelation. "He is not ashamed to have so many daughters and only one son?"

Once again, Sam was enthralled by her innocent charm, her desire to understand and learn whatever he could teach. "No, he is very proud of them. All of my sisters are married. The youngest wed only days before I set sail for China."

He waited. She fidgeted with the frayed edge of her tunic and tucked a stray wisp of hair behind her ear, while her gaze remained fixed upon the worn sandals covering her tiny feet. "And you? Have you taken a wife?" she asked, her voice a mere whisper.

"Not yet, although gifts have been exchanged. My mother feared I would not marry unless she became involved in the engagement process. She insisted Li Laan was waiting for me. We have known each other since childhood, and our parents planned for us to marry from the time we were babies."

Why was he rambling on? And why did he feel such a need to defend his engagement to Li Laan?

Once again it was quiet between them. "So marriages are arranged in your country—just like in China?" she ventured, finally breaking the silence.

"Not always. Two of my sisters had arranged marriages,

but both of them loved their intended husbands. My youngest sister chose her husband—or I should say, they chose each other."

"How could your sisters love their intended husbands? Were they also childhood friends?"

Sam laughed and shook his head. "No, their husbands attended the same church. They first became acquainted with them at the church services. In America, young men and women are permitted to know each other before marriage. They go to dinner and attend activities together. It is how they become better acquainted and find out if they are suited for a lifetime with each other. Not all Chinese people permit their children this opportunity, but my parents wanted happy marriages for their children, so they have given their permission."

She appeared to be contemplating her next question, so he waited, wondering if she would ask if he loved Li Laan. "How was it possible for your sisters to meet their husbands at the temple?"

Her eyes were filled with confusion. Sam had prayed for an opportunity to tell Qui Jin about his faith. Unlike his mother and sisters, who never wanted to miss an opportunity to share the gospel, Sam and his father both waited, hoping to find God's perfect timing for sharing their belief. Perhaps it was merely the fact that his sisters followed their mother's enthusiastic zeal for sharing, while Sam followed his father's thoughtful consideration and careful planning.

He measured his words for several moments before speaking. "I am what is known as a Christian. Have you ever heard that word before?"

She shook her head. "No. What is a Christian?"

Her question gave him the freedom to speak the words he had longed to share with her for days. He issued a silent prayer of thanksgiving before speaking. "A Christian is someone who believes that Jesus Christ is the Son of God. The Bible is God's message to us. It tells us Jesus was conceived of a virgin, lived here on earth, and was crucified to save us from our sins."

"So your Jesus is dead?"

"No. He died, but three days later He arose and once again reigns in heaven with God the Father. When Jesus returned to heaven, he left the Holy Spirit here to comfort and be with us. Do you understand?"

Qui Jin's face was etched with confusion. "You don't pray to Buddha?"

"No, I pray to the one true God, the Creator of the universe. Whom do you pray to, Qui Jin?"

"I don't pray to anyone. My father did not speak of gods or religion. He believed he was cursed since he had so many daughters."

Sam nodded. There was a crushing sadness in her voice, a tender ache that revealed wrenching pain, for she believed she was a disappointment to her earthly father. "Qui Jin, you need to believe that you are exactly the person God intended you to be. He has a plan for your life, and He is delighted with you. Most of all, I want you to know God loves you very much. Can you believe that?"

She shook her head. "No. I don't think any god could love me if my own father considers me a curse."

Sam stretched out his arm and lifted her chin with his finger. "Look at me, Qui Jin. Look into my eyes. You are not a curse; you are a child of God. He loved you so much, He sent His own Son to die on a cross—just for you. I pray that one day this will become clear to you."

"If my new Chinese family believes as you do, perhaps they will teach me," she replied. "Do you think that is possible?"

"It may be very possible," he said, while jumping to his feet. "Go below. I must talk to the captain," he ordered.

"I have offended you?" She backed away from him.

He was such a fool, jumping up and ordering her about. His actions frightened her. She probably thought he was some sort of lunatic. He needed to assure her everything was all right. But when he moved toward her, she ran across the deck and down the stairway. He wouldn't follow her—not now. Instead, he would find the captain.

Chapter 4

Sam knocked on the door leading to the captain's quarters. He had searched the deck and questioned the crew, but no one had seen the captain for several hours.

"Who's disturbing my peace and quiet?" Captain Obley roared from the other side of the door.

Sam hesitated for only a moment. "Sam Ying. I need to speak with you when you have a few minutes."

He waited. Finally, he heard a chair scrape across the wooden floor, followed by the thud of footsteps. The door swung open. The captain filled the small doorway, his bloodshot eyes squinting to focus in the bright morning sunlight.

"Get in here," he snarled, pulling Sam inside and slamming the door. "Sit down," he ordered, pointing to a wooden chair as he fell into another. "What's on your mind?"

"The girl, Qui Jin. I wanted to discuss her future."

The captain licked his lips and leaned across the small table by his side. "I thought maybe that was it. You're wantin' her, ain't ya?"

"Not in the way you're thinking," Sam answered, "but I am concerned about your plans for her. You mentioned at the beginning of the voyage that you might need my help getting her off the ship."

"My plans are to sell her and make a tidy profit. What's your plan?"

"There is no way you'll be able to get her past the immigration inspectors. There is no plausible reason for you to have a female Chinese peasant on board this ship. We both know that."

"Some of my mates have told me the inspectors can be bribed," the captain argued.

Sam remained unmoved by the captain's words. "Possibly, but that would certainly cut into any profit on the girl. Besides, I've heard stories of the inspectors taking bribe money, then arranging to seize a ship and its captain for breaking the law."

The captain glared across the table at Sam before running his broad hand against the stubble that splotched his beefy jowls. "You got this all figured out, ain't ya? You think I'll just give her to you so's I don't have to worry about losing my ship. I'm right, ain't I?"

"No, I don't have it all figured out. That's why I'm here. I thought we could reason this out together. I'll be honest with you, Captain Obley. I think the girl deserves better than a life of prostitution. What if she were your daughter?"

"Don't be trying to turn the tables on me, Sam. She ain't my daughter, and it was her own father who was so willing to get rid of her. And remember, it's your own people who are using these women as prostitutes."

"I know that, and it shames me greatly. That is why I am here."

"Then make me an offer I can't refuse. You can afford to buy her, and we both know you can get her past the inspectors. You're a businessman; the law permits you to return to the United States with a Chinese wife." The captain slapped his knee in delight. "It's a perfect way out of this mess—for all of us."

"Except for the fact that I do not believe in buying and selling human beings."

"Oh, I get it. You want me to give her to you. That would be mighty nice, now wouldn't it? I'll take my chances sneaking her by the inspectors before I give her away. I could even keep her on board and let my men have at her. They'd be willing to pay for the use of her. I'd have my money back in no time."

"You know better than that, Captain. You'd have more fights on board this ship than you could handle if you did such a thing."

"Well, pay me for what I've got in her. That's the least you can do. Don't think of it as buying her. Think of it as a creative settlement of a difficult situation."

Sam wasn't sure how to resolve the matter. On the one hand, he knew bartering in human flesh was morally wrong. Yet to turn his back would mean that Qui Jin would surely be doomed to a life of misery. "Give me time to consider your offer," he finally replied.

"If the winds stay with us, I'd say you've got about six days to decide. Just remember: If you don't take her, I'll find some way to get rid of her."

Sam nodded as he left the room. He knew the captain meant to frighten him—and he had. It was obvious that the captain regretted purchasing Qui Jin, but he also knew Captain Obley would want a fair return on his money. Sam leaned his arms along the railing of the ship and thought of his parents and sisters. How would they handle such a situation? Most likely, his sisters and mother would immediately pay the money and consider it well spent. His father, on the other hand, would look for another way. He would insist that correcting one wrong with another was not a proper way to proceed. *Look to the ways of Jesus,* he would advise. "Look to the ways of Jesus," Sam said aloud. Immediately, he rushed to his cabin and opened his Bible. Surely his answer must lie within these pages. "Give me wisdom, Lord. Show me how I may please You," he prayed.

Sam rose early the next morning and made his way to Captain Obley's cabin. Sometime during the night his answer had come. Now he must see if the captain would agree. Sam rapped on the door and waited.

"Made your decision so soon?" the captain inquired as he pulled open the heavy door.

"I have a proposal to place before you. I do not know what you paid for the girl."

"Well, I. . ."

Sam held up his hand to stave off the attempted interruption. "Please do not tell me. I have sought the Christian way to handle this matter, and here is my offer to you: I will pay for the girl's passage from Canton to

San Francisco. I can give you the same amount I paid for my own passage. Although you may choose to believe you are selling the girl, please understand I am paying for the cost of her journey—nothing else. Do you agree?"

The captain grinned and spat on the floor. "You got a deal. Hand over the money and she's yours, or she's free—whichever you want to call it."

Sam placed the money in the captain's outstretched hand. "Please let me explain this transaction to Qui Jin."

"I wasn't planning on telling her anything. Haven't said a word to her since the day after we set sail and don't plan to start now. Guess you know I would have sold her for a lot less," the captain said as Sam walked toward the door.

"Perhaps. . .but I didn't purchase her; I paid for her passage on the ship," Sam replied without looking back.

His plan had worked. It didn't matter what the cost or what the captain thought. Qui Jin was free.

Chapter 5

Qui Jin made her way down the hallway and up the steps to the deck, her heart quickening when she saw Sam watching for her. He motioned to her and smiled. Apparently, she had misinterpreted his actions the day before. She had been certain that he was angry when he sent her off to her cabin.

"You are not annoyed with me?" she questioned in a barely audible whisper.

"Of course not. Come closer—I want to talk to you."

She moved by his side and returned his smile. "I heard the sailors talking. They say we will soon be in San Francisco. Is that correct?"

He nodded his head. "Yes, possibly five or six days. That's why we need to talk. You misunderstood the captain's plans for your future in America, and he permitted you to believe whatever you wanted. He had no plan for you to become a servant to a Chinese family. In fact, there are laws that prohibit him from bringing you into the country."

She felt confused. Why would the captain purchase

her if she was not allowed into the country? "I don't understand."

"I know. It is difficult. The captain thought he might be able to smuggle you past the inspectors. If he had been successful, he planned to sell you to one of the Tong leaders, who would use you as a prostitute."

His voice grew so quiet, she needed to strain forward in order to hear him. As he completed his explanation, she jumped back. "I am to be a. . ."

"No, listen—I went to the captain and agreed to pay for your passage if he would give you your freedom. He agreed. You are now free."

She stared at him in disbelief. "Free to do what? I will die in this country of strangers." Uncontrollable fear welled up inside her, a giant volcano threatening to erupt at any moment.

"I am going to help you. My family will help you. It's going to be all right—you'll see." He gently wiped away a tear that glistened on her cheek. "Trust me."

"What else can I do?"

He smiled. "I don't know that you have many choices right now, but one day you will. I hope when that time comes, you will have wisdom to make all the right decisions."

"I hope so also. You were reading your Bible?" she asked, pointing toward the book in his hand.

"Yes. I was looking for answers."

"And did you find them?"

"Some of them. A few questions still remain unanswered. I am hopeful that with prayer and God's help, the answers will come when they are truly needed."

Qui Jin nodded. "Perhaps if we continue to search your Bible, we can find the remaining answers. You said we have five or six days until we arrive, didn't you?"

Sam gave her a broad smile. "Why didn't I think of that?"

Unable to hide her enthusiasm, Qui Jin clapped her hands together. "Let's begin!"

Sam handed her the Bible. "You choose what you would like to read."

Thumbing through the book, Qui Jin looked at Sam in dismay. It was difficult to make a choice among so many pages. Finally, she shrugged her shoulders, looked heavenward, opened the Bible, and handed it back to Sam.

He gazed down at the page. "The tenth chapter of Romans." He contemplated the passage, then began reading the plan of salvation aloud to Qui Jin.

With deliberate determination, Sam handed the Bible to Qui Jin each time they began their Bible readings. On every occasion, she looked heavenward and opened the Bible. They read the seventeenth chapter of John, the thirteenth chapter of Luke, and the third chapter of John. And so it continued. Sam would read; she would listen. He was sure she understood, and yet she gave him no indication of her own willingness to accept Christ as her Savior.

He prayed for the words to speak—to convince her. None came. And so he remained silent, handing her the Bible, waiting to read the Scripture. On their final day at sea, Qui Jin handed him the open Bible. "Luke, chapter twelve," he read, surprised at the choice, for he knew the Scripture spoke more of hypocrisy than of salvation.

"Wait, wait. . . ," Qui Jin interrupted as he finished reading the seventh verse. "God cares not just for people but for even a tiny bird?" Her eyes were filled with wonder.

Sam nodded his head. "Yes, every creature, even a tiny bird."

"And surely if a tiny bird is of value to God, a girl-child must be of some worth also—wouldn't you think?" she timidly questioned.

"Oh, yes, Qui Jin. You are worth His life. He died for you—that's how much He loved you."

"I think what you have been trying to teach me has now become clear, Sam. I, too, want to belong to your God."

That afternoon, the *Falcon* docked in San Francisco. "Go to your cabin and put this on. We will be going ashore in about an hour," Sam instructed while handing her a yellow silk dress.

Qui Jin eyed the costly garment and looked back at Sam. "Is this for your betrothed?"

"No, it is for my mother. I never return home without a gift for her. I thought she would like a new dress."

"It is beautiful. I cannot wear such an expensive piece of clothing."

"We haven't time to argue, Qui Jin. You must trust me. If I attempt to take you off this ship and you wear your tattered clothes, we will be questioned and possibly thrown in jail. Please do as I say."

He kept his voice firm and gave her a stern look that made her rush off with the dress under her arm. When she reappeared on the deck, Sam's breath caught in his throat. She had braided her hair and fashioned it into two large coils that rested at the base of her head. The dress fit her perfectly, and the red embroidery along the neckline emphasized the pink tinge in her cheeks. The captain was right—the few extra pounds she had recently gained turned her into a beautiful young woman.

"Am I presentable?"

"You are more than presentable. You are lovely."

The color in her cheeks heightened with his praise, and she immediately looked downward. "Do you think they will notice my shoes?"

"I doubt it, but if they ask questions, let me answer. You must act as though you understand nothing they say. I don't expect any problems, but keep this with you." He pulled the golden cord he used as a bookmark from his Bible and placed it in her hand. "Should we become separated, find some trustworthy person and ask him to bring you to the Tongantang Apothecary. My father owns the shop, and generally some member of my family works there. If for some reason the man is afraid to escort you, ask him to deliver the cord to the shop and say it is for me. Do you understand?"

Sam watched the fear begin to etch itself upon her face as he spoke, yet he needed to protect her. There were too many of his fellow countrymen who would be delighted to take advantage of her, should the opportunity arise.

"I understand, but I will stay close to you," she

promised as she took the cord from his hand.

"Good. I am praying God will go before us and give us a clear path."

She nodded. "Tell Him I would like that also."

"I will. Now come along; it is time." Sam turned toward the captain. "Thank you for providing us with a safe journey, Captain."

"Glad to have you aboard anytime, Sam. Good luck to you. Your cargo should be unloaded in a few hours," Captain Obley replied while gesturing toward the dock.

Sam nodded, then led Qui Jin down the gangplank and into a dilapidated building at one end of the dock. A weatherworn sign had come loose from one of its hinges and now balanced precariously over the door as they entered.

"Papers?" one of the officials barked while holding out his hand.

Sam complied and said nothing. "What about her?" the inspector asked, using his club to turn Qui Jin's face toward him.

"She is with me," Sam replied.

"Went over there and brought back a wife, did ya? She ain't half bad for a slant-eye. Go on! Get outta here. Just what we need—another Chink," the inspector muttered before he turned back to continue his game of cards.

"We are safe now?" Qui Jin whispered as they turned away from the ocean and began to make their way down a narrow street.

"I'll get a carriage to take us to my home," Sam replied. He motioned to a Chinese man standing down the street.

Moments later, a shiny black carriage pulled by two brown mares came to a halt in front of them. Slowly, they moved down Jackson Street and then Dupont. They passed the corner of California and Montgomery Streets and continued onward, each street lined with its share of red-and-green barber stands, bazaars, and emporiums, along with a Chinese theater, and the large, granite-faced Wells Fargo Bank.

"That is one of my father's apothecary shops," Sam remarked. "Now tell me, what do you think of our little city?"

"It is larger than I thought it would be, and there is much to see. Most of all, I enjoy seeing so many of our people, especially the children." She pointed toward two small children toddling alongside their father. "It makes me feel more at home to see familiar sights; yet at the same time, it makes me long for home. Does that make any sense at all?"

He smiled. She was so lovely in the yellow silk with her velvet brown eyes staring up at him as though he had all the answers to every problem in the universe.

"Yes, it makes sense. I feel a bit the same way when I visit China."

"But you know you will come back home to what you love, to a family who is waiting for you. That is a huge difference."

"Qui Jin, what would you have me do? If you want to return to Canton, I will purchase a ticket on the next ship. Is that what you want?"

"In here," she said, placing her hand firmly on her

chest, "that is what I want. But here," she continued, pointing to her head, "I know I cannot return. Yet what is to become of me? I have no home, no place where I belong. I don't mean to sound ungrateful. You have been very good to me."

"You need not apologize for anything. Just know for now, you belong with me. We'll figure out the rest later."

"I hope your family will feel the same way," Qui Jin replied, though a note of trepidation caused her voice to falter.

Chapter 6

Ying Kum Shu stared at his son in disbelief. "You purchased this girl and brought her home? What were you thinking? What happened to your values and beliefs? I cannot believe my son would stoop so low as to buy another human. Did you think this girl was no different from glassware at the bazaar? You just pay your money and bring her home?"

"No, Father. Please permit me to explain. I did not purchase her. I merely agreed to pay her passage. I don't own her. She is free and she knows that, but where was she to go? I prayed about her situation and what to do. I believe I was meant to help her. We both know that if she had left the docks alone with no money and no place to go, she would have ended up in one of those cages on Bartlett Alley, working as a prostitute. Tell me, Father, what would you have done?"

Kum Shu shook his head. "I do not know. There is truth to what you say. It would be tragic to have her end up in a brothel, and yet. . ."

"He did the right thing," Sam's mother interrupted.

"Your mother has been away from the homeland too long. Not only does she interrupt her husband, but she now disagrees with him."

Their gentle laughter broke the tension and released the mantle of gloom that had cloaked their conversation over the past hour. Sam leaned toward Kum Shu, his arms resting on his knees. "You know my heart, Father. I would not intentionally do anything to disgrace you, and I try very hard to live by God's Word."

"I know you do, my son, and I am sorry for my hasty remarks. Sometimes I need to spend more time in thought and prayer before I open my mouth. Your intentions and your heart were in the right place. But what do we do with this girl?"

Ying Ah Ching fervently shook her head. "Such foolishness! You make it sound as though there is no need for a beautiful young Chinese woman in all of this city. Most likely, you could have her betrothed by nightfall—but that is not what I recommend."

Kum Shu's lips turned slightly upward as he listened to his wife. "I am sure you have already decided upon the perfect plan for Qui Jin's life."

"Since you asked, I think she should remain with us. She can work here in the house. You know there is more than enough work for two women in this house. It would be a pleasure to have another woman here with me, now that all of our daughters are gone."

"You already have another daughter to help you. Li Laan will be here tomorrow," Kum Shu reminded.

Sam turned toward his mother. "What?"

"While you've been off to China, Li Laan's mother received word that her parents are ill. Naturally, Li Laan's parents wanted to return to the homeland and offer their assistance. They sail at daybreak. Li Laan did not want to leave her teaching position at the school. Of course, she could not remain alone in their house. . . ."

The words hung in the air, begging for completion for several minutes. Sam looked back and forth between his parents. His father finally spoke. "Your mother suggested Li Laan come to live with us until her parents return to San Francisco."

"I see." Sam nodded his head. "Well then, Mother, having Li Laan and Qui Jin in the house will be very similar to the days when my sisters were living at home, won't it?"

"Exactly! You see, this is not a problem. I managed to keep three daughters busy for many years. Besides, Li Laan will be teaching at the school most days."

"As you wish, Wife, but you may find that you can't control Li Laan and Qui Jin in the same way you controlled our daughters."

"You need not worry. I'll take care of the household, just as I always have. I think I'll go upstairs and see if Qui Jin is rested and would like to join us for some tea."

A smile played at the corner of Sam's lips as he watched his mother walk from the room.

"You are pleased that Qui Jin is going to be close at hand, aren't you?" Kum Shu asked.

Sam stiffened at the question. He hesitated a moment while glancing down at the floor. "I am pleased she is going to be safe."

"I see how you look at her, Sam. It is not the look of someone seeking safety for a stranger. I fear your eyes betray your true feelings for the girl. Can you tell me otherwise?"

"I do care for her, Father. We were companions throughout the voyage. Her life has been difficult, and it brought me pleasure to help her. I told her about life in California and began teaching her English. She is bright and wanted to learn. Is that so wrong?"

His father's dark brown gaze remained fixed upon Sam for several minutes. "If that is all that you truly feel, there is no need for concern."

"Here we are," Sam's mother said as she led Qui Jin into the room. "You two continue your conversation. We're going to make tea, and we'll be back to join you in a few minutes."

Kum Shu smiled at his wife. "That would be very nice. I trust you find your room adequate?" he asked Qui Jin.

"It is lovely—much too nice for me. The sleeping room you have provided is larger than the entire house where my family lives. I am in your debt." She kept her head bowed.

"I am pleased we can help you in this difficult time, but you need not bow to me, Qui Jin. This is America, and my family no longer adheres to some of the Chinese customs practiced in the homeland. Most of those rituals have been replaced by our religious beliefs. I am sure my son spoke to you of our faith?"

Qui Jin nodded. "We studied much about God. Sam used stories from the Bible to help me learn English. I accepted Jesus as my Lord only a short time before we arrived. I still have many questions, there are matters that still confuse me, and the Bible has many words to learn."

"Yes, it does. I'm sure my wife will be happy to assist you. And Li Laan, Sam's future wife, is a teacher at the Christian school. She can answer many questions for you also."

"Sam told me that Li Laan is a teacher. I look forward to meeting her."

Kum Shu returned Qui Jin's smile, then turned back toward Sam as the two women left the room.

"Your eyes sparkle when she enters the room; you watch her every movement, entranced by her beauty and grace," Kum Shu accused.

"You think she has beauty and grace also?" Sam flinched at his father's stern look of disapproval. Why had he asked? But it was too late to snatch back the words.

"Sam, have you forgotten that you are engaged to marry Li Laan?"

"Not for a moment, Father." It was the truth, but he dared not elaborate upon the answer. His father would not be pleased to hear Sam's particular thoughts about his engagement to Li Laan. Those distressing thoughts had been in the forefront of his mind on both the journey to China as well as his return.

"Your wedding date is set. You will not bring shame upon me, will you?"

"If it is in my power, I will never do such a thing. But tell me, Father, why are you willing to let some rituals die yet insist that others live on? Why are you willing to accept your wife as an equal but continue to choose the marriage partners of your children? If you have trained us properly, surely you must trust our ability to choose a life partner."

"We arranged marriages for only two of your sisters, but they are happy with the husbands we chose for them. And you are so involved in work, I doubt you would have ever chosen a wife. I thought Li Laan an excellent choice for you. You are well suited, both born in this country, educated, Christians; and our families hold each other in high regard—what more could one desire? You never voiced such concerns before meeting Qui Jin. Until now, you seemed satisfied with our decision. Your question serves only to reinforce my concerns."

"It is not my intent to cause you concern, but I can answer your question in one word, Father. Love—that is the one word that you leave out of your equation for a good marriage."

"As a flower blooms in its season, love blossoms with time. I did not know your mother when we married, but I grew to love her over the years. With time and patience, you will learn to love Li Laan. Don't cause me to regret showing kindness to Qui Jin. I fear I've already made a mistake by giving my permission for her to stay—"

"Here we are with the tea," Sam's mother interrupted.

Qui Jin watched from the doorway as Ah Ching carried a teakwood tray containing the gold-embossed teapot and fragile, porcelain cups into the room. "I am not feeling very well. May I be excused to go upstairs?"

Sam rose from his chair and began to walk toward

Qui Jin, but she motioned him away. He stopped, hoping she realized that he only wanted to help.

"Do not concern yourself, Sam. I think I need to rest awhile longer. I'm not hungry or thirsty, just weary. I believe it would be best if I went to bed. Thank you for your hospitality," she said, once again bowing her head to Kum Shu. Not waiting for a reply, she rushed down the hallway and up the stairs.

Ah Ching waited until she heard the door latch before she turned to her husband. "We could hear you talking as we came down the hallway," she said, her voice a hoarse whisper. "What were the two of you thinking, to have such a conversation within earshot of the hallway?"

"I suppose I wasn't thinking," Kum Shu replied. "It is my fault. I am the one who pursued the discussion. It should have waited until we were out of the house. Perhaps she didn't hear everything. Perhaps she truly is overtired from the journey."

❦

Qui Jin closed the door and leaned her weight against it. Sam's father didn't want her in his home. She had heard his words: He regretted his decision. There was no choice; she must leave. Once it grew dark outside, she would sneak from the house. She would not remain in a place where she was unwelcome.

Carefully, she spread the yellow silk dress on one side of the bed; she then donned her tattered blue shirt and pants. Laying down on the other side of the bed, she folded her hands and quietly awaited nightfall. Darkness finally descended, and the household noises and conversations came to a halt. Carefully, she turned the doorknob and peeked into the darkened hallway. With her heart pounding, she tiptoed down the stairs, out the heavy wooden door, and into the moonless night.

Chapter 7

Blackness shrouded the streets. Qui Jin fell on the cobblestones in her haste to escape. Perhaps it would be best to retrace the path she and Sam had taken, if only she could gain her sense of direction. The shadowy buildings all looked alike in the disquieting darkness, and she silently reprimanded herself for not paying more attention to the route they had traveled. Instead, she'd been busy gaping at the fortune-tellers and peddlers hawking their wares along the streets.

"I must decide," Qui Jin muttered while turning to look back down the street she had just crossed. Continuing to weave back and forth among the streets, she moved onward. The smell of the ocean made it possible to discern that she was growing nearer to the docks. She slowed her pace and looked over her shoulder. Were those footsteps behind her? The moonless sky made it impossible to see for any distance. Once again, she hastened her steps. Palms sweating, heart racing, she strained to listen for distant footsteps as she scurried past one building and then the next.

Too late she heard him. A scream of fear rose in her

throat. An arm encircled her waist and an open hand slammed over her mouth. Her teeth jammed into the tender flesh of her lower lip. She struggled against the arms that now held her in a viselike grip, his jagged voice hissing curses into the night air as she stomped his left foot.

"You vile little—"

She twisted hard to free herself from the powerful hand that covered her mouth. From the very depths of her being, Qui Jin screamed for help. For the second time, she felt the rough palm slap across her face, thrusting her head back into the muscular chest of her assailant.

"You cannot get away from me. If you know what's good for you, you will cooperate," the man snapped while twisting her head.

He would break her neck—of that she was now certain. Reluctantly, she ceased fighting and allowed her body to go limp.

"That's better. I am going to take my hand away from your mouth, but if you scream, I will kill you. Do you understand?"

He loosened his grip ever so slightly, and she nodded her head in agreement. Slowly, his hand dropped away from her mouth. He pulled her arms back and quickly bound her wrists, the leather strap cutting into her soft flesh. She winced but was cautious to remain silent.

"Listen to me carefully. We are going to walk to my home, where you may remain until morning. Who are you running from? Don't you realize these streets are unsafe? You need my protection."

"You have a strange way of protecting people. If my welfare concerns you, why did you hurt me?" she whispered.

"If I had merely called out for you to stop, would you have done so?"

"No."

He shrugged his shoulders. "You see?"

She wanted to believe him. Perhaps he could help her find work and a place to live. Sam had told her of factories where cigars and shirts were made. She wondered if women were permitted to work in such places. Surely this man could tell her. When they arrived at his home, she would ask him.

He pulled her along until they reached a narrow alleyway. The sun had not begun to rise, but the approaching daylight hour had driven away the deep shroud of blackness that loomed overhead only a short time ago. However, nothing seemed familiar. She struggled to see the address printed on a building above her head. A cold shiver ran down her spine, for it was one of the names Sam had spoken: Bartlett's Alley. She was being taken to one of those places where men paid for sexual favors. She had to get away from this evil man. Without thinking, she jerked her arm from his loosened grip and began running. She heard him laugh as he began chasing after her. With her arms tied behind her, she was easy prey.

She landed with a thud, her face hitting the ground as he tackled her. "You stupid girl!" he screamed, yanking her by her tethered arms. A deep, overpowering wail escaped her lips and echoed through the predawn silence.

Searing pain surged through her arms and upward into her shoulders as he jerked her to a standing position. "Did you think you could get away from me? Look what you've done to yourself!" His condemnation was followed by an angry glare as he turned the left side of her face toward him. "Your face is scraped and bleeding. Within the hour, you will be swollen and bruised."

Her face ached, and she could feel the warmth of her own blood beginning to trickle downward, stinging as it seeped from the open wounds on her face. A sharp pain in her left knee caused her to yelp as the man once again pulled her forward. "Why are you so angry? You don't care about me!" she sobbed.

"I care about the money you will be making for me. The way you look right now, I would be lucky to find any man willing to bed you. I have principles. The men who use these Chinatown brothels know that the first time I put a woman in one of my cells, she will be worth top dollar. I treat my women better than the rest of these men—feed them well, make them wash themselves at least twice a week, provide medicine. I know how to protect my investment."

"I am not your investment. I am free."

His look of contempt was followed by a scornful laugh. "You are my investment, because you now belong to me. Now get over here." He placed his key into a heavy lock hanging from one of the doors that lined the alleyway.

Metal bars slashed across a square opening in the wooden door the man now unlocked and pulled open. He jerked her inside, shoving her onto a mat on the floor while he lit a candle that sat atop a small, scarred table.

"This," he said, gesturing with his arm, "is your new home. I will return in a short time with some salve and herbs to tend to your wounds." He grabbed her chin and pushed her head back against the cold brick wall until he was looking directly into her eyes. He spoke to her from between clenched yellow teeth. "For now, sit there and be quiet, or you will incur my wrath. Believe me, you do not want that to happen."

She remained on the mat, listening as he carefully locked the door and scurried back down the alley. Once assured that her assailant was gone, Qui Jin limped to the window and pressed her bruised face against the bars.

"Psst. Can anyone hear me?" she asked in a hoarse whisper.

Silence. She waited for a few moments, then tried again. "Anyone—is anyone awake? Can you hear me?"

"Who are you?" a woman called back. It sounded as though it came from the door to her right.

"Suey Qui Jin. I came here from Canton—just yesterday," she added. "Who are you?"

"My name is Tien Fu Lin. Did Kem Chinn smuggle you into the country?"

"No. I am free. I was walking down the street when a man attacked me and brought me to this place."

"Free? You'll never be free again. Believe me, there is no escape from this wickedness. I have been here for three years. Kem Chinn came to China, saying he wanted to take a wife. In fact, he made grand promises to my parents and spoke of his wealth, telling them we would be married in California. Once we arrived in California, he placed me in this alley. This room is where I have remained ever since. When I asked him why he had lied to me, he said that in order to become prosperous, he needed more women for his business. I am fulfilling his need to acquire more wealth. So will you." Her words were spoken in a sad yet matter-of-fact tone.

"I will not do such a thing," Qui Jin replied firmly.

"That is what I said also. But you will soon find there are no choices for us. I saw you attempt to run away. I was silently cheering for you, hoping you would gain your freedom," Fu Lin replied. "Where are you injured?"

"My face is swollen and bleeding, and I injured one leg. I don't think he damaged my arms, although his leather strap cut into my wrists."

"Kem Chinn will be primarily concerned about repairing your face. The men who frequent the brothels are willing to pay extra money for attractive girls. He prides himself on having the most beautiful, well-dressed girls. If you are a virgin, he will obtain triple price for your first night. That will make him very happy."

"I should never have run away from Sam's home," Qui Jin mournfully murmured as she lowered herself onto the mat. Exhausted, she lay down and dropped off into a fitful sleep.

The sun was streaming through the bars when Kem Chinn reappeared inside the cell, this time with an old woman in tow. "Fix her. I will return for you later," he snarled at the old woman. He glared at Qui Jin, turned, and departed.

The woman squatted down and motioned Qui Jin closer. "You made a mistake wandering out in the night, didn't you?" She didn't wait for an answer but turned to her basket and pulled out a white cotton cloth along with a bottle of clear liquid. After dousing the piece of soft fabric, the old woman gingerly dabbed Qui Jin's swollen cheek.

"You are hurting me." Qui Jin winced and shoved at the woman's hand.

She leaned back on her haunches and cackled. "Stings, doesn't it? But it will heal these cuts without leaving scars on your face, which will please Kem Chinn. Where did he find you?"

"He didn't find me—he chased me down and tied me up. I am free."

Once again the woman laughed. "You may have been free before he captured you, but you are now the property of Kem Chinn and will turn a nice profit for him." She observed Qui Jin's face more closely. "At least once you are healed. Until then, he will consider you a liability."

"And do you belong to Kem Chinn also?"

"Yes, but I am too old to work in the alley any longer. Now I work at the house, preparing meals, keeping you girls in good physical condition, and teaching proper behavior to the new arrivals, girls just like you."

"Proper behavior? I am locked inside four walls. How can I behave improperly?"

"You already have. Look at the damage you have caused your beautiful face and well-formed body. It will be at least five days before you are healed, and Kem Chinn will not place you for bid until he can obtain the highest price. You are a virgin?"

Qui Jin stared at the woman, her mouth stretched with disgust.

"If you do not answer, I will be required to examine you. You don't want that, do you?"

"Yes, I am a virgin," Qui Jin quickly responded.

"You see? It is much easier if you cooperate. You will find that is true in all things, especially when you are with the men. You must do whatever they request of you, and you must do it as though it pleases you to make them happy. If Kem Chinn receives complaints from his customers, you will suffer his rage. He is a cruel man. He will injure you, but not in ways that will prohibit you from servicing his customers. Do you understand what I am telling you?"

Bile rose in Qui Jin's throat, and she swallowed hard before nodding. She knew it would do her no good to disagree with this woman.

"Good. Take off those clothes. I will see that they are burned. You must wash yourself," she said, pointing toward the basin and pitcher of water. "Wear this dress. I will leave the necessary items for you to fashion your hair," she ordered as she pulled a green silk dress from her basket.

Humiliation and modesty caused Qui Jin to shrink into a far corner while she disrobed and began washing her body. The old woman seemed to sense her embarrassment and busied herself rearranging the basket of supplies.

When she had completed bathing herself, Qui Jin pulled the dress over her head and moved to the center of the small room.

"Even with the scratches and cuts, you are quite beautiful," the woman stated as she scooped up the worn blue clothing.

"Stop!" Qui Jin shouted.

Startled, the old woman dropped the clothing into a pile on the floor. Qui Jin rummaged through the inner pocket of her pants and pulled out the twisted gold cord and closed it into her palm.

"Give me that," the woman commanded.

"It is nothing of value, merely a keepsake."

"Let me see it," the old woman insisted. She grabbed Qui Jin's hand and attempted to pry open her fingers.

"You see?" Qui Jin asked as she voluntarily opened her fist.

The woman grabbed the cord and dangled it from one finger. "Quite right. This tiny piece of twine is of no value. It is too short to braid into your hair, and certainly too flimsy for use in hanging yourself. You wait and see. In a few days, you'll be willing to trade that piece of thread for a nice strong rope." Cackling, she shoved the cord back into Qui Jin's hand.

"Kem Chinn is coming. Behave yourself in his presence, or we will both be punished," the old woman hissed.

"Are you done, old woman?" Kem Chinn called out.

"Yes, yes. She is doing well."

"How long before she will be ready for bidding?" Kem Chinn asked as he opened the door and moved inside.

Kem Chinn leered in her direction for a moment, then began walking around her like a hungry tiger circling his prey. Qui Jin shivered in disgust as he prowled about, first touching her arms, then running his fingers down her leg. He turned toward the old woman. "She will make me much money. How long until her face is healed?"

"Four days, maybe five."

"No more than four days. You have her ready," he commanded.

Qui Jin fingered the golden cord as she watched Kem Chinn and the old woman scurry away. "Perhaps the old woman is right. I may be hoping for a rope long enough to hang myself within the week," she murmured, no longer able to stave off the fear that loomed within her.

Chapter 8

Horror filled Ah Ching's eyes. "Qui Jin is gone!" Sam's jaw went slack as he stood silent, staring into his mother's eyes. When the words finally registered, he pushed past her and vaulted up the steps two at a time. He had to see for himself. Surely his mother was mistaken. His fingers dug into the wood molding that surrounded the doorway. This was a cruel joke, for Qui Jin could not be gone. He had been able to protect her throughout their entire voyage to California, managed to answer questions posed by the inspection officials, gained permission for her to stay in their home, and now she was gone. How could he have ultimately failed so miserably?

"You'll not find her up there," his father called. "Go to the school. Ask Li Laan if there have been any new girls admitted to the mission home. Hurry! I'll go to the shop and gather a group of men to help search. Come on, Sam!"

Retracing his steps, Sam returned to where his father stood waiting. "I should have checked on her last evening." It was all he could manage to say.

"Had you told her about the mission home?" his father asked as they reached the street.

"Only that Li Laan worked at the school."

Kum Shu shook his head. "Then it's doubtful she went there, but it is at least a possibility. Ask Li Laan to report Qui Jin's disappearance to the head of the mission council. Perhaps they will be able to assist in some manner."

Sam forced himself to concentrate on his father's instructions. He needed to keep his wits about him and remain calm. Otherwise, he would be of little assistance. "You think the worst has happened?"

"I don't know. We'll need to check the docks. Perhaps she wanted to return home and thinks she can smuggle herself onto a ship. Who knows what she may have been thinking."

Sam fought back the words he wanted to speak. They both knew what Qui Jin had been thinking when she slipped away. Now was not the time for blame. It wouldn't bring her back, and it would only slow their search.

"Come to the shop after you've talked to Li Laan," Kum Shu called out as he rushed down the street, his long black queue slapping back and forth as he ran.

Sam headed off in the opposite direction, wondering if finding Qui Jin was the primary reason his father sent him to the school.

After entering the gate, he ascended the four steps leading to the front door of the Chinese Christian Mission School. Why was he hesitating? Perhaps once he saw Li Laan, these feelings he had for Qui Jin would disappear and life would return to normal. But how could life ever be normal again? Qui Jin was gone, and he felt responsible for her well-being. What if he never found her? How could he live? Guilt washed over him. He was betrothed to another, yet he wondered how he could live without spending his life with Qui Jin.

"Does no one answer the door?"

Startled, Sam turned to see a man accompanied by a young boy standing beside him. "I just arrived. I haven't rung the bell." Sam quickly reached toward the brass bell and pulled the thick, hemp cord.

"Sam! I didn't know you had returned," Clara Ludwig greeted as she opened the door. "You may go to your classroom," she said to the little boy as his father pushed him forward before rushing back down the steps. "It is good to see you, Sam."

"Thank you, Mrs. Ludwig. I need to speak to Li Laan."

"She's not here, Sam. I'm sure you know her parents are sailing on Friday. She said she needed time off to assist her mother at home prior to their voyage."

He bent his head and placed his right hand on his forehead. Something was wrong. Hadn't his mother said that Li Laan's parents were sailing at daybreak today? They should already be gone. His mother must have confused the dates.

"You did know her parents are leaving for China?"

"What? Yes, yes, but my mother said they were sailing at daybreak today. She must have been mistaken. May I come in and talk to you, Mrs. Ludwig?" he asked, attempting to regain his composure.

"Certainly." She led him into her small office, indicating

he be seated in a straight-backed wooden chair. "What can I do for you?"

Without going into great detail, Sam hastily explained Qui Jin's current plight and his growing concern for her whereabouts. "Have you had any new girls come to the house?"

"I'm afraid not, Sam, but I'm attending a meeting with the other mission school leaders this morning. I can spread your inquiry among them. If there's any information, I will send word."

"Thank you, Mrs. Ludwig. You do understand our concern?"

"Of course. Unfortunately, if she wandered off during the night and made her way into the wrong part of town, I fear you may have a struggle gaining her back, even if she should be found."

He wouldn't permit himself to think of Qui Jin in such circumstances. They would find her. Surely God would not allow more pain into this young woman's life. Not now—not when she was searching to find Him and accept the truth. Would Qui Jin think to pray? Ashamed, he admitted to himself that he had not. Instead, he had looked only to his earthly father to solve the problem. Perhaps his mother and father had prayerfully sought guidance in finding Qui Jin.

Sam rose from the chair and moved toward the front door. "Would you pray for her safe return, Mrs. Ludwig? And ask the others also?"

"Yes, Sam," Mrs. Ludwig said. "Please keep us advised of any news—and when you see Li Laan, tell her she will be missed this week. The children love her very much."

"I will do that, and thank you."

He knew that his father expected a report from him, but he must return home first. Surely his mother had been mistaken about the departure date of Li Laan's parents. Or perhaps he had not listened carefully.

Hurrying as he neared the house, Sam pushed open the door and called out, "Mother, where are you?" No answer. Where was she? Rushing about the house, he continued calling out as he moved from room to room and then up the stairs. All the women in his life seemed to be disappearing. Sweat beaded on his forehead as he ran back down the stairs.

"Why are you yelling?" his mother called out from the back of the house.

Relief washed over him as he ran toward her and pulled her into his arms. "Where were you? I need to talk to you."

"I was in the garden, praying."

He smiled while a sense of calm began infusing his spirit. "I should have known."

She returned his smile and took his hand. "Come join me."

Walking side by side, they entered the small garden and sat down on a narrow metal bench. "I went to see Mrs. Ludwig at the mission home—"

"I thought you went to see Li Laan."

"Exactly. I did go to see Li Laan, but she wasn't there, so I talked with Mrs. Ludwig. They have not seen Qui Jin, although Mrs. Ludwig is going to inquire of the other mission leaders this morning. Perhaps one of them will have—"

"Have you told your father?" she interrupted.

"No, not yet. I needed to talk with you first. Mrs. Ludwig said Li Laan requested time off from the mission school to help her parents before they sail for China."

His mother sat listening, nodding approval at the remark. "That was a sweet gesture. Li Laan is a good daughter. But why did you need to tell me this now?"

"Mrs. Ludwig said Li Laan asked to be gone until the end of the week—that her parents sail on Friday. I thought you told me they were sailing today."

He could see the confusion begin to etch itself upon his mother's face. "They should have sailed early this morning. I saw Li Soon at church on Sunday, and their plans had not changed. You say that Li Laan is not at the mission?"

"No, she is not expected back until next Monday."

"This is very strange. She was to come here this afternoon when her last class was finished. Perhaps she is ill. I'll go to the house and see if she is there."

"You know Father would not want you traversing the streets unaccompanied. Besides, I doubt she is ill. She arranged to be away from school all week. I'll go and report to Father. One of us will stop at Li Laan's house today."

Ah Ching took Sam's hand in her own. "Why don't you take a few moments to pray with me? I think you will find it time well spent."

Sam lowered his head, and together the two of them prayed for the safety and protection of Qui Jin and Li

Laan. When they had finished, Sam rose from the bench and embraced his mother. "Thank you for reminding me where I should place my trust."

"You must remember that they are both in God's care. Now, go and talk to your father. Perhaps he has some good news."

"Let's hope so, Mother."

Hurrying down the street, Sam broke into a run once he had crossed the street. By the time he entered the apothecary shop, he was gasping for breath. "Any news?" he cried out when he finally spotted his father near the back of the store.

Kum Shu beckoned, and Sam propelled himself toward the rear of the store. His father must have found Qui Jin.

Chapter 9

S am glanced about the rear of the store, quickly looking first in one direction and then the other. "Where is she?"

Kum Shu shook his head. "We have had no success, but I am hopeful."

"I stopped at the house before coming here. Mother and I prayed. When you motioned to me, I was certain Qui Jin was here."

"I assume that Li Laan has heard or seen nothing of a new girl?"

Sam hesitated for a moment, embarrassed that he had not immediately told his father of Li Laan's disappearance. "I was unable to speak with Li Laan. She was not at the mission school today."

"Is she ill?"

Sam recounted his conversation with Mrs. Ludwig as well as the discussion later with his mother. "It appears that I have yet another mystery to solve, Father."

"So it does," Kum Shu agreed. "Ten men have been dispatched, searching in teams of two. They agreed to send someone back here each hour to report on their progress. They've reported nothing substantial thus far, but I remain confident. These men will leave no stone unturned."

"It is gratifying to have such friends."

Kum Shu nodded in agreement. "All these men are from the church. Some of them closed their businesses in order to assist us. Knowing that each of them is praying for Qui Jin's safety while they conduct their search is even more gratifying."

Tears glistened in his father's eyes, which surprised Sam. His father was not a man who had ever displayed his emotions to others—particularly his children. "It is difficult to realize that, even in the midst of this adversity, we still have reason for thanks," Sam said.

Kum Shu cleared his throat. "I think you should go to Li Laan's house and see if she is there. If not, talk to the neighbors. Isn't there another Chinese teacher at the school? Perhaps she knows something."

"You're right. Lon Yoke—they are friends. I'll go to the house first, then on to the school."

"If you are unable to gain any information at her house or from the neighbors, go directly to the school. Otherwise, come back and report your findings. If I do not hear from you, when the other men come back here to report, I will request they add Li Laan to their search."

Sam shouted his agreement as he hurried out the front door and rushed off toward Kearney Street. Arriving in front of the Tin Fook Jewelry Shop, Sam stopped to regain his breath before ascending the steps that led to the upstairs rooms where Li Laan and her parents lived. When he finally reached the second floor, Sam knocked on the door and waited before he knocked again. No answer. He pressed his ear to the door, hoping to hear some sound of life—anything—but he heard nothing. He knocked one more time.

"There's no one down there," a woman called from one floor up.

Sam loped up the stairway. "Wait, I need to talk to you," he called just as the woman's door was closing. "I am Sam Ying. I am betrothed to Li Laan," he added quickly.

The woman observed him through the narrow opening between the door and the doorjamb for a moment. Apparently satisfied he meant her no harm, the woman returned to the hallway.

"I am searching for Li Laan. Her parents were to sail this morning—for China."

The woman shook her head, agreeing as he spoke. "Yes, I know. They told me they were going. They left very early this morning, before daybreak."

"Have you seen Li Laan today?"

"No. Her mother said she was not going with them, that she would continue teaching at the school and was staying with your parents. She is at the school during this time of the day."

"Yes, I know, but I went to the school, and they have not seen her. That is why I'm here." A hint of exasperation was creeping into Sam's voice as he struggled to remain calm.

The woman shrugged her shoulders. "If she's not at

the school, I have no idea where she could be. I thought I heard her leave this morning, perhaps a little earlier than usual, but I may have been mistaken."

"If she comes home, will you tell her of my concern? Tell her it is important she go to the home of my parents, please."

"She is probably sitting and drinking tea with your mother as we speak," the woman said, then quickly added, "but I will tell her if she comes back."

Sam thanked the woman and returned down Kearney Street. If he hurried, he could make it to the school in fifteen minutes, but somehow his sense of urgency had subsided, so he slowed his pace. His compulsion was replaced by a gnawing sensation deep in the pit of his stomach as his mind wandered back to the day of his departure for China. A picture returned to his mind of Li Laan's parents insisting the family accompany him to the dock and his inability to deter their desires—except for Li Laan, who posed no objection to remaining at home. Her parents, however, persevered. Now he recalled the look of detachment in Li Laan's eyes while they discussed the projected date for his return. . .the appearance of disinterest as she assured him there was no need to hurry his voyage. Her parents were engrossed in every imaginable detail of his journey while Li Laan sat in the carriage, strangely quiet and aloof. He hadn't noticed, hadn't even thought about it—until now.

He continued onward, nodding at the occasional passerby, his thoughts focusing on his relationship with Li Laan in the weeks that preceded his voyage. There had been the conversation when she informed him her beliefs regarding arranged marriages differed from those of her parents, her declined invitations to dine with his family, and her seeming lack of interest in their wedding preparations. Her behavior had been a bit unsettling.

Mrs. Ludwig opened the front door. "Sam! I'm surprised to see you again so soon. Did you locate Qui Jin or Li Laan?"

"No, Mrs. Ludwig. In fact, that is why I have returned. There is no one at Li Laan's home. Except for you, everyone I have spoken with tells me she should be here teaching. Would it be possible for me to speak with Lon Yoke?"

"Of course. I didn't think to suggest that you speak with her earlier today. Li Laan and Lon Yoke spend so much time together in the classroom they have become closer than sisters. Let us hope she can help. I'll go and fetch her. I shouldn't be long," Mrs. Ludwig replied as she hurried off.

The sound of footsteps in the hallway caused Sam to turn. He stood still as Mrs. Ludwig entered the room, with Lon Yoke following close behind.

"I must leave, or I'll be late for my meeting. However, please stay and use my office. I'll leave the door open," Mrs. Ludwig stated while hastily running a hatpin through her flower-festooned straw hat.

"We shouldn't be long," Sam replied. He turned toward Lon Yoke. "What can you tell me of Li Laan's whereabouts? She is not at home, and she is not here."

Lon Yoke immediately began twisting her embroidered handkerchief. "I have not seen her today," she whispered.

Sam nodded. "But do you know where she is?"

"Now?"

"Yes, now."

Lon Yoke gazed down at the highly-polished oak floor. "No, I do not know. May I return to my class now?"

"No!" Sam shouted. His voice was louder than he'd intended. Lon Yoke cowered back in her chair. "I'm sorry. I should not have raised my voice. Please understand that I am under a great deal of strain. Not only am I searching for Li Laan, but there is another Chinese girl we fear has been abducted. Perhaps Mrs. Ludwig mentioned the disappearance of Suey Qui Jin."

Lon Yoke raised her head ever so slightly, her eyes still focused upon the floor. "Do you fear Li Laan has been abducted?"

"I don't know what to think. The only thing I know for certain is that Li Laan is missing, and nobody seems to know her whereabouts. I think you can help me."

He remained silent—waiting.

Finally, Lon Yoke shifted in her chair, moving forward to the very edge as she reached into the pocket of her shirtwaist. Pulling out an envelope, she extended her arm and handed it to Sam. "I was not to give this to you until she was gone for two days. I told her I would not lie, that surely someone would come looking for her before two days had passed. I truly do not know where she is right now, but I do know she has left the city. She hopes you will not follow her, Sam. I am sure Li Laan is safe, but I doubt the same is true of Qui Jin. It appears Qui Jin is the one who needs your immediate attention."

Sam ripped open the envelope, unfolded the letter, and quickly read the message. He could feel Lon Yoke staring at him, obviously awaiting his response. After neatly refolding the letter and returning it to the envelope, Sam looked at Lon Yoke. "Thank you for providing this information," he said quietly. He tucked the letter into his pocket.

"You have nothing else to say?"

The envelope rustled as he patted his jacket pocket. "No, Li Laan has said it all."

Chapter 10

Y ou are healing nicely. I think you will be ready sooner than I imagined. Kem Chinn will be satisfied with my work," the old lady announced proudly.

"Would you consider telling him I need more time to heal?" Qui Jin begged. "This is only my second day."

The old woman looked directly into her eyes, and Qui Jin thought that for a brief moment she saw a flicker of kindness. "We shall see," she replied after a moment. However, the woman's voice lacked commitment, and her words gave Qui Jin little encouragement. Soon Kem Chinn appeared to take the woman away. Qui Jin sighed with relief when he didn't enter the room to examine her.

The hours passed slowly. Occasionally, a man would be escorted to one of the cells during the early evening hours, but most of them came under cover of darkness. The clanging of the locks and noises that filtered into her room from the alley made it impossible to sleep. She covered her ears to muffle the sounds, then she began praying to Jesus. All through the night she uttered prayers, urgent pleas that Jesus would rescue her from this place.

"Qui Jin!" the girl in the next cell called out.

Qui Jin moved to the barred window. "Yes?"

"I heard Kem Chinn tell my customer he would have a virgin up for bid in two more nights. He spoke of your beauty and asked that my customer share the information with his friends."

The words struck fear in her heart. Lacing the golden cord through her fingers, she stood staring out into the ugliness of the alleyway. Was this to be the end of her life, living in a brothel, making money for Kem Chinn? Did Jesus die on a cross to save her from her sins in order for her to live out her days as a prostitute? *Surely not,* she prayed.

"You should be pleased. He will treat you better, give you more food and prettier clothes to wear," the girl continued.

Qui Jin ignored the comment. Clothes that men would force her to remove at their pleasure—clothes to wear within the confines of a tiny cell. What did she care about pretty clothes? She stood at the barred window of her room and stared across the narrow street. "Across the alley on that far cell—what is hanging from the window?" Qui Jin called to Fu Lin.

"Sometimes Kem Chinn will move us to different rooms. He says he does it to be kind, but I'm sure there is probably some other reason. For a short time after he moves us, a few of the girls hang a piece of silk or a scarf from their cells so that their customers know where to find them."

"They want the men to find them?"

"Of course. Some of the girls are working here until they repay their debt to Kem Chinn for passage to the country. For those like you and me who will never get away, it is not as important. However, if we don't make enough money for him each day, he withholds our food or punishes us in other ways."

"How much more could he punish us? We are already prisoners."

"You do not want to know. Believe me when I tell you that you do not want to anger Kem Chinn. But if you are as beautiful as I have heard him say, you will have many customers."

Once again, a shiver of fear coursed down Qui Jin's spine. She tucked her hands into the pockets of her dress and paced. Back and forth, back and forth she walked, her fingers wrapping in and out of the tasseled cord until finally she stopped pacing and pulled the cord from her pocket. The fringed tassel appeared to glisten in the sunlight as she held it to the barred window. She would use the cord to mark her cell—not so that men would know her whereabouts and come to abuse her, but so she could tell them the golden cord was from a Bible that spoke of God's love. Carefully, she wrapped the twisted length and then drew the tassel through, pushing the loop down the bar until it hung outside the window, with the fringed end blowing in the warm afternoon breeze.

Qui Jin smiled. There was a bit of comfort in knowing that the same cord that had marked God's Word now identified her cell. On the final days of her and Sam's voyage, she had read a story of Rahab, a woman who had marked her home by hanging a rope out her window. Perhaps someone would come down the alley and see the cord. . .perhaps that person would know it was a Bible marker. . .perhaps that person would realize she believed in Jesus. . .and perhaps that person would save her. "Probably not. Why would a Christian come down one of these alleys?" she murmured in a dejected whisper. The spoken words caused her fear to return anew.

Sam rushed toward Dupont Street. His father would already be on his way home for the noonday meal. Explaining the facts surrounding Li Laan's disappearance would be less complicated with both of his parents together, for there would be less chance of confusion and misunderstanding. At least, that was his desire as he loped into the small courtyard where his parents were beginning their midday meal.

Their joy at seeing him was evident, his father rising as Sam drew nearer. "I have news," he panted.

His father nodded. "Take a moment to catch your breath, then tell us."

After several moments Sam regained his composure. What he was going to say would be unpleasant. There was no way he could paint a lovely picture. Simple and to the point would be the best method, he decided. "Li Laan has run off with another man. She says she loves this man and intends to marry him."

Perhaps his simple and to-the-point words were not the best decision after all. His mother gasped for breath, her arms flailing as she reached out toward Kum Shu.

There was a look of horror in her eyes that was quickly replaced by a glare of accusation as she glanced in Sam's direction.

As Sam had expected, his father remained calm. He'd reveal his thoughts through his words, not with an emotional reaction. Sam watched as his father comforted and calmed his mother until her breathing started returning to normal.

His mother now turned and looked directly into Sam's eyes. "What have you done?"

The words stung. Each one was a punctuated stab that caused surprising pain. "I did nothing, Mother. I honored your wishes in regard to Li Laan and our marriage," he responded in a hushed whisper. "It is Li Laan who has chosen to break the commitment." He pulled the letter from his pocket and thrust it into his mother's hand. "Read for yourself."

"You must go after her." Urgency filled his mother's voice as she quickly scanned the page. "There is no time to stand around talking—you must hurry!"

Kum Shu shook his head. "No! He will not go."

"What? We will be disgraced! Every gossip in Chinatown will be speaking of our shame."

"I care little what the gossips will say. As to shame, Sam did nothing to cause us dishonor. Besides, I doubt he could find Li Laan—and if he did, she would probably already be married."

"But what if he finds her and she hasn't married? He could bring her back, and things would return to normal. They would be married. She would learn to love Sam instead of this other man," his mother argued.

Once again, Kum Shu shook his head. "Hear me, Wife. Even if Sam could find Li Laan, they would both be miserable. It serves no good purpose for Sam to chase after her."

"Sam would not be miserable. He loves Li Laan. Over time, he would win her love in return."

Sam looked toward his father, seeking approval to say what Kum Shu already knew. His father smiled and nodded at Sam. "Tell her," he instructed.

"I do not love Li Laan, Mother. I never have. I, too, love another."

"This is impossible. How can any of this be happening? What have I done to deserve such turmoil and horror in my life?"

Kum Shu laughed. "I am sorry, my wife, but you are creating drama worthy of the theater with your weeping and self-pity. If we compared this incident with the injustice that daily occurs on the streets of Chinatown, I think your turmoil and horror would be infinitesimal. Are you not at all curious whom your son loves?"

A spark of interest gleamed in Ah Ching's eyes. "I am sure I already know. It is Sing Lee Lo. She is attracted to you; her father spoke to us regarding her desire to wed with you. You are secretly meeting with her, aren't you?"

Sam smiled at the smugness in his mother's voice. Confidence etched her face. "No, Mother, Lee Lo does not capture my interest. It is Qui Jin I love."

His mother's eyebrows arched and her tiny lips gathered into a bow. She stared at him momentarily, then nodded her head. "I should have known."

"Did you not notice the way he looked at her?" Kum Shu asked.

"You knew?" Ah Ching directed an accusatory glare at her husband.

Kum Shu smiled, obviously pleased with himself. "Women are not always the first to see a spark of love. Sam and I discussed his feelings for Qui Jin, but he agreed to honor his betrothal to Li Laan. There is no need for further discussion. I now believe Sam is right; God directed their paths, and they are intended to unite."

Ah Ching stared at her husband in disbelief. "You are giving permission for Sam to wed a peasant girl? Perhaps I could more fully understand if you would reveal what caused you to believe Sam's marriage to Qui Jin is a divine arrangement."

"I will be pleased to do so—but at another time. Right now, we must concentrate on locating Qui Jin." Turning back toward Sam, he shook his head. "I am sorry, but there is nothing positive to report from any of the men searching for Qui Jin. We did become excited for a few moments when one of the men reported seeing an un-escorted young woman near the docks. After investigating, our man discovered she is the wife of a merchant returning from China. Her husband explained business detained him and caused his late arrival at the wharf. There is nothing else of consequence to report."

Sam paced back and forth in front of the small stone pond in the courtyard. "Has anyone gone to the alleyway brothels to inquire?" The words stuck in his throat. He did not want to think of Qui Jin in such a place. The very idea caused a wave of nausea to wash over him.

"Yes, but the owners of those despicable places reported there were no new girls. Of course, they tried to interest the men in purchasing services from the women. After declining the invitation, Wing Chew attempted to share God's Word with one of the owners. Unfortunately, Wing Chew didn't have any more success converting the brothel owner than he did finding Qui Jin," his father related.

Sam smiled. He admired Wing Chew's tenacity, for not many would go into the brothels and share Christ. "I doubt there is any reason to check with Mrs. Ludwig at the school, either. I'm not sure where I should search, but I can't sit here waiting. Pray that God will direct my feet. I fear that time is our enemy."

⁂

Walking down Sacramento Street, Sam attempted to squelch his feelings of apprehension. *Talking about faith is much easier than putting it into practice,* he decided, bowing his head against a salty breeze. The sound of pounding feet caused Sam to turn and look over his shoulder. Wing Chew was rushing down the street waving his arm.

"I have news," Wing Chew called out. "A report of a girl. I believe it may be Qui Jin."

⁂

Angry, arguing voices awakened Qui Jin. She turned her back to the door and placed a finger on each ear. If only they would go away and permit her the luxury of escaping back into her dreams of the homeland and her family. Instead, the noise grew louder. Someone banged on her door, and Kem Chinn screamed vile profanities into the night. There was a clanking noise—the sound of a key in the lock at her door. Qui Jin shrank back into the corner. It was too soon for Kem Chinn to bring men to her cell. Why was he coming into her room?

"Get up, Girl!" Kem Chinn screamed as he lit the candle stub. "This man says you are not free—that you belong to him and I have stolen you." He grabbed Qui Jin's arm and pulled her into glow of the candle.

"She belongs to me. Her name is Suey Qui Jin, and I brought her from Canton. I paid for her passage to California. Captain Obley of the *Falcon* will verify I speak the truth. We sailed on his ship. The girl is somewhat insolent and misbehaves—she ran away during the night. I've been searching for two days. When I saw this cord," he said, "I knew she was here. This marker is mine."

She could not see his face, but her heart filled with unabashed joy at the sound of Sam's voice. How she longed to look into his eyes and beg him to forgive her. She ached to be the woman of his desire, to feel his arms wrap around her in love and protection for the rest of her life—but that was impossible! Still, she determined, if he rescued her from this place, she would offer her abiding friendship—both to him and Li Laan.

"Speak up, Girl, and do not lie. You told me you were free, did you not?" Kem Chinn yelled, his words pulling her away from rambling thoughts of love and friendship.

"Yes," she whispered. "But this man speaks the truth. I belong to him."

Kem Chinn's face was wrenched with anger as he

paced about the small cell. "What of my investment in this girl? I have spent much money for her medical care, fed and clothed her, and now you want to just walk out with her. It is unjust."

Qui Jin began to feel courageous in Sam's presence. She doubted Kem Chinn would attempt to strike her with Sam close at hand. "You were the cause of my injuries, pushing me down into the street and dragging me by my arms. And I did not ask for food or this dress. You told me that if I did not eat and do as I was told, you would punish me."

Kem Chinn leapt in front of her, leaning down until his face hovered only inches from hers. "You do not speak!" he screamed. "This is between men. What you have to say is of no importance to either of us."

"It is of importance to me," Sam replied in an even tone as he stepped closer to Qui Jin.

Kem Chinn's mouth dropped open at the unexpected comment. He shifted, moving away from Qui Jin. "You must pay me," he insisted.

"I think the opposite is true. You have damaged my property."

Kem Chinn began to sputter. "But if I had not captured her, she would most likely be aboard a ship to China. I have performed a great service for you."

Sam appeared to be contemplating his rebuttal. "On the one hand, you have managed to keep my property in Chinatown." A wry grin spread across Sam's lips as Kem Chinn bobbed his head up and down in agreement. "On the other hand, my property is now damaged. It appears the best solution is that I take the girl and leave this place."

Kem Chinn's head moved back and forth in vigorous disagreement. "You know that if it weren't for me, she would have escaped. You must pay me."

"I don't know if she would have been successful in boarding a ship," Sam replied. "Perhaps she would have become frightened and returned to my home. In that case, she would not have sustained these injuries. I would like to settle this without intervention of the Chinese Six Company. We both know how they feel about your 'business.' "

Qui Jin watched closely as the men bantered back and forth. She had never heard of the Chinese Six Company, but Kem Chinn cowered at the mention of the name.

"Take her. You know I cannot withstand interference by the Chinese Six Company. Get out of here."

Kem Chinn pushed Qui Jin forward. Rage had returned to his face, and his hands were trembling. Yet he stood fast as Sam moved forward and claimed Qui Jin.

Sam took Qui Jin's elbow and guided her from the cell. "Say nothing and do not look back," he whispered.

Suddenly Qui Jin stopped. Sam was urging her forward, but she remained steadfast. "We must go back to the cell. I forgot the cord from your Bible."

"I will get you another one. We must go," Sam replied.

She shook her head. "Another one will not be the same. I must have that one. It saved my life."

"That piece of cord didn't save your life. I did. Come on," Sam urged.

Qui Jin stopped in her tracks. "You are right, Sam.

The cord did not save my life, but it makes me remember where I should place my trust. You see, I now realize Jesus truly saved my life. It is in Him I must always place my trust, not in myself or in others."

How could he possibly argue with such truth? Sam nodded his head. "You wait here. Do not move. I will retrieve the cord."

Once again, Qui Jin heard Kem Chinn shouting, but she did as Sam had directed and did not move. Soon he returned and placed the cord in her hand.

"Thank you," she murmured.

"You are truly welcome, but we must hurry. If we don't soon get out of this place, I fear that Kem Chinn will change his mind."

She remained silent, scurrying along as she attempted to keep pace with Sam. Only when they were a short distance from Bartlett Alley did Sam slow his steps. "This way," he said, while leading her across the cobblestone street.

They had walked only a short distance, both of them quiet, Sam obviously intent on his own thoughts. "You are angry with me?" Qui Jin finally asked, breaking the silence.

She waited. Finally he spoke. "No, Qui Jin, I am not angry. Fear, disappointment, sadness—those words more adequately explain how I felt. Somehow, I should have found a better way to handle matters. I know you heard my father's words and you were hurt by what he said. However, I never imagined you would run away."

"All my life I have been a burden, first to my father and

now to you and your family. I doubt you can imagine such a thing. After all, you are a son, and sons are the beloved children—always a privilege, never an obligation."

Sam stopped and turned toward her. "There is something I must explain to you, Qui Jin. No matter what your earthly father may think of you, you are a child of God. When you accepted Jesus as your Savior, God became your Father. God treasures you more than all the riches you could ever imagine. I know it may be difficult for you to believe yourself worthy of such love and adoration, but our God loves all of His children equally. He more than loves you; He adores you." Sam hesitated for a moment and looked into her eyes. "Do you believe me?"

Qui Jin listened intently to Sam's words. She knew he would not lie to her, yet she had to speak the truth. "I believe what you say, Sam, but such a concept is difficult for me to accept."

He nodded and took her hand. "Consider this: You accepted Jesus as your Lord only a week ago. When you asked Him to come into your heart, He saved you from your sins and granted you eternal life. You were born again. At this time, you are still a baby in God's family. A girl baby."

Could this be true? A baby once again? She smiled at the thought.

Sam returned her smile as he continued. "Remember these things. You were on a ship that does not normally carry passengers, yet I was aboard. Captain Obley gave permission for me to spend time with you on the voyage. I was able to gain your freedom by paying for your passage rather than purchasing you. We were able to pass through the inspection without having to tell one lie. You were given protection in a Christian home, and God directed my path to find you when you left the security of the home He provided for you. Can you honestly question God's complete love for you after all He did?"

"It is true that God has done much for me in a short time. I am undeserving of such goodness."

Sam shook his head. "None of us, male or female, deserves God's generosity. We are all sinners, yet God's grace abounds to all of His children. I pray you will learn to accept His unconditional love in your heart as well as in your mind."

"I will pray about this also," Qui Jin agreed as they continued onward.

A short time later, while they walked together in a comfortable silence, she spied Sam's home and began to slow her pace. Kum Shu's words echoed in her mind. How could she return to Kum Shu's home? She had heard him say he regretted having her as a guest.

She stopped and touched Sam's arm. "Is there someplace you could take me other than your home—someplace where I would be safe? You must understand that I do not want to remain where I am not wanted. I don't hold your father's words against him. He should not be required to accommodate unwanted guests. I believe it would be better for all of us."

"I think you will find my father a willing host, Qui Jin— if you will just give him the opportunity. He deeply regrets his behavior. I'm sure he wants to offer his own apology."

The thought of a man apologizing to her was almost as frightening as returning to unfriendly surroundings. "Before we go in, can you tell me what I did to offend him? If I know, perhaps I will not repeat my error."

"You did nothing wrong. My father and I had been having a discussion about you. He feared that I had grown to love you and would dishonor my pledge to marry Li Laan. Although I told him I would never do such a thing, he continued to interrogate me, convinced my love for you would eventually triumph over my honor. You walked down the hallway then and heard him say he regretted inviting you into our home. My father no longer has reason for concern. He will be most pleased to see I have found you."

She thought about Sam's words. Kum Shu was convinced Sam loved her, and the thought made her heart sing with joy. Even if he married another, she would know he returned the love she held for him. Still, she didn't understand how any of this made a difference in the welcome she would receive from Kum Shu, unless—

"You and Li Laan were married during my absence?" she ventured.

Sam laughed, a loud belly laugh. "No, I have been too busy searching for you, and Li Laan has been too busy running off with another man."

"Truly? She has married another and brought disgrace upon your families? Your father and mother will be distraught. I cannot go in there."

He urged her forward. "You can. They will be most relieved to know that I have found you. Trust me. They will be anxious to welcome you home."

Once again she pulled back. "Wait one moment. I have another question."

"Yes?"

"You said your father feared your love for me would overpower your honor."

He nodded in agreement. She swallowed hard. She had to know. "Was your father correct? Do you love me?"

"More than you can imagine," he replied tenderly. "It is my deepest desire to make you my wife."

She could see the adoration in his eyes. No man had ever looked at her in such a manner. Qui Jin struggled to suppress the mix of emotions rising within her.

Sam raised his finger to her face and carefully wiped away the tear that had spilled over onto her cheek. "I have made you unhappy. You do not share my feelings of love."

"I do share your feelings, Sam. These are tears of joy, not sadness. I am overcome with sensations I cannot begin to explain," she murmured. "I would be honored to become your wife, if your parents do not object. But I have no gifts to offer."

"You have everything I need. I have no desire for worldly gifts from my bride, only her pledge to love me as I love her," he whispered. He gathered her into his arms. "Can you give me your love, Qui Jin?"

"Yes," she whispered. "Now and forever."

JUDITH MCCOY MILLER

Judy and her husband make their home in Kansas, although their grown children have begun scattering off to other locales throughout the country. She works for the legal division of the Kansas Insurance Department as a compliance analyst. Judy is ever thankful God has blessed her with the privilege of writing Christian fiction. Her first two books earned her the honor of being selected **Heartsong Presents'** favorite new author in 1997. She has had three more Heartsongs and two Barbour novellas published since.

The Crimson Brocade

by Susan Downs

Dedication

To my mother,
who blessed me with a wonderful Christian heritage
and inspired me to see each day as a new adventure.

Peace I leave with you, my peace I give unto you:
not as the world giveth, give I unto you.
Let not your heart be troubled, neither let it be afraid.
JOHN 14:27

Preface

In the winter of 1937–38, Japan's Imperial Army launched a fierce military campaign for control of China's capital city, Nanking. Historians refer to the resulting civilian atrocities inflicted upon hundreds of thousands of the city's citizens in such graphic terms as The Nanking Massacre or The Rape of Nanking. The days leading up to this time of unspeakable terror may seem an unusual backdrop for an inspirational romance. I chose the locale for this story with fear and trepidation, not wanting to trivialize the true-life horrors of war but rather to heighten awareness of a largely overlooked chapter in history.

Love often blooms amid the most unlikely of conditions. Faith frequently sprouts in life's most adverse circumstances. By setting Shiren and Dewan's story in the weeks preceding one of history's most appalling episodes of man's inhumanities to man, I hope to illustrate as much.

"And we know that all things work together for good to them that love God, to them who are the called according to His purpose" (Romans 8:28).

Susan Downs

Chapter 1

August 1937
A Village along China's Yangtze River

Han Shiren pulled back the faded gray hopsack curtain and allowed her mother to pass ahead of her from their living quarters into the family sewing shop. "But, Mother, Sunday worship services seldom last more than a couple of hours or so, and I will work twice as hard when I return. You have my word."

Shiren stepped over the doorjamb and let the curtain fall. The draft from the curtain carried the oily odor of their fish and tofu breakfast. While her mother, Chang Chinchuan, unlatched the front door and flung open the window shutters, Shiren followed close on her heels, fumbling with the frog closure at the neck of the jade green *qipao*. Her throat chafed against the hot, stiff collar, but the long silk gown comprised the full extent of her wardrobe's proper church attire. The steamy August heat moistened her hands and impeded the most simple task of dressing, even though the sun had yet to reach the treetops on the horizon.

Pleading with her mother so she could attend church had become a course of habit since her father's death a year ago, but today Shiren felt a particular sense of urgency. "When I went to market yesterday, I learned from Aideh that our missionaries may move up the date of their departure for furlough in light of the reports of advancing Imperial Army troops. Please, Mother. This may be my only opportunity to tell them good-bye before they leave—" Shiren pushed her wire-rimmed eyeglasses up the broad bridge of her nose, but they slid back down before she could lower her hand from her face.

"And, Mother, might I respectfully mention—" Shiren bowed so as not to appear too bold. "I worked most of the night. See? I cut out all of the pieces we need to complete the last twelve coats in Uncle's order. We shouldn't have much trouble finishing the job before tomorrow's promised delivery date." She pointed to the neat stacks of quilted fabric pieces beside a treadle sewing machine. Unable to still her fidgeting hands, she pushed her glasses up the bridge of her nose again, then ran her fingers like a comb through her freshly cut, chin-length hair.

Shiren fell quiet in obeisance when her mother paused in front of her prayer table and lit a fresh stick of sandalwood incense. Mother kowtowed and mouthed a rote prayer to the spirits of her ancestors, petitioning them to appease the gods on her behalf. But Shiren stood tall. She meant no disrespect. Quite the contrary, she revered and cherished the memory of her kind and gentle father and honored the venerable ancestors from whose lineage the Han family sprang. Even so, she refused to pray to anyone or anything but the one true God.

Dear Jesus, Shiren silently pleaded while her mother went through her daily religious ritual, *in Your time, please grant me the blessing of marriage to a Christian man who dwells in a Christian home so that I might escape this constant spiritual conflict.*

An unwelcome pang of selfishness washed over Shiren as her thoughts winged heavenward in prayer. She knew if she married and left home, her mother would be alone—devoid of any Christian influence. Still, she feared she wasn't yet to such a point of selflessness that she could accept a life of spinsterhood for her mother's sake. *Lord, I am ready to be made willing,* she conceded. *That is the best I can offer You right now.*

Shiren raised her head to see Mother offer a final, prayerful nod and back away from her altar. Then she turned and, without acknowledging Shiren's earlier request, took her place at the sewing machine. Shiren waited, knowing silence and prayer would be her chief advocates.

Her mother matched the front and back panels of a coat at the seams, pausing just long enough to shoot an impatient look over her shoulder toward Shiren. "What with these rumors of war, the pilot of the junk I hired is charging me nearly double the fare to carry us and our shipment to Nanking tomorrow. We cannot afford to be late and risk missing the boat." Her shoulders rose and fell with a deep sigh. "We have so much work yet to be done before we go. I must say, I am surprised at your asking today. Most certainly, if your grandmother were here, she would put a quick end to your pleadings."

If Grandmother were here, she would be enveloped in an opium cloud, grousing about anything and everything. . .not just my church attendance. At that insolent thought, Shiren bit the inside of her lip to punish herself. Yet, as she did, her mind replayed the weekly Sunday-morning mantra her crotchety grandmother, Long Yifang, would recite whenever Shiren headed out the door to worship services.

"How can you continue to follow after the foreigner's God in light of the catastrophes such worship has brought upon our lives?" Grandmother would waggle her finger in Shiren's face when she spoke. "I would put an immediate stop to your going, had your mother not foolishly vowed to my eldest son on his deathbed that we would not refuse your impudent desire to follow these radical, rebellious teachings." She accented each adjective with a staccato punch of air. "Now I must honor the dying request of my son lest an even greater tragedy befall us."

The very memory of her grandmother's nagging rankled Shiren, like fingernails scraping down the chalkboard at school.

From the time Shiren was a little girl and her grandfather marched off to fight as an officer under Chiang Kai-shek in the Kuomintang forces, her grandmother had lived with them. Last year, nine months after Shiren's father died, Grandmother went to stay in the capital city of Nanking with her only living offspring, second son, Han

Fulei. Neither Shiren nor her mother had ever said as much, but Shiren saw her grandmother's move to Nanking as the only benefit resulting from her father's death. However, before Grandmother left, she had filled Mother's head with such suspicion and fear, Shiren still found it necessary to plead with her for the privilege of going to church.

Mother snapped the presser foot down on the fabric, and the sewing machine's needle bobbed up and down, mimicking the movement of her feet on the treadle. When she reached the end of her seam, she swiveled in her seat to look at Shiren.

"Well, what are you waiting for? Go on!" Her mother's angry tone belied her action as she shooed Shiren toward the door with a free hand. "You know, thanks to the promise I made your father, I cannot refuse you. Run along. But hurry back. The junk sails at six tomorrow morning, and we have plenty of work yet to be done—"

Shiren bobbed her head in a humble show of gratitude as she walked backward through the shop's door. Her bicycle leaned against the crumbling plaster of a once-white wall, but she took one look at the rutted road, still muddy from yesterday's rain, and decided she'd get there faster if she walked.

While she picked her way down the miry lane, Shiren recalled the many Sundays she'd traveled this route with her parents on their way to church. All about her, happy neighbors were leaving their homes and embarking on a weekly family day or, in the case of the village's few Christians, heading off to worship. The bucolic scene made Shiren wish her mother would accompany her to church again soon, but nothing short of a miracle could bring such a hope to pass. If only they could go back to the way things used to be, so many years ago.

Ten years had passed since Shiren's father became a Christian and stripped their home and tailor shop of all things related to ancestral worship or pagan gods. He forbade anyone in his household, his mother included, to practice offering ritual sacrifices to the spirits of their forefathers. Instead, Father insisted such adoration belonged only to the Christian God introduced to him by the American missionaries.

In humble deference to her husband's wishes, Shiren's mother complied. As any dutiful wife would, she attended the mission church along with Kuanghan and Shiren. Chinchuan's heart seemed tender toward the gospel in those days, despite the fact that she never did profess to accept her husband's new religion. Yet, even then Shiren's grandmother refused to accept her son's conversion. Although she dared not argue with the head of the household and her firstborn son, Yifang refused to ever set foot inside their village church. To add fuel to the fire of their quarrels, each time the family prepared to leave the house to attend worship services, she fearfully scolded, "The gods will punish us all for ignoring them and favoring the God of the big-nosed foreigner."

As if assuring her prophecy, Grandmother Yifang sought to make life difficult for her daughter-in-law whenever her son's back was turned. Each time, Shiren wished she could step in between the two women to protect her poor mother; but the dictates of convention forced her, as a young girl with no authority in the family, to stand by helplessly and watch.

After Shiren's father's death, her grandmother badgered and belittled her daughter-in-law for wasting time in churchgoing when she needed her help with the never-ending chores. Chinchuan, who all along had sought only to follow her husband's wishes, finally conceded to the household matriarch and stayed home to work alongside her.

Shiren stood at the corner and looked down the path that led to the place on the Yangtze where the family houseboat of her childhood friend, Dju Aideh, was docked. She'd spent many happy hours as a child playing on board their *sampan* with Aideh; but something, perhaps the same sticky weather, triggered a most unpleasant memory. The recollection of that day still sent shivers bristling down Shiren's spine. She had been playing with Aideh on the deck of this very boat the day her grandmother's piercing screams sent Shiren scurrying back home.

Soon after Shiren's father, Kuanghan, converted to Christianity, word came of his father's battlefield death. When Grandmother Yifang learned the tragic news of her husband's demise, her shrieks rang throughout the village and split the placid river air. Before Shiren even left the river path, she could make out the vindictive words of her grandmother's cries. "My rebellious son's religion has made a widow out of me!"

On that mournful day so many years ago, Shiren caught her first whiff of opium as Grandmother sought solace from her grief in a long-stemmed *hookah*. . .and the old woman had depended on its vaporous comforts ever since. Yifang's bitterness and vocal opposition to her son's religious faith grew louder and stronger with each passing year, and Shiren saw the remaining peaceful remnants of her childhood home erode until it became a place of friction and discord.

In order to avoid her grandmother's tirades, Shiren took to working long hours in the tailor shop after school during her teenage years. Regardless of how hard she worked or how honorific her manners, Shiren also found herself the object of her grandmother's caustic tongue. "My crazy son spoils his worthless girl-child," she would lament.

With no consideration of the fact that Shiren could hear her every word, Yifang grumbled to her son on countless occasions. She insisted Kuanghan's unnatural doting on his daughter would result in a whole new generation of misery. "To raise a daughter like a son is like trying to make a stallion out of an ox," she made a habit of saying. "If Chinchuan can't provide you an heir, you should seek a concubine."

"I am outnumbered by women three to one in my own home already." Shiren's father always responded to his mother with a laugh and summarily dismissed the idea. "Besides, Shiren's mind is sharper than that of any of my friends' sons. I am proud such a daughter bears my name."

Each time Shiren heard her father brag on her, she applied herself to her studies all the more.

Today, from her vantage point at the top of the path, Shiren could see Aideh's mother hanging her wash out to dry across the bowline. They exchanged waves. Undoubtedly, Aideh would have already left for church. She made it a habit of arriving everywhere she went at least five minutes early, while Shiren never showed up anywhere on time. This was just one of the many idiosyncrasies that made their friendship interesting and their years as college roommates challenging.

She and Aideh had shared the honors of being covaledictorians of the 1933 graduating class at their village mission school, and they had both received scholarships to attend the Christian Women's College in Nanking. The scholarships not only provided the two friends with the rare opportunity to become educated women; it also allowed Shiren the chance to escape the pervading tension in her home for nine months out of a year.

Unfortunately, a fresh agony ended her formal education near the end of her junior year and cut short Shiren's reprieve from Grandmother Yifang's harassment. When malaria struck her father during plum season over a year ago, Shiren took an indefinite leave of absence from her studies in order to help her family any way she could, while Aideh finished her education and went on to become the primary teacher at the mission school.

Over the course of Shiren's father's infirmity, Grandmother stayed in the shadows and remained unusually quiet. Shiren spent many long hours at her father's bedside, reading the Scriptures and praying with him while her mother tended to his physical needs. During those moments when Father was strong enough to speak, Shiren gleaned a lifetime of wisdom and advice from him.

Of course, when her dearly loved father and only Christian ally breathed his last breath, Shiren grieved his loss; but she had confidence she would see her father again someday, if she held true to the same faith he had professed. However, her heathen—and hopeless—mother and grandmother reacted to Kuanghan's death with loud wails of anguish and wretched, pitiful moans. His spirit had no sooner left his diseased body than Grandmother's heathen altar and icons resurfaced, along with her zealous adherence to all her former worship customs.

Shiren's grandmother also refused to entertain the idea of allowing Shiren to return to the university run by the American Christians, even after a proper time of mourning. The financial hardship brought on by her father's death was not the only reason she found herself forced to withdraw indefinitely from school to work alongside her mother in the tailor shop.

"See here, what calamity you and your father have brought upon our household by listening to the foolishness of the foreigners." Grandmother had charged as they prepared for the ceremonial cleansing of Father's body. "You can't possibly expect us to support your continued brainwashing by the Americans. Look what's happened to my son! We have already so angered the spirits of our ancestors, we may never regain their favor. A curse covers us, thanks to you—"

With her father no longer there to defend her, the full brunt of the blame for their family's troubles now rested on Shiren's shoulders. No one dared to defile the honor of the deceased by questioning the judgments and decisions he made while on earth. Shiren certainly couldn't count on her mother to stand up for her. Chinchuan had quickly cowered under the dictatorial rule of her mother-in-law. She obediently followed Yifang's lead in returning to the time-honored religious traditions and Confucian customs of their past, lest she further incite the wrath of the family ancestors from the other side of eternity.

So Shiren now stood alone in her faith, and she walked to church by herself.

She hadn't traveled very far down the village's main thoroughfare when a familiar coolie pulled his rickshaw alongside and called out to her. "You're late for church again, Han Shiren. And you'll never get there jumping from one dry patch of ground to the next." He lowered the poles of his carriage, flipped his long queue over his shoulder, and bowed. "Please, climb in and I'll have you there in no time. This ride is on me."

When her father was still alive, he would pay the coolie's small fare to carry them to church by rickshaw each week. Now that Father was gone, Shiren's mother refused to shell out what precious few *yuan* they had for such a frivolous expense. But not even her mother could protest the price of being carried this trip. Shiren offered repeated words of profuse thanks as she scrambled into the rick-shaw, taking care not to rub her muddy shoes on the seat.

When they rounded the corner of the street leading to the mission compound, breathy squeaks and squawks from Mrs. Williams's accordion bellowed from the open church windows and filled the air with the strains of the morning's congregational hymn. Missionary William's off-pitch monotone carried above the soft voices of his Chinese parishioners, and Shiren winced in gleeful distress. *When our missionaries leave, I may not hear such happy music for a very long time. . .if ever again.* Her shoulders rose and fell with a melancholy sigh, but she refused to dwell on the sad prospect.

The coolie pulled up in front of the church as the song ended and Missionary Williams began to speak. From the few words she could make out of his American-accented Mandarin, he seemed to be introducing someone. Shiren yearned to hurry inside, but she lingered just long enough after disembarking from the rickshaw to offer her proper gratitude to the coolie for the free ride.

While the missionary continued with his words of introduction, Shiren eased into a rough-hewn pew toward the back of the "women's side" of the simple sanctuary and lowered her head to offer a customary word of prayer. Breathing an amen and pushing her glasses back into place, she raised her head again to see her friend, Aideh, seated two rows ahead. She had twisted in her seat to look at Shiren, and Aideh's eyes sparkled as if she had a secret she was dying to tell. Shiren exchanged a quiet nod of greeting before pursing her lips into a playful frown. She gave her head a diminutive shake in a lighthearted show of disapproval at her ill-mannered friend. Then, she made a deliberate point of turning toward the pulpit to indicate to Aideh she should turn her attentions to the front as well.

From this particular angle, the pulpit hid the face of the guest speaker from Shiren's view, but she guessed him to be a foreigner by the looks of his Western-style business suit. Missionary Williams seemed to confirm her suspicions with his final words of introduction. "In light of China's present escalating military tensions with Japan, I doubt any of us would have faulted this good man had he chosen to remain in America upon the completion of his theological training. Yet, with a true servant's heart, he hastened to China in order to join in the work of evangelizing the lost and building the church. Please pray for our brother as he assumes my duties during our family's time of furlough, and open your hearts for the spiritual wisdom he shares with us this morning. Reverend Shin, won't you come?"

At the mention of the man's family name, Shiren jerked to attention. She squinted to get a clearer view of the towering man who rose from his seat. Dragging a stiff left leg behind him, he crossed the platform toward the pulpit.

Perspiration moistened Shiren's palms. She'd been mistaken. The special speaker was not an American. He was Chinese and she knew him. Even from this distance, and notwithstanding her poor vision, she immediately recognized Shin Dewan's distinct Asian features and halting gait. After four years of study in America, her betrothed had returned.

Chapter 2

Dewan stepped behind the pulpit, opened his Bible to his chosen text, and smoothed the creases from his sermon notes. Then he gripped the sides of the pulpit with both hands and took a deep breath.

He'd preached often to the congregation at the Northern California Chinese Christian Fellowship where he had served as an intern and associate pastor throughout his years of seminary. From personal experience, he knew a queasy stomach and shaking knees should be expected when a preacher entered a strange pulpit for the first time; but such knowledge did little to relieve his present nervousness—perhaps because his jitters stemmed from more than the preaching.

"Before I begin, won't you please join me in prayer?" He threw a cursory glance toward the parishioners, then he bowed his head and closed his eyes.

"Our Father in heaven, I pray as did the psalmist, 'Let the words of my mouth, and the meditation of my heart, be acceptable in Thy sight, O Lord, my strength, and my redeemer.'" Dewan's audible prayer bore a distinct formal tone. Yet, as he quoted the familiar Scripture, his heart's silent, heaven-bound supplication took on a far more urgent quality. *Dear Jesus, You've got to help me! Keep me focused right now on worship and the proclamation of Your Word rather than on what may follow afterwards.* He closed his prayer with a loud amen and took another gulp of air. When he finally raised his head, he determined not to look any farther than the first few pews occupied by the elderly.

Missionary Williams assured him before the service that Han Shiren would almost certainly be there. He said she rarely missed worship—in spite of her mother's protests, so Dewan had searched for her when they stood to sing the hymns.

He hadn't really expected to recognize Shiren. He'd not seen his betrothed for four years, and she'd no doubt blossomed into a full-grown woman since then. However, his careful scan of the sixty or so congregants revealed only one qualifying candidate within Shiren's age range.

A thick-waisted, moon-faced girl looked straight at him in a way most brazen and ill-mannered for one raised in the Confucian traditions of showing elders utmost honor and respect. Her simpering grin revealed a mouthful of decayed teeth. Perhaps she had been told of their betrothal as well, and that was why she greeted him in such a casual fashion. Even so, Dewan's heart sank. He had hoped to see the same shy, sparkling smile he remembered from his last trip to the village, just before he set sail for America.

Since Dewan's teenage years, he'd known of his parents' prearranged commitment to join him in marriage to the daughter of a business associate and fellow Christian friend, although Dewan had been told neither the girl's family nor her given names. Under normal circumstances, he wouldn't have learned the identity of his betrothed until both sets of parents met to officially seal the engagement in a final session with an intermediary or matchmaker. However, in light of his impending lengthy absence, his father thought he ought to know what prospective joys awaited him when he returned home.

On that long-ago day, Dewan first learned the details of his future union with Han Shiren as he and his father made their way down from Nanking to deliver a textile order to the Han family's tailor shop. While his father and Han Kuanghan conducted their official business, Dewan, armed with the secret knowledge of his betrothal, studied Shiren with a bolder scrutiny than he normally would have dared. He remembered thinking how sweet and pretty she appeared as she quietly went about her task of serving them tea and rice dumplings. If truth be told, his memory of the fair Shiren and the promise of their marriage played a major part in his recent decision to return home to war-torn China.

Regardless of Shiren's outward appearance, Dewan remained honor-bound to fulfill the promise his father had made. He was ready to take her as his wife.

Had he cared nothing about his parents saving face, he could have accepted the offer to stay on as a fulltime associate pastor at NCCCF and followed the American custom of choosing a mate on his own. Despite the clash of cultures he faced after living abroad these past four years, the ingrained customs of his youth would not allow him to consider such a disgraceful act. Besides, he trusted his parent's judgment in such matters much more than he trusted his own.

This morning, as he had discussed the day's tentative plans with Reverend Williams, Dewan found his resolve to follow through with his marriage to Shiren further bolstered when the missionary vouched for Shiren's deep faith and serving spirit. "Shiren would make a wonderful wife for any clergyman," the missionary said with firm assurance.

Now only one overriding worry about his intended bride continued to nag Dewan. Even though the family elders had all agreed to this union a decade ago, he wondered if, in light of Shiren's Christian father's death, the Han family would still honor their commitment to offer Shiren in marriage to a crippled minister. The next few hours would reveal the truth. His only recourse was to wait. He needed to get through this sermon first.

Dewan forced his focus back on his page of notes, and with one last silent plea for divine guidance, he began. "Dear friends, in times like these, we have a mighty Ally." He looked out over the congregation, training his eyes on the men's side of the sanctuary as he spoke. "That Ally is none other than the Lord Jesus Christ. Let me read to you from the New Testament book of Hebrews—"

While he launched into his well-rehearsed sermon, his gaze drifted to the back door. He tried to keep from looking toward the moon-faced young lady he'd decided must be Shiren, but the shimmer of jade green silk drew his attention to the pew two rows behind her. A young woman sat with her head buried in her Bible. Her shiny black hair fell forward like a shroud to conceal her features.

He hadn't noticed her earlier. She must have slipped in after the singing.

Once again, Dewan shifted his thoughts back to his preaching. Yet he couldn't keep from snatching quick glimpses of the lady in the green silk gown. Fearing disappointment, he hated to hold out any hope for the possibility that this woman, rather than the moon-faced one two rows ahead of her, might be Han Shiren. If only she would raise her head, he felt certain he could confirm or deny his wishful thinking. He wanted desperately to see her face. With his every glance, he tried to will her to glance his way—but she never stirred.

At an alarming speed, Dewan reached his sermon's third and final point. He still hadn't managed to get a good look at the mysterious woman. He'd given up on her raising her head. The truth would be disclosed in a matter of minutes anyway, when Missionary Williams pulled the real Shiren aside.

In his last official act before he left on furlough, the missionary had agreed to serve as the Shin family's intermediary. After the worship service, he planned to ask Shiren to deliver a note to her mother which contained the Shin family's request to meet this week with the honored elders of the Han clan. A special gift wrapped in bright red paper would accompany the note as a token of their good faith.

"In conclusion, my dear brothers and sisters," Dewan said, pulling a white handkerchief from his back pocket and mopping the sweat from his brow. "I want you to know that even in such dire times as these, I count it a great honor and privilege to minister among you during the absence of your beloved missionary family. I covenant to do my best to serve as an instrument of His peace, with the grace and help of our Lord. Now, won't you stand as Sister Williams plays our hymn of benediction?"

He backed away from the pulpit and bowed deeply, tucking his Bible under his arm. To the accordion accompaniment of "O God Our Help in Ages Past," Dewan followed Missionary Williams down the center aisle. When he reached the pew where the moon-faced woman sat, she nodded a greeting and gave him another black-toothed grin. The only movement made by the bowed head of the lady dressed in green silk came when she parted her hair just far enough away from her face to push her glasses into their proper position on her nose.

Dewan made his way to the back door with the missionary to greet the exiting parishioners as they filed past. He took care to position himself at such an angle so as to observe both young women when they turned to leave, but the one in the green silk dress seemed bent on frustrating him. She remained facing forward while her moon-faced peer came alongside her and chittered into her ear behind a cupped hand.

A gaggle of stoop-shouldered grandmothers circled around Dewan, pulling him out of the doorway and into the summer sun. By the way they patted his cheeks as though he were a toddler, Dewan knew he'd have his work cut out for him if he hoped to be treated with much respect in the missionary's absence. The dear old saints rubbed their callused fingers along the crisp seams of his American-made suit, and Dewan laughed aloud when someone asked if all the Chinese in America were as wealthy as he. This question served as a springboard for a host of rapid-fire questions, and the venerable women badgered him until he regaled them with several tales about his life in the United States.

By the time Dewan managed to send the last of the elderly women on their way, he stepped back into the church to find the sanctuary empty. There was no sign of either of the two young ladies or the missionary and his wife.

He wondered if someone had decided to play a cruel joke on him. His sliding footfall sounded through the empty hall when he made his way back to the platform. His anxiety rose with each step.

Even though he'd convinced himself that he'd be happy with whichever woman turned out to be Shiren, in his heart of hearts, he hoped to learn the woman dressed in jade silk would be his promised bride. He had no need to see her face to understand she possessed a certain gentle gracefulness and diminutive charm.

He only knew of one way to wrestle his selfish desires back into submission. He knelt at the step in front of the pulpit. Setting his Bible down, he closed his eyes and turned his thoughts to prayers.

"I promise you shall know the answer before you depart today for Nanking." An angelic voice floated over the quiet and brought an abrupt end to Dewan's prayer.

His eyes flew open.

"We may leave as early as three o'clock this afternoon." The missionary's familiar, deep bass timbre dispelled Dewan's momentary notion that he'd heard from a heavenly messenger. From their increasing volume, he judged them to be nearing the end of the hallway leading into the sanctuary from the missionary's study. He scrambled to his feet and sat on the front pew. He feared appearing weak and anxious to Shiren should she catch him on his knees, and he wanted to make a strong impression on his future wife.

"Now, Papa, don't rush the girl," Mrs. Williams interjected in English as she stood in the doorway. "We're not in such an all-fired hurry to leave that we can't wait an extra hour or two." She paused and turned back toward the hallway, shifting her speech with ease back into Mandarin. "Shiren, Honey, if your mama can't send her response to our note by then, the three of us will just wait until sunrise tomorrow to travel up the Yangtze."

Shiren's voice drifted from the dark, windowless hall. "I will deliver your note and package to my mother as fast as I can make it home. Of course, without knowing the nature of your business, I cannot say for sure what her response will be. If, as you say, she must give no more than a brief answer to your inquiry, I think I should be able to deliver her reply within the hour. I am just so sorry—" A small sob broke her words, and she paused to regain control of her faltering emotions. "I am just so sorry you have to leave China earlier than any of us anticipated."

Dewan decided, then and there, he no longer cared which of the two women Shiren turned out to be. Anyone with such an exquisitely sweet and tender voice must possess an angel's heart to match.

Her speech wavered again and soft sniffles accompanied her speech. "I feel certain I could not have made it this past year without your help." She cleared her throat and seemed to speak with renewed resolve. "I am more than happy to do whatever you ask if, by being of assistance to you, I can in some small way repay your many kindnesses to me."

Dewan found himself in the awkward position of being an eavesdropper as he listened to Shiren's tender discourse, but he saw no graceful way to escape. At this point, he thought it best to make his presence known. He rose from his seat, making as much of a commotion as he could.

"Oh, there you are, Reverend Shin." Mrs. Williams reverted back to English as she addressed Dewan. She held her hand high in the air and fanned her fingers to indicate for him to come. "I promised our young school teacher, Miss Dju Aideh, I would extend her greetings and welcome you to the mission on her behalf. She wanted so very much to meet you, but she had pressing matters to tend to back on their family's *sampan* at home so she had to leave. However—" Dewan alone could see the exaggerated wink she gave before she reached into the shadows of the hall and urged Shiren into the light. "There is someone else here I want you to meet."

Dewan heard no more of Mrs. Williams's words of introduction. His rapid pulse pounded in his ears, rendering him all but deaf, as his full attention riveted to the vision in a jade green *qipao* standing right in front of him.

"Zao chen hao, Han Shiren. Ni hao ma?"

Shiren raised her head for a splinter of a second and allowed him a glimpse into her sparkling eyes. He found their stunning beauty further magnified by her wire-rimmed spectacles and the dark hue of her gown. Her ebony hair contrasted the pale softness of her skin in a most becoming way. Over the course of time since they'd last met, the childish features of her face and form had blossomed to full and splendid maturity.

"I am well; thank you, Shin Dewan," Shiren answered, lowering her gaze and tucking her head in strict adherence to traditional Chinese etiquette for the rare occasion when a young woman met a man.

The thought of this demure woman possibly becoming his bride before week's end made Dewan's heart pound even harder in his chest.

With her chin resting on her bodice, she said, "Please allow me to welcome you back to China. I pray the Lord shall grant you many days among us, filled with peace and happiness."

Shiren edged away with her head still down. She pinched a strand of her raven hair between her thumb and finger and rolled it back and forth as she spoke. "Excuse my rudeness, but I must beg your leave. I have promised to run an errand for our honorable missionaries, which they say is a matter of some urgency." With one arm, she clutched to her chest the wrapped parcel sent by his parents as a harbinger of the large wedding dowry they were prepared to give, should Shiren's mother agree to honor the marriage covenant made a decade ago. Dewan wondered if she realized the significance of the item she grasped or if she knew from whom the package came.

Bowing her good-byes, Shiren backed a respectable distance, then spun on her heel and hurried out of the church.

Chapter 3

Shiren ran as fast as she could down the muddy road, but her long skirt tangled around her legs, impeding her progress. The humid heat sapped her energies. By the time she reached the open-air market in the village center, she had to stop and catch her breath. She leaned against a stall displaying an extensive selection of pig heads and other porcine parts. The merchant didn't even bother to look up from the game of *mah-jongg* he played with the proprietor of the next booth.

Her hands full, Shiren used her arm to swipe at her perspiring brow and push her glasses back into their proper place. As she did, she squeezed the thick, soft, twine-tied parcel wrapped in red paper tighter to her chest. She deduced, with a fair degree of certainty, the package contained a fabric of some kind. With an almost equal measure of assurance, she believed she knew the meaning behind the mission with which she'd been charged. A shudder of sheer giddiness ran through her, and she buried her head in the package to stifle her laughter.

The day her father foretold more than a year ago had finally come to pass.

In a rare, lucid moment, when her malaria-stricken father lay on what would become his deathbed, he motioned for Shiren to come close. He said he had a secret he wanted to share.

"I hope the knowledge of this future happiness might ease your coming grief," Father whispered, burrowing deeper into his quilt to stave off another chill. When his shivering stopped, he lifted his chin over the covers and continued his discourse. "Your grandmother would never let me rest in peace if she were to learn I'd made you privy to these plans, but I believe that in my telling and in your keeping of this confidence, we share a special bond."

He paused long enough for Shiren to dampen his parched lips with a bud of water-soaked gauze.

"When you were but a child of nine, I promised you in marriage to an ideal mate. . .the son of a weaver whom I've done business with for years."

With gentle strokes, Shiren smoothed her father's salt-and-pepper hair away from his fevered face. He thanked her with his weak smile. "Your betrothed's family possesses a goodly sum of earthly wealth. They'll provide well for you. More importantly, they follow the same God you and I profess—"

Shiren watched, powerless to help, when another tremor swept over her father's body with such force, his teeth began to chatter violently. At last, his shaking ceased, but the lengthy discourse had taxed him to the point that his whispers came slow and barely audible. In order to catch his words, Shiren leaned in so close, her father's lips brushed her ear. His sentences came in punched phrases, divided by labored gasps.

"Your intended is five years your elder. . .a learned man. . .studies in America to become a minister. . .but his father assures me. . .upon completion of his schooling. . . his son will return and take you as his wife."

At her father's mention of America, the image of a certain scholar from Nanking popped into Shiren's head. Her hands began to tremble in anticipation of the name her father would soon divulge.

"I doubt you would remember. . .but on occasion he used to come here with his father. . .from Nanking. . .to deliver shipments of silk. . . ."

Shiren tried to maintain a befitting air of aloof composure, but she found it impossible to keep a smile from tugging at the corners of her lips. If he gave her opportunity, she could finish her father's pronouncement and spare his waning strength. Yet, even in his grave condition, he seemed to find some small delight in building the suspense of his declaration to a climactic end.

"His family name is Shin. . .son of Jihong, the one who first told me about the Christ. . . The boy walks like a cripple. . . But his body is strong. . . He bears the name Dewan. . . Means virtuous and amiable. . . Name fits him well. . . He'll make you happy, Shiren. I'm most sure of it." Father raised an arm as though to reach out for her, but the movement required more energy than he possessed. His head sank into his pillow and his eyes closed.

Father lay silent for such a long time, Shiren thought he must be sleeping, but when she moved to leave, he stayed her with a lifted hand. His voice seemed empowered by the brief rest.

"Do not let the sorrow of my passing overwhelm your soul. Let today remind you of my deep love and my pride in you." He reached up and caressed Shiren's cheek with the back of his quivering hand. She stared long into his eyes, soaking in the significance of his words. "When you see these things come to pass, find comfort in this knowledge. . ." His eyes misted, and Shiren had to look away to stay the sob that threatened to break loose. "Even though your earthly father may not escort you to your bridal sedan, your heavenly father continues to watch after you. He will accompany you on that happy day."

Spurred on by her precious memories and the imminent expectancy of her father's words coming true, Shiren ran the rest of the way home.

She no sooner opened the shop door than her mother rose from her place at the sewing machine and took a step toward Shiren with her hands on her hips. "You insolent child! What took you so long? You knew full well the amount of work we have yet to do. I suppose you hoped I'd finish it all myself while you lazed around at the mission with your foreigner friends. I have half a mind to refuse you permission to go there again. . .no matter what promises I made to your father. Such impudence!"

"My honorable mother, I humbly apologize and beg your forgiveness." Shiren lowered her head in submission, and with both arms outstretched, she extended the package she'd been charged to deliver. "Yet I must implore you. Please grant me opportunity to explain my tardiness." Chinchuan took the parcel from Shiren, and the corners of her eyes crinkled in curiosity as she examined the bright wrapping.

"The missionaries detained me and asked that I deliver this message to you." Shiren tapped the sealed envelope attached to the gift. "They are waiting for my return with your reply before they travel to Nanking. They plan to leave from there for America on the next ocean liner."

Chinchuan laid the package on the sewing machine table and plucked the envelope from off the top. She turned it over and back, intently studying the characters which comprised her name. Then she broke the envelope's seal and withdrew a one-page letter. Her expression screwed into a look of bewilderment. Shiren, her eyes downcast in a show of deference, still managed to catch quick glimpses of her mother as she studied the document.

Finally, she shrugged her shoulders and shoved the letter toward Shiren. "You're going to have to read it to me. I can't make any sense of this. Your foreigner friend's Chinese characters look like nothing more than chicken scratches to me."

Shiren accepted the outstretched note. After a hurried scan, she guessed the writing to be that of a well-schooled native Chinese scholar. . .perhaps Dewan himself—even though the red-inked chop imprint bore the Chinese version of Reverend Williams's name. The impeccable calligraphy appeared perfectly legible to her. Shiren knew her mother's difficulty in reading the letter did not lie in its poor penmanship but rather in her lack of a formal education and inability to read anything other than the simplest words. To allow her mother to save face, Shiren dared not make an issue of her criticism or try to contradict her. Rather, Shiren simply began to read aloud.

" 'To Chang Chinchuan, Most Honorable and Noble Wife of the Late, Venerable Han Kuanghan.' " Out of the corner of her eye, Shiren saw her mother nodding her head in approval at the flowery salutation.

" 'I, Randolph J. Williams, as a duly authorized representative and intermediary, am writing on behalf of the humble textile merchant, Shin Jihong and his wife, Wu Yiching. The Shin family wishes to respectfully present the accompanying gift as a meager expression of their good faith, and they most kindly request your gracious consideration of the following petition.' "

Shiren paused in her reading and looked first at the package, then out the open window. She thought she ought to tell her mother about Dewan's return, but she knew her eyes would expose her excitement, so she diverted her gaze. She feigned particular interest in a barking mongrel across the road, which tormented the neighbor's tethered rooster.

"Speaking of the Shins," said Shiren, trying to restrain the enthusiastic lilt in her voice. "Their son Dewan preached the sermon in our worship service this morning. He's completed his studies in America and plans to take over the missionaries' duties during their year of furlough." Shiren turned back to her reading without even taking a breath, allowing no time for her mother to process or respond to this news.

" 'The pervading climate of military conflict precipitates this writer's imminent departure from China. However, as the intermediary hitherto agreed upon by both family patriarchs, there is a matter of some urgency which, if possible, must be resolved before I leave.' " Even Shiren stumbled on the formal wording of the letter, and she read in halting fits and starts. She found little wonder in the fact that her mother couldn't decipher the meaning of these characters.

Shiren hesitated and shot a darting glance at her mother. All color had drained from Chinchuan's face. She teetered on wobbly legs like a dowager on tiny bound feet, but before Shiren could express her concern, her mother waved her hand in a circular motion to indicate Shiren should continue.

" 'T–therefore,' " she stammered and cast another worried look toward her mother, " 'in light of reports that the honorable widow and daughter of Han Kuanghan shall travel to the capital city in regards to business on Monday morning, August 13, 1937, the Shin family seeks a meeting to discuss a matter of mutual concern with the Han family elders. If such plans seem agreeable, and you feel so inclined in these anxious days of war, our meeting may convene on this same day, during the hour of afternoon tea, at our Nanking mission compound. Just prior to the appointed hour, an escort shall be sent to collect you and provide safe passage.' " With one hand, Shiren pushed her glasses back into place. With the other, she lifted the letter in the air and brought it back down. "That's the extent of it. He ends the letter by writing, 'I eagerly await your response before we set out for Nanking this afternoon on the Yangtze.' Then he signs it, 'Your humble servant, Reverend Randolph J. Williams.'"

The color had not yet returned to Chinchuan's washed-out complexion when she eased herself into the chair and scooped the red package into her lap. Mystified by her mother's reaction to the letter, Shiren watched her pick at the twine that crisscrossed the parcel. She had to be aware of the impetus behind the meeting request, even though no mention of wedding plans appeared in the note. Shiren thought her mother would have been at least a little happy at this portent of seemingly good news. Instead, a crackling tension flashed between the mother and daughter while Shiren waited for her to offer a response.

For a fleeting moment, Shiren wondered if she should tell her mother all she knew, but she forced herself to swallow the words of confession that threatened to spill from her lips. Since the letter did not divulge any specific details, Shiren still remained honor-bound to keep silent about her father's forecast of her marriage to Dewan until such time as her mother saw fit to reveal the arrangement to her. At last, the older woman raised her head, but her continued fidgeting with the parcel added to Shiren's mounting nervousness.

"If you'll pen my response, I'll send a coolie to deliver it." Mother spoke with such softness, Shiren had to lean forward to catch her words.

"I can't spare you any longer today. I've no business with your missionary, and the only matter I need to discuss with Shin Jihong and his wife concerns a new order of silk." Like a child caught in a lie, she quickly dropped her gaze away from Shiren's perplexed stare. "Even so, for the sake of propriety, I'll agree to meet with them, if only to return the gift in person." She snapped the twine against the wrapping. "There's no sense in my opening this. I must return it anyway."

"B—b—but. . ." Shiren couldn't stay the stammer of protest. However, the simple word had no sooner left her lips than she wished she could retract it. Her mother's eyes narrowed, and she studied Shiren with a disconcerting intensity. Another lengthy span of silence ensued. The heat of the tense moment added to the already unbearable August humidity, and Shiren could feel her glasses slipping down on her perspiring nose, but she dared not move to push them back into place.

"Your father told you, did he not?"

Shiren suspected her face betrayed her guilt of prior knowledge even before she admitted as much with a slight dip of her head. The movement nearly sent her slipping eyeglasses to the floor, and she had to poke them back into place. When she dared to look up once more, she saw her mother's stern expression had softened.

"For your sake, I wish he had not done so." Mother drew a deep breath, then slowly exhaled. "I have dreaded this day for months and hoped against hope Dewan would choose to stay in America so long his family would be forced to be the ones to break our contract. The marriage arrangements we discussed with the Shins happened a very long time ago. So much has changed since your father left this world. I cannot possibly give my consent for you to marry anyone right now. . .let alone Shin Dewan."

"I–I do not understand." In spite of her best efforts to maintain control, Shiren's voice cracked with emotion and she had to clear her throat. "Father spoke as if everything was settled. I needed only to wait for Dewan's return."

"Child, listen—" Her mother left the package in her seat and came alongside her, then with an unfamiliar gentleness, she began to stroke Shiren's hair. "I know you are well into your marriageable years. Perhaps in another year or so, if these current uncertainties are resolved, maybe then we can see to arranging an appropriate marriage partner for you. What with the threat of approaching war and all, we face such turmoil in our lives. This just is not the right time." Her hand rested on her daughter's arm, and though she looked in Shiren's direction, she seemed intent on avoiding her gaze.

"Besides, your grandmother disapproves of you marrying into the Shin family. No matter how much we dislike the idea, with your father gone, Grandmother Yifang's opinion must be considered in such important matters. She claims the Shins are even more fanatical about the foreigners' religion than your father ever was. She also couldn't understand why we would promise you to a crippled boy when there are so many other strong and healthy matches we could make, such as the son of Chen Liwu."

At her mother's mention of the short and chunky son of the village cobbler, Shiren tasted a nauseating surge of bile. She determined she would run away before allowing herself to be matched to such a nasty, lewd man. In fact, she wanted to run away right now, rather than be forced to listen as her mother laid waste to all her future dreams.

Only fervent prayer quelled her rancor toward her grandmother's unwelcome interference regarding her future mate.

Only fervent prayer stayed her while her mother continued to add to her list of reasons why Shiren could not marry Dewan.

"Even if I chose to ignore your grandmother's advice and agreed to your marriage to Dewan, I no longer have sufficient resources to match the dowry demands of a bride worthy of the Shins." Chinchuan rubbed her palm up and down on her forehead like she always did when she felt a migraine headache coming on. "Your uncle barely provides us with enough money to subsist, and the only extra we have comes from the odd tailoring jobs that come to us off the street. Even in the best of times, if you were to marry and leave me to join another family, on my own I would be hard-pressed to produce the quantity of garments your uncle requires to stock his store in Nanking. I could not possibly do all this work alone." She waved her hand over the stacks of finished coats waiting to be tied in bundles for the trip to Nanking. "Would you see your mother starve?"

Shiren didn't trust herself to speak, so she shook her head slowly from side to side. She stared at the package her mother had left on the chair. Its contents would forever remain a mystery, its hidden treasure returned to be offered to another. No matter how compliant she appeared on the outside, her heart screamed, *Unfair!*

She knew a good Christian ought always to place the needs of others above one's own selfish desires, and she really did want to aid and comfort her mother; but down deep in her soul, Shiren balked at her mother's demand that she sacrifice her own happiness. Almost every girl she knew was either already married or betrothed. All but Aideh. A panicked thought raced through Shiren's mind. Perhaps if she weren't allowed to marry him, Dewan's parents would pick Aideh for his bride. The thought of seeing her best friend married to the man to whom she'd been pledged was almost more than she could bear.

She'd heard enough. A swell of bitterness toward her mother swept over Shiren, and she struggled to stay her stinging tears. Still, Mother continued her catalogue of reasons why she couldn't marry Dewan.

"Our neighbor came by while you were gone to church to report that the Imperial forces invaded Shanghai the day before yesterday. If the Japanese troops reach Nanking as they're threatening to do, your uncle may well decide to flee the capital city and return with his mother here to their family home. Should that happen, with both you and your father gone, they might very well decide simply to turn me out, since I'm no blood relation. . ."

Her mother fell silent so abruptly, Shiren set aside her own simmering emotions long enough to look at her. Never, not even when her father died, had Shiren seen her mother cry, but there was no mistaking the glistening evidence of tears welling in her eyes. In a gesture of comfort, Shiren laid a hand on her mother's arm.

"Even if they allowed me to stay, I would be treated

no better than a slave, tending to the needs and whims of your grandmother and her coddled son. When I had your father and you, I was able to bear the torments of my mother-in-law. If you were to marry and leave me alone, I do not believe I could bear her cruelty—"

All remaining fragments of Mother's reserve crumbled. She covered her face with her hands and began to sob. Shiren embraced her mother, and they wept on each other's shoulders until all their emotions were spent. When Mother pulled away and wiped her eyes on the broad hem of her shirt sleeve, the animosity Shiren had felt only minutes before had evaporated, and in its place sprang genuine concern. In that moment, Shiren saw her mother in a different light than she ever had before. They were kindred spirits who shared a common bond of vulnerability. Her mother needed her. A flood of compassion washed over Shiren and swept away her mounting bitterness and anger.

"Don't worry, Mother. I will honor your wishes and stay with you as long as you have need of me. I trust my God enough to work out His perfect plan for my life in accordance with what is also best for you. When. . .or if. . . I am to marry, the timing will be right for both of us."

Chapter 4

Long before their ferry pulled into Hsiakwan port late Sunday evening, Dewan knew something was amiss. Heavy traffic on the river stretched the usual journey of three hours into five, and although the Yangtze teemed with watercraft, their own junk appeared to be among a select few traveling toward Nanking.

When they docked at Chung Shang Mato wharf, Dewan stopped a roustabout and asked him to explain the reason for this frenzied exodus, while the missionaries hurried to the street corner to hail a rickshaw. As soon as Dewan gathered what details he could, he pushed his way through the crowd to join up with the Williamses.

The missionaries had already settled into a carriage and piled their luggage at their feet. Dewan hoisted himself into the rickshaw next to the Reverend Williams, but just as the coolie moved to maneuver his way into the mainstream of traffic, Dewan ordered him to wait.

"I think you should hear the news before we leave the wharf. You may want to revise your plan of going to the mission compound." Dewan spoke in English so the missionaries could clearly understand his report. "From what I could gather, the moment we've all feared has come to pass."

Mrs. Williams poised herself for the worst by gripping her husband's hand and covering her lips with her fingertips.

"This afternoon at two o'clock, the Japanese launched their first bombing raid on Nanking," Dewan said. "They attacked again at five."

The implications of his own words hit him full force. For a fleeting moment, fear overwhelmed him and left him powerless to speak. Only after pausing to pray was he able to wrestle his fright into submission and find his voice. "Many people on the streets didn't know to seek shelter. They were killed when heavy machine-gun fire rained down on them from the planes."

Dewan wanted to race to his parents' home and confirm with his own eyes that they were unharmed, but he viewed the safety and well-being of the missionaries as his first responsibility. "Do you think your ship's departure date has been changed? Should we try to get you on a vessel headed for a safer harbor tonight?"

"No, no." Missionary Williams gave a resolute shake of his head before Dewan finished his inquiry. "The civilian casualties are most regrettable, but I suspect the Japanese are just saberrattling at this point. With the battle raging in Shanghai, they aren't likely to deplete their forces right now by sending ground troops here to the capital. Judging from the large number of our Nationalist soldiers I've seen since we landed, I'd say the chances of the city falling into enemy hands this week are slim." The missionary motioned for the coolie to proceed down the dark street toward the inner-city mission compound. "Before we jump to any conclusions, we need to discuss the situation with the Nanking mission director. He will counsel us as to the best course of action."

In a blatant attempt to bring a bit of levity to the tense mood, the missionary playfully jabbed his elbow at Dewan's ribs. "Besides, Son, I have some important business to finish prior to my leaving town. Knowing what I do of Shiren's mother, she and Shiren will be arriving tomorrow morning, according to plan. She lives in fear of those in-laws of hers, so if they're expecting her to make a delivery for their store, you can bet the farm she'll be here."

Dewan winced at the missionary's mention of Shiren and her mother. After seeing the lovely woman his future bride had become, he wanted more than ever to speed up their wedding plans. Yet he wrestled to reconcile his desire to take her for his wife with the need to follow every precaution to insure the safety of all those involved.

As the pandemonium of war unfolded before his eyes, tomorrow's meeting seemed rather foolhardy. If he had any way of sending word back to the village, he would tell Shiren and her mother to stay home, but he was powerless to stop them at this late hour. He didn't want to be the least bit responsible for placing Shiren or her mother in harm's way. Likewise, though he wanted Missionary Williams to preside over the prenuptial agreements and—if things worked out as he hoped—to officiate over the wedding, Dewan questioned the wisdom of detaining the missionaries in China for a single day.

The circumstance was totally out of his control. Dewan knew, as difficult as he found it to do at times, he had to leave the matter entirely in the Lord's hands and trust Him to watch over them all.

❈

The next afternoon, Dewan pounded his fist on the steering wheel when the flow of traffic came to yet another standstill. For the past half hour, he had marked his progress in inches rather than miles, and his frustration had simmered in this oppressive heat until his ordinarily long-suffering temper finally reached its boiling point. The distinction Nanking shared with Hankow and Chungking as being one of China's "three ovens" most aptly applied today. Although he'd shed his suit coat and loosened his shirt collar before leaving the mission compound, the effort provided him little relief. Added to the skin-prickling discomfort of the heat, his bum leg throbbed from the strain of working the clutch.

He hated driving—especially someone else's car. However, none of the mission's hired hands were available to escort Shiren's mother to her meeting with his parents and the missionary.

Dewan had planned to see his parents safely to the mission compound, then wander the grounds in search of a secluded place to have his daily quiet time; but when he and his parents had arrived, they found the facility in turmoil. An official statement had just been received from the American embassy which called for all American women and children to report there this evening for evacuation to either Kuling or Hankow. Only those who had responsibilities or difficulty leaving town would be permitted to remain. Since Sister Williams was already scheduled to board an ocean-bound freighter with her husband on Wednesday, she would be allowed to stay behind until then. All the other women of their mission were hurriedly packing and had pressed into service all available hired hands to assist with their preparations to leave. The best the Nanking mission director could offer was the use of his car, so Dewan reluctantly volunteered to be the one to escort Chinchuan.

After going to all this effort, he may very well arrive at Shiren's uncle's place to find that, for whatever reason, Shiren and her mother weren't there. Without going in person, he had no other way of confirming whether or not they had arrived in town. Shiren's uncle, Han Fulei, didn't own a telephone, and no messengers could be found today—no matter the price one was willing to pay.

Dewan massaged his thigh, just above his right knee, at the place where he'd fractured it as a kid. The bad break and a doctor's bungled job of setting the bone had left Dewan with a pronounced limp and unrelenting pain. He opened the car door, stepped onto the running board, and stretched to his full height. Then he dangled his sore leg over the side in an attempt to work out some of the stiffness. While he performed the simple exercise, he craned his neck to see up the street.

Judging by this gridlock, half of Nanking's populace had decided to start their frantic exodus to safety at the same time. The crush of evacuees clogged Chungsan Road as far as Dewan could see. Pedestrians, the sum of their worldly goods balanced on bamboo poles, darted in and out among an assortment of trucks, rickshaws, cars, bicycles, and *mashaws*—or horse-drawn carriages.

From this point, he needed to travel only a few more blocks; but at this stop-and-go pace, he would arrive long beyond fashionably late. *I might as well relax,* he told himself. *There's no way I can pick up Shiren's mother on time.*

Dewan lowered himself back into the driver's seat and closed the car door. Then he propped his elbow against the open window and nested his chin in his cupped palm. Rather than focusing on the tense street scene in front of him, he looked to his left and studied the serene landscape of nearby Purple Mountain. He couldn't help noticing even the lazy clouds moved past the bluffs at a faster clip than he was able to travel by car.

As he waited for the traffic to move, his thoughts drifted back to the events of yesterday afternoon. He had no real reason to suspect anything other than a busy schedule had kept Shiren from personally delivering her mother's response regarding today's meeting. Yet a hundred questions and a thousand worries assailed him because she failed to return as she said she would. What if her mother made her privy to the contents of the note and Shiren flatly refused to consider him for a spouse? Had they opened the package his parents sent and found it lacking somehow?

Dewan hoped he would have the chance to catch another glimpse of Shiren when he picked up her mother today. He felt sure he could dispel the worst of his concerns with just one glimpse of Shiren's expressive face. The very memory of her grace and ethereal beauty made his heart pound.

"*Shegoan*—out of my way," barked the driver of a wagon that had wedged in between him and a truck to create a third lane on the two-lane street. The command jolted Dewan out of his reverie, and he looked ahead to see a slight break in the traffic.

He inched his automobile forward, steering around a pack-burdened young lad who led a blind grandmother along the side of the road. Although the airspace over Nanking had remained quiet thus far today, fear lined the faces of both the boy and the old woman.

Dewan had to admit, no matter how hard he prayed and reminded himself of Jesus' words, "Fear not," he, too, felt downright scared. He'd grown up hearing talk of warlords and battle, but never had the fighting come so close to home. He wondered if he would have signed up for his new assignment so quickly if he had been fully aware of the serious threat the Japanese army posed. He'd felt so certain back in San Francisco that his return to China was what God wanted him to do. Now he worried his conviction stemmed more from a selfish desire to wed than a divine commission to serve and minister back in his motherland. He would not turn back from his commitment to the church, yet he couldn't help but question if this was the time to be marrying. In light of the present circumstance, he wasn't at all sure he ought to be taking a wife and assuming responsibility for another's life.

A disturbing whistle began as a soft, deep whir and

rose to an earsplitting crescendo, rupturing through the clamor of the street. From behind him, a woman's scream made him jerk, and he tightened his grip on the steering wheel.

"*Ying bao!* The *Ying bao* has sounded!" Dewan looked back to see the blind grandmother flailing her arms in panic. "We must take cover. Grandson, find us a place to hide!"

The street around Dewan exploded into total chaos. All craned their heads to look skyward for signs of enemy planes, and a good many accidents occurred as a result. Those on foot darted into storefronts. Horse-drawn wagons disappeared down narrow alleyways. Coolies abandoned their loads curbside and fled the street in droves.

Before the shrill warning call of the air-raid siren tapered off again, Dewan discovered an open path in the traffic ahead of him. He floored the accelerator and sped down the street.

Alarmed at what sounded like the distant drone of an engine above, Dewan squinted toward the sun. He studied the skies in search for enemy aircraft, but he saw nothing resembling a plane. If any planes were there, the clouds hid them from view.

He steered around several abandoned vehicles and dodged the few pedestrians who had yet to find their way to safe haven. Though he still couldn't see any signs of a plane, the rumble from on high sounded ever closer. He knew he should heed the air-raid warning and seek shelter in a nearby store immediately, but he grappled with the idea of leaving the mission director's car in the middle of a busy and unfamiliar boulevard. He needed only to turn right at the next intersection and he would be within a block of Shiren's uncle's store and home. If he could just make it that far, he could park close by and wait out the bombing raid there.

However, when he navigated the turn, he had to stomp on the brake. The car screeched to a full stop. Deserted vehicles blocked the base of the side road, which led up a steep incline. He tried to think, to decide what he should do, but the screeching, squealing whine of what sounded like a diving plane filled his ears.

Immobilized by fear, Dewan squeezed the steering wheel with a white-knuckled grip when an odd flickering light in his driver's side mirror caught his attention. Dewan twisted in his seat and looked out the rear window.

There he could see the surreal sight of a single airplane flying along the center of the street, bearing down on him. The nose of the plane erupted with red flame, followed a split second later by the staccato popping sound only a machine gun could make.

His terror-stricken mind took it all in, as he watched the macabre scene unfold. Strafed! A Japanese plane was strafing this very street! He had no way of escape. In a reflex action, he hunkered down in his seat, although he knew the move provided him little to no protection from an attack by enemy aircraft.

Oddly, time seemed to slow down. Dewan closed his eyes. Yet, even with his eyes closed, he winced over and over again as the terrible sounds ripped toward him. Dewan squeezed his eyes shut more tightly. Gravel, clods of earth, and other debris dislodged by the passing volley of bullets bounced off the side of his car. He winced and caught his breath.

A sharp crack made Dewan jump. He opened his eyes to see a pebble pass through his open driver's window and bounce to the floorboard. The rain of gravel had also struck the windshield and chipped the glass.

Looking up through the pitted windshield, Dewan saw a quick, bright flash overhead. Like an angry, fiery hornet, a spent tracer bullet whirred across his line of sight over the car's hood.

The drone of the airplane's engine increased in volume, becoming so loud it made the car shake. With a roar, the fighter spliced through Dewan's field of vision. The aircraft passed so close, he could make out the blood-red "Rising Sun," the symbol of the Japanese Empire, on the underside of its wings.

He raised in his seat just far enough to peer out the open car window. A jagged line of small craters, road rubble, and spent shell casings from the fighter dotted the lane next to his car. The plane had passed so low over Dewan's head, he could smell the cordite from its machine guns.

"That was close," Dewan said aloud. "Too close."

He gulped for air to assuage his light-headedness, but he had no time to savor his survival of such a close encounter with the enemy. His pulse thundered. Dewan watched in horror as, far overhead, dark objects dropped from the bottom of other aircraft and plummeted toward the general vicinity of Shiren's uncle's home and store. Bombs littered the horizon. His stomach clenched when a cloud of smoke mushroomed just over the hill's sharp rise. He couldn't see which buildings took direct hits. A cloud of debris and smoke mushroomed over the rooftops upon the impact of the bombs. The ground trembled and shook from the blasts' concussions, and he grabbed the steering wheel.

Somewhere in the blackness ahead lived Shiren's uncle. Shiren!

Dewan disregarded his previous concerns over the security of the car. He set aside any consideration for his own safety. Scrambling out onto the street now littered with deserted vehicles, he staggered up the steep road on foot as fast as his crippled leg would allow him to travel. He couldn't wait for the all-clear siren to sound. Bombs were exploding all across the city's southern quadrant, and he had no idea how long the raid might last. Wherever those explosives had detonated, someone might be trapped inside—in desperate need of help. That someone just might be Shiren.

Shiren! He had to find Shiren.

He braced himself, but nothing could have prepared him for the scene which lay before him when he crested the rise.

His stomach's contents lurched to his throat, and he fought back a wave of nausea. He could feel the blood drain from his head. Cold beads of sweat erupted on his upper lip.

The second-story residence of Han Fulei, Shiren's uncle, had received the full impact of one of the bomb blasts. It had imploded into the family's first-floor clothing store. A pile of rubble filled the place where the building once stood.

Dewan traversed the several meters' distance between him and the wreckage, yelling for help as he went. Evidently, fear kept the neighbors from leaving their safe sanctuaries. The only other person in sight was rummaging through the remains of a butcher's shop across the narrow street. Still wearing the stained apron of his trade, the old proprietor appeared dazed and confused. He waved a live chicken in his left hand and picked through stacks of toppled cages with his right. He didn't seem to hear Dewan's shouts for aid but instead proceeded to push his hen into a wooden crate and secure its wire latch.

Every second could prove crucial in the race to rescue Shiren and her family. Dewan couldn't waste precious time begging for help. He had to do what he could by himself.

Stumped as to where or how to begin, he stared for a moment at the mountain of crumbled mortar and splintered timber which used to be Han Fulei's clothing store. Shards of broken glass from the display window and pieces of roof tile mixed in with multicolored clothing scraps to create a morose kaleidoscope. The bomb had not created the blazing inferno Dewan expected to see in the aftermath of such a blast. The sheer force of the explosion's concussion must have blown most of the fire out. Nevertheless, acrid fumes permeated the air. A ribbon of smoke spiraled from the center of the rubble to form a sooty cloud. When he listened closely, Dewan could hear the crackle of burning wood.

No one trapped beneath such carnage could survive. Dark and dreadful horror stabbed at the back of his consciousness. Too terrified to fully articulate his plea, a simple prayer streaked through his mind over and over again. *O, God! Please, God! Help me, dear Jesus. Please!*

Dewan stood on what used to be the store's threshold and yanked at a fallen crossbeam. When the resulting rain of falling rubble stilled, he thought he picked up on the faint, soft sound of a moan coming from his immediate right.

He froze and stared at a jumbled mound of parcels, wrapped in lengths of muslin and tied with strips of cloth. Judging by their location just inside the door, he guessed they were part of the shipment delivered by Shiren and her mother hours earlier. He willed the sound to repeat. . .to no avail. Dewan wondered if his ears were deceiving him. He had about decided he was imagining things when the heap moved and groaned.

With a burst of superhuman strength, he pitched aside the beam he held aside and began ferreting through the bundles. Quilted coats spilled from their wrappings as Dewan raced to unearth the source of the noise.

A flash of red sprang from the sea of drab gray jackets first. Then the bank of debris started to squirm. He tossed another soft package of coats aside and suddenly, Shiren's mother, Chang Chinchuan, emerged. She raised herself up onto one elbow and squinted at Dewan.

"Where am I?" she asked, confusion and bewilderment written on her face. "What happened?"

He saw no blood or obvious signs of serious injury. She appeared to have use of all her extremities, but he worried that Chinchuan may have suffered a slight concussion from the blast. With a passing burst of curiosity, he noted she clutched a familiar red-wrapped package in her right arm.

He slid his arms beneath her and struggled to stand amid the tangled mess with her cradled in his arms. "You're. . .you're in. . .you're in Nanking—Nanking." He stuttered, stopped, and began again. "A b–b–bomb. . ." He stuttered and stopped and looked toward the smoldering ruins. He couldn't bring himself to tell her what he feared.

He looked back at Shiren's mother and their eyes met. Chinchuan's brows knitted in consternation, and she shook her head violently from side to side. "I cannot understand a thing you're saying with this awful ringing in my ears."

Still cradled in Dewan's arms, she looked past him and surveyed the appalling devastation. "I was waiting by the door for you to come. . ." Horror washed over her face. Her eyes widened in alarm. A startled cry escaped her lips.

"Put me down," she screamed.

Dewan instinctively followed Chinchuan's line of vision to see the cause for her hysteria. He had to swallow hard to stifle his own outcry when there, on the edge of the building's ruins, he spied a dangling, lifeless arm.

"Put me down!" Chinchuan wrested herself from Dewan's hold. "I will be fine. But the others. . ." She started to shiver uncontrollably and cuddled the red package close to her chest. "You must save the others! They were upstairs when. . ." She shrieked and tightened her grip on the red package when the all-clear signal began to blare.

Chapter 5

I do wish you didn't have to rush off so soon," said Miss Vaughn. "Although I'm glad you haven't far to go." The president of the Nanking Christian Women's College led Shiren along the covered walkway past the school's chrysanthemum gardens on the way to the main entrance of the campus. Their walk through the hallowed halls and familiar grounds had reignited Shiren's burning desire to study and learn, but she had long since come to terms with the likelihood she would never complete her degree. Still, she was grateful for the opportunity to see her former teacher again.

"I must be getting back to Uncle Fulei's." Shiren paused when they came to the wrought-iron gate. "My mother wants me to stay close by while we're in the city. I'm grateful she allowed me to come see you at all. When I left her, she was waiting for her ride to take her to the meeting with Dewan's parents and Reverend Williams at the mission. She didn't expect to be gone long. Of course, that's assuming she wasn't long. She was probably caught at the mission compound during the bombing raid."

Shiren tipped her head and looked through her slipping eyeglasses as she addressed the American.

"For my own sake, I am happy to learn that you convinced the authorities to allow you to stay in China for the time being." Shiren fell silent until after she and Miss Vaughn exchanged greetings with a passing group of women. "I have said more than my share of good-byes of late. Even so, I fear for your safety. These bombing raids seem awfully dangerous. I hate to think of what may follow in the coming days. If you ever sense the risk is too grave for you here in Nanking, please know our village home is always open to you."

While enduring her first air raid by sitting next to Miss Vaughn in a cramped space under the central building's basement stairs, Shiren's fear of the enemy had increased immeasurably. Yet the university president didn't seem nervous or scared at all.

"Thank you, Shiren," Miss Vaughn replied, leaning heavily on her walking stick. "I appreciate the offer. The air raids are frightful, aren't they? But I could not have chosen a more delightful companion with whom to share my stairwell today. Believe me, I'll take every precaution for my safety, but beyond that, I have to trust the Lord to watch over us. I won't leave my charge here at the university unless I see no other choice. I am still hoping we can just postpone the start of the semester rather than have to cancel classes altogether."

The iron gate squeaked on its hinges when Shiren pushed it open. "Thank you for listening to all my problems, President Vaughn. I did not come here intending to weigh you down with my burdens."

Shiren studied the westerner's care-worn face. Except for her round eyes, after twenty years in China, she looked more Chinese than American. She wore the typical everyday attire of baggy trousers and long overshirt, and she walked with the aid of a stick that was worn smooth. An oilpaper umbrella rested on one shoulder to protect her from the sun. No hint of a foreigner's accent tinged her Mandarin.

"Oh, Honey. I'm so glad you felt free to share your situation with me." Miss Vaughn raised her walking stick and gave it a shake to punctuate her words. "Now I know how best to pray for you. In our human understanding, your marriage to Dewan sounds like a match made in heaven. I know how disappointed you must feel at your mother's refusal to agree to the union. It's in times like these your faith is put to the test." Her expression testified to her utmost confidence in the Almighty. "Remember, Shiren, even in the face of cataclysmic events like war, God knows you by name and cares about your individual needs. He loves you, Shiren. If you trust Him, He will work this situation out for your good."

"Yes, Ma'am. I know what you say is true. I just need to be reminded time and again. Thank you." Shiren dipped at the waist in a deep *kowtow* and dismissed herself from the older woman's presence with a promise to keep in touch. Exiting the gateway, Shiren headed south on Ninghai Road, but a few yards down the street, she looked back to see Miss Vaughn still standing at the gate.

You are a saint if ever there was one, Miss Vaughn, Shiren thought. Her former teacher had willingly forsaken any hope of a comfortable, married lifestyle back in America and had chosen a life of solitary service on the mission field. When Shiren considered such devotion, she felt guilty for wallowing in self-pity like she had been doing since yesterday. She certainly had a lot of growing to do before she ever reached such a level of spiritual maturity. She exchanged waves with the missionary, then started off again.

Once Shiren left the tranquil confines of the campus, the atmosphere grew steadily more onerous and oppressive. A government decree had ordered all of the red-tiled roofs on city buildings and landmarks to be painted to make them a less conspicuous shade to protect them from the enemy. The once colorful Drum Tower now stabbed upward from the city's eastern skyline in a depressing shade of gray.

Earlier, during the air raid, the rumble of enemy planes and their unleashed weapons' explosive impact rattled the walls of Shiren and Miss Vaughn's hiding place under the stairs, but neither of them could pinpoint the precise direction or locations of the bombing targets. However, the farther southward Shiren traveled, the more frequently she witnessed the evidences of war. In the few blocks she had to walk to get to her uncle's place, she saw several destroyed homes and businesses.

Like a morbid carnival, throngs of curiosity seekers clustered around each bomb site and hindered rescue efforts. Shiren had no desire to linger at these scenes of destruction, but the crowds made it hard for her to pass.

At one leveled residence, an assemblage of women stood over a shroud-wrapped form and tried to shush a squalling toddler. A foreboding chill spread over Shiren as she witnessed this heart-wrenching scene. She felt a sudden sense of urgency to rejoin her mother and leave Nanking. With dogged determination, she pushed her way through the mob.

Her grandmother had been ready to leave the city as soon as Shiren and her mother arrived. She wanted all her family to return to the village on the next available boat, but Uncle Fulei made it clear he would leave his shop only as a last resort. Sunday's air raids had been frightening enough to convince Grandmother Yifang that she didn't want to stay in Nanking, no matter what her number two son chose to do. From the time Shiren and Chinchuan walked in the door, Yifang started in complaining about her severe case of nerves brought on by the Japanese and their dropping bombs.

She smoked her opium pipe openly and without apology.

Only when Chinchuan explained to Yifang about her afternoon appointment with the Shins did the old woman cease her unending whining and nagging. "For once you're thinking with your head on straight, Daughter-in-law," she said upon learning of Chinchuan's plan to return the betrothal gift and sever all prenuptial agreements. "That's a reason worthy of postponing our journey home to the village." She proceeded to launch into a lengthy gripe session about the Shins and the missionaries. Approaching this fresh theme with a renewed burst of negative energy,

Yifang besmirched the intelligence and religion of both Dewan's family and the Williamses.

Shiren supposed her grandmother's stinging remarks provided the catalyst behind her mother's granting her permission to visit the university. She even saw her mother grimace at some of Yifang's barbs. When Shiren left to see Miss Vaughn, her mother followed her to the door, and they exchanged an unspoken commiseration at the prospect of Grandmother Yifang returning to the village with them.

"I think I'll wait right here for my ride to the mission," Chinchuan said in a raspy whisper. "I need a few minutes of peace and quiet to gather my thoughts." Her mother laid a gentle hand atop Shiren's own hand as she reached for the doorknob.

As she contemplated that simple act, Shiren believed her mother was trying to signal her sadness and reluctance over having to follow through with terminating the betrothal.

Reluctant or not, her mother's deed was likely done by now.

Shiren harbored no vengeful malice toward her mother for thwarting her hopes and dreams of marriage to Dewan. God had worked a true miracle in her heart yesterday in that regard. Still, she yearned to put all of this mess behind her and leave Nanking. After today, she would forever associate only negative, fearful feelings with the big city. Like her grandmother, she wanted only to hurry back home to the village.

Her reed slippers slapped against the hard ground as

she wormed her way through the shoulder-to-shoulder crowd. Shiren started up the hill to her uncle's, shuffling in short, quick steps to save her slippered feet from a trampling. When a teenage boy rather forcefully bumped her, her eyeglasses nearly went flying. From that point on, she held onto one stem with her left hand to keep them in place.

The closer she came toward her destination, the denser the crowd became. A heavy smell of sulfur hung in the air.

When she topped the incline, Shiren gasped to see the field of destruction spread before her. A scream of terror lodged in her throat and refused to budge. She froze in her tracks. Her chest heaved as she gulped for breath.

There, in front of what had been her uncle's home and business, two men struggled to lift a covered figure into the back of a cart and lay it beside two other cloth-draped human forms.

My family!

Shiren hugged herself. She fought to stand on weak, trembling legs. She found no words to pray, but an agonizing groan rose from the very depths of her soul.

The nudging, prodding, goading sea of humanity faded from her awareness. Shiren pushed her way forward and came alongside the heavy-laden cart.

Myriad reasons to panic exploded in her thoughts.

One lone possibility tempered her utter hysteria.

She clung to a solitary hope. If her mother's meeting took place as scheduled, she would likely have been away when the air raid began. She couldn't possibly be one of the three corpses in the back of the *mashaw*.

Even so, she may have very well returned ahead of me. Shiren scanned the ruins of her uncle's home in search of her mother but didn't see any signs of her. Her hunt was cut short, however, when she caught a line from the conversation between the workers who had just lifted a body into the cart.

"We'd better make room," one man said as he hoisted himself up onto the bed of the cart and held out his hand to help his coworker up. "When we were pulling this one from the rubble, I heard someone say there is likely to be one more body—a woman—still buried in there."

Shiren grabbed onto one of the wooden side slats to steady herself, then she turned toward the men who towered over her from the cart. "A fourth victim?" She couldn't keep the note of panic from her voice. "Tell me. Who said that? Who's in charge here?"

Could Mother have possibly returned before the bombs fell? Did she not go at all? She dreaded the thought of having to look underneath the cerements to identify the bodies. If only a neighbor or someone on the scene could confirm for her who had been recovered from the wreckage and tell her for whom they still searched.

The stockier of the two men eyed Shiren suspiciously. "Why does it concern you?"

"I'm Han Shiren and my family lives—" She looked at the destroyed building then back to the motionless shapes, which filled the wagon bed. "My family lived here."

The idea that the final death toll might include the sum total of her family was more that she could bear. She'd be orphaned. Totally, absolutely alone. Without even the hope of marriage to Dewan, or any other man, to look forward to. No one would marry a penniless, orphaned spinster as the likes of her. Tears spilled unchecked down Shiren's cheeks.

To lose a single relative would be horrible enough in and of itself—but to lose them all! Especially since none of them believed in Jesus or had accepted Him as Savior. They would enter eternity separated from God, apart from Him, their road to judgment paved by their wickedness and selfish, demanding ways.

The hearts of Grandmother Yifang, Uncle Fulei, and his wife had been cold and hard toward the things of Christ. They had never shown an interest in Christianity. In fact, they had been vocally opposed and downright mean in most regards. While she would mourn their untimely deaths with all the respect and honor due any relative, she found it hard to feel deep personal sorrow for the loss of her father's family. They had all played an active part in making both her mother's life and her own miserable—particularly Grandmother Yifang. Yet Shiren's mother had once been so close to becoming a Christian. Shiren felt certain that, if the Lord would just give her mother one more chance, she would see the light. *Please, Lord,* she *pleaded, please don't let my mother die!*

"See the tall guy over there," said one of the men in the cart before anguish totally overtook Shiren. He pointed toward the building's remains. "The one who walks with a limp."

Before her mind had time to process his description,

Shiren saw Dewan. He was digging through the rubble with the wild and frantic motions of a desperate man. Soot irreparably blackened his white dress shirt. A rip in his suit pants exposed one knee.

Dewan happened to look up at just that moment. His gaze met Shiren's. Without a moment's hesitation, he dropped the roof tile he held and hurried toward her.

"Why are you. . . ? What happened. . . ? Do you know where my mo. . . ?" Shiren bombarded him with a string of half-finished questions. He didn't answer a single one. Rather, he swept her into his arms and hugged her close to him.

"Shiren! You're alive! You're safe!" Dewan buried his face in her hair. "Oh, thank You, Jesus!"

She could not fathom what business brought Dewan to her uncle Fulei's. Whatever it was, he must not yet be aware of her mother's decision to break off their betrothal. Otherwise, he would not be so free with his affection— even in such an emotional circumstance. Shiren had no clue why he happened to be there at the time she needed comfort most, but she did not want the moment to end.

Never had Shiren experienced such a public display of emotion by a man. Nor had she ever been held in another's arms. She knew the dictates of society demanded she push away from him. Even now she could sense the disapproving stares of those passing or standing nearby. Still, she longed to commit Dewan's touch to memory. In the midst of this nightmare, she found solace in his embrace. She needed his consolation almost as much as she needed breath itself in this abyss of stench and death. She closed her eyes for a moment to allow herself to dream of a permanent togetherness with Dewan. As she did, she savored his strong tenderness for as long as she could. The remembrance of what she was feeling now would have to last her a lifetime.

Yet she felt guilty for finding even the smallest pleasure in the shadow of such horrible calamity. She pushed away and wiggled from his arms. As she did, she struggled to hold back her burning tears.

"Shin Dewan, you have to tell me if you know." Her voice started to tremble and she swallowed hard. "I'm strong enough to handle the truth, no matter how terrible." She glanced over her shoulder at the wagon, then back to Dewan. A bead of perspiration traced down his cheek like a tear. She grimaced as she braced herself for a confirmation of her fear. "Is my mother among the dead?"

"No, no." When Dewan saw the look of profound dread in Shiren's eyes, he hastened to alleviate her fear. "Your mother is alive. She's got a few bumps and bruises, but she's going to be fine. Neighbors from up the street rushed over to help as soon as the all-clear siren blew. The lady insisted on taking your mother into their home to tend to her needs while her husband and two sons stayed to help as we searched for other survivors. If you'd like, I'll take you right away and you can see with your own eyes that your mother is all right."

Dewan watched as the palpable tension that lined Shiren's face eased. She removed her glasses with one hand, and with the other she wiped away her tears. Then she slid her spectacles back into place and tipped her head to look up at him again.

He despised the thought of having to inform her of the deaths of her relatives, although he suspected she already knew. Without stopping to think about the forwardness of his act, Dewan stroked Shiren's cheek with the back of his hand. Shiren did not pull away from his touch, but her cheeks pinkened, and she tucked her head. Her shyness reminded Dewan that, despite the shock of the afternoon's events, Shiren still possessed the reserved demeanor of a young, unwed Chinese woman. Her behavior served as a graphic reminder of the fact he was no longer in America. Dewan cleared his throat and crossed his arms over his chest.

His gaze drifted toward the cart. "I don't know how to break this news to you any other way than to just come out and say it. I am sorry to have to tell you this, Shiren, but your grandmother, your uncle Fulei, and his wife did not escape."

As he spoke, Shiren studied her hands. Even against this ghastly backdrop, her plain and simple beauty caused his heart to pound. He wanted to embrace her again, to protect her from further suffering for as long as he lived. When she became his bride, he would do everything within his power to fulfill this wish.

"When I first saw you standing here, Shiren, I thought my mind was playing tricks on me. After the bomb hit and I found your mother buried under rubble near the front of the store, I had the impression you were trapped with the others in the ruins. Seeing you here now; well, I've never been happier to learn I was wrong."

She raised her head for a fraction of a second and looked at him before lowering her gaze again. "I am sorry to have added to your duress in any way."

He started to protest her claim, but she shot another fleeting glance his way and continued on. "I can't tell you how grateful I am for all you have done. There is no way Mother and I can fully repay you for your many kindnesses."

Dewan let his gaze travel to the smoldering remains of the building. When he saw the crew of coolies and neighborhood volunteers still digging through the debris, his mouth dropped open. "Excuse me for just a second, Shiren," he said. "I need to get the attention of the other men. I should have given them word as soon as I saw you were alive."

He cupped his hands around his mouth and yelled, "Halt the search!" The band of men stopped their excavation and turned toward Dewan. He pointed to Shiren. "The one you're looking for is here. Unharmed." The coolies began to scramble down from the pile of smoldering ruins, and with waves and nods, they dispersed into the crowded street to return to their rickshaws. The neighbor man and his sons started toward Dewan and Shiren.

As they approached, the *mashaw* driver called out to Dewan from the front of the cart. "Where are you wanting us to go, Mister?" He clutched the horse's reins in his hand, poised to set the animal in motion with the flick of a wrist. The man's assistant occupied the seat beside him.

Before Dewan could answer, the elder of the three

neighbors said, "Excuse me for my rudeness in interrupting." He bowed low and nudged his sons to do the same. "However, I understand that the other family members of the deceased are from out of town. Our family would count it an honor if you would let us prepare for the necessary arrangements from our home."

"Oh, no," Shiren exclaimed. "You are extremely gracious and abundantly kind, but we cannot accept such an offer. That is much too much of an imposition. We could not possibly—"

"I most humbly insist. All I am proposing is but a bit of Christian charity." The neighbor dipped in another deep bow.

"Might we assume you are a believer, then?" When the man answered in the affirmative, Dewan matched his kowtow with one of his own. "God bless you, Sir, for all you have done and are prepared to do." Dewan turned to Shiren and tried to choose his words with care.

"The decision is yours and your mother's, of course. Perhaps, for your mother's benefit, we should consider his offer. She has been awfully shaken up today. I don't know how much more she can stand. We can return tomorrow morning, but I would like to recommend that you allow me to drive you to the mission compound now. I am certain they can put you up there for the night. I think we probably ought to get your mother settled someplace quiet and away from here, so she can rest."

"I do not need any more rest."

Dewan started at the sound of Shiren's mother's voice. He turned his head to see Chinchuan coming around the other side of the cart.

"But I would be most grateful if you would take us to the mission compound." Chinchuan squeezed a tattered red package to her chest when she stepped between him and Shiren. "I am horribly late for my appointment to meet with your parents and the missionary. If they are still available, it is urgent that I speak with them right away. What we have to discuss cannot wait another day."

Chapter 6

When Dewan turned into the drive and parked, his parents and the Williamses stepped out on the front porch of the Nanking mission director's two-story, Western-style home. Shiren disembarked from the backseat of the car and followed the others into the wide foyer.

While Dewan pulled his parents and the missionaries aside and, in discreet whispers, explained all that had transpired over the course of the afternoon, Shiren worriedly guided her mother toward the parlor. The cumulative effects of the day seemed to be taking an extreme toll on her. She'd been distant and nonresponsive in the car, as though drowning in her suffering. Shiren breathed a silent prayer. She needed divine guidance to know how best to minister to her.

Mrs. Williams's voice broke through the somber stillness that had descended on them all. "You poor dears. You've been through an awful experience today." According to Chinese etiquette, she skillfully avoided the mention of the word death. "Why don't you let me show you both to the guest room so you can rest." She nodded toward Dewan's mother, who stood in the wide doorway. "Wu Yiching and I will bring you a dinner tray. Since the mission director has gone to the pier to see his wife and children off to Hankow, he left me in charge of the household until he returns."

"Please. Wait." The urgent note in Chinchuan's voice surprised Shiren. She feared her mother might be feeling sick, so she moved closer to her side. Her mother paid her no heed but rested her chin on the bedraggled red package she had clung to all afternoon.

"I seek in every way to respect and honor my venerable husband's family." Chinchuan's gaze traversed each person in the room. "I know this is an odd request in light of. . ." Her words trailed, then her voice came back strong. "Yet I need to resolve a matter of pressing urgency."

Chinchuan looked over at the missionary. "Reverend Williams, the Japanese warplanes delayed our meeting scheduled for earlier this afternoon. I hope you do not consider my request a dishonorable act, but I would be most grateful if we could convene that meeting now— before any more time goes by."

Shiren felt her cheeks flush with heat. She wanted to run. At this moment, she felt so embarrassed, she would have considered trading places with her grandmother to end her misery. Her life's most supreme humiliation had begun. She could not believe her mother would chose to set this degradation in motion while she was present in the room. She'd held out hope that her mother, given time, would reconsider her decision and consent to her marriage to Dewan.

To Shiren's way of thinking, the single redeeming outcome of today's tragic events had been the unforeseen delay of the meeting at which her betrothal to Dewan would be dissolved. Apparently, in spite of everything, her mother still insisted on following through with the course of action she had outlined yesterday.

Shiren understood her place. She had no authority to argue with her mother or speak a word of protest. She could do nothing more than hang her head and study the floor.

"Shall we take a seat, then?" asked Dewan's father, Shin Jihong. "Dewan, perhaps you should retire to the kitchen until we are done."

"I realize my request is most unusual, but if you have no objection, I would like for the children to remain. I want my daughter to hear what I have to say."

The intonation of her mother's voice sounded controlled and her speech rational. Even so, Shiren could not believe the words coming from her mother's mouth. She wondered if her ties to sanity had snapped. She knew of no other reason why her mother might choose to disgrace her publicly.

From the corner of her eye, Shiren watched Dewan's father and the missionary exchange shoulder shrugs. Judging by their faces, they were as perplexed as she by this break with convention, but Shin Jihong merely pointed Shiran toward a chair.

Shiren selected the parlor's window seat as the least conspicuous spot in the room. She also hoped the open window would afford some relief from the heavy heat, but without the slightest breeze to stir the air, the curtains hung like blankets on either side of her. Turning sideways, she instinctively scanned the horizon for enemy planes. Only wispy clouds crossed the evening skies, casting long shadows over Lion Hill. For a moment, the peaceful scene allayed her fretfulness.

When Shiren returned her attention to the room, she caught her mother studying her. When their eyes met, her mother gave her a sad smile; but Shiren could neither interpret her mother's expression nor guess her thoughts.

Rather than choosing to sit in one of the chairs, Mother had dropped to her knees on the floor in a posture of humble supplication. Her clasped hands rested in her lap. On the Oriental rug in front of her lay the package from the Shins, its once bright red wrapper now dingy and rumpled, with one corner torn.

"I beg your forgiveness for my doing away with the usual formalities and directly addressing the matter at hand," Chinchuan said while the others were settling into their places, "but something is burning within me and I must speak."

Shiren watched her mother's shoulders rise and fall with a deep sigh. She sensed Dewan willing her to look his way, but she dared not return his gaze. She knew her eyes would reveal the humiliation she felt at what was about to occur, so she focused on the rug instead.

"I implore you all, as followers of the same God served by my revered husband, Han Kuanghan, to help me. Please! I am in desperate need of spiritual advice and counsel."

At that unexpected request, Shiren's eyes opened wide. She raised her head and pushed her creeping glasses back into place. Her mother's lower lip was quivering. A sudden shame washed over Shiren for fretting about her own selfish concerns. She could see how her mother struggled to hold her emotions at bay, and Shiren had to swallow hard to stay a rising cry of empathy.

"Many years ago, I approached a crossroads in my journey toward eternity. I had to choose between two diverging paths—one, the ancient way of tradition, paved by generations of my ancestors; the other, a narrow road of faith shown to our family by strangers from a distant land." When Mother paused and drew a deep breath, only the call of a nightingale from the tree beside the open window broke the utter stillness of the room.

"I came within a hairsbreadth of reaching the end of my chosen path this afternoon. When I stood at that portal which separates life from death, I realized I had followed the wrong road." Shiren's mother shook her head slowly from side to side. "Had I entered eternity through the broad gateway of our ancestors, neither my husband nor his God would be waiting to greet me there."

Her voice took on a note of pleading as Chinchuan looked to the missionary. "Reverend Williams, long ago you pointed my husband to the one true way to find eternal life. You tried to show me too, but I turned my back and would not listen. I rejected what you had to say, refusing to believe that generation upon generation of my forefathers could be wrong. Shiren, I want you to know, I saw today where the path of ancestor worship ends."

Shiren's respect for her mother swelled—she'd included her, a female offspring, in her confession. Such humility commanded an even greater measure of reverence and esteem. A chill rippled through Shiren as her mother continued to speak. "I no longer want to travel in the steps of Yifang. Please, before you leave China, can you show me how to change my course and follow the way of Christ?"

The missionary left his seat and lowered himself to the floor beside Chinchuan. "My child," he said, "you have already taken the first step by recognizing your need of a Savior. Whenever lost travelers on life's road call out to Him, Jesus runs to meet them where they are. He promises to walk with you on your journey. If need be, He'll carry you the rest of the way home. You only need pray. Are you ready to do that now?"

Tears welled in Shiren's eyes when her mother answered with an enthusiastic yes. Shiren joined the others as the small band of Christians gathered around her mother. Reverend Williams instructed her to repeat his words and make them her own, then he began to pray.

Even though the prayer did not originate with her mother, Shiren noted an unmistakable sincerity resonating in her voice—so unlike the monotone chant she used when she would recite her rote petitions to their ancestors. Chinchuan asked Jesus to forgive her and to cleanse her from her sin. She promised to follow wherever He would lead and devote the remainder of her days to serving Him.

When her mother echoed the missionary's amen and

raised her head, Shiren saw a new light sparkling in her eyes. Joy sprang from her own heart with such intensity, she wanted to ignore social decorum and throw her arms around her mother's neck. Only her deep, inbred sense of propriety kept her from doing so.

Across the circle, Shiren caught a glimpse of Dewan, and the memory of their earlier embrace sprang to her thoughts. She could still feel the warmth of his arms. Before she could shift her gaze away, he nodded and smiled at her. She had to hide her mouth behind her hand to conceal her spreading grin.

Mrs. Williams reached across and patted Shiren's mother's arm. "This day of sorrow has become a day of rejoicing as well. Welcome into the family of God, Dear."

Dewan's mother, Wu Yiching, leaned toward Chinchuan. She flicked open her folded rice-paper fan and waved it in front of her face in swift strokes. Her gruff whisper filtered out just loud enough for Shiren to hear. "We may soon be family in more ways than one."

Chinchuan reached down in front of her and slid the red-wrapped package up into her lap. "Yes, I suppose we do have another important item to discuss, do we not?"

Shiren's smile dissolved. She braced for her mother's reply.

"We might as well speak freely. I have the feeling it is no secret among anyone here as to why this meeting was originally arranged." Chinchuan let her gaze rest briefly on each member of the Shin family, stopping at Dewan's father. He signaled his agreement with a tip of his head.

Shiren balled her hands in her lap and kept her head

down. She couldn't keep from holding her breath as her mother's voice shifted to a more formal tone of address.

"Shin Jihong, Wu Yiching, nothing would honor the memory of my venerable husband any more than to fulfill the contract he made with you. I gladly grant my approval and consent for my daughter to wed to your son."

Shiren's head jerked toward her mother, who confirmed her change of heart with an almost imperceptible nod and a smile. Unable to stop herself, Shiren looked to Dewan. Despite his mussed hair and soiled clothes, his beaming face made her heart pound wildly in her chest. This time, she did not bother hiding her grin behind the palm of her hand.

Chinchuan faced Missionary Williams. She raised up on her knees and bowed. He matched her movements and waited for her to speak. "Please know, I mean no disrespect whatsoever to my husband's family by what I am about to recommend." She cleared her throat and seemed to be struggling to formulate her words. "But nothing would pay greater tribute to Shiren's father than for you, his closest spiritual brother in this life, to conduct his daughter's marriage ceremony. Therefore, if the family of Shin Dewan would agree—" She paused and acknowledged Dewan's parents by tipping her head. "I suggest we address the matter of the dowry and, if all agree, proceed with the wedding tomorrow, before you leave our country."

Reverend Williams bowed again to Chinchuan. "You greatly honor me with your request," he said softly. "However—and please excuse me if my thoughts are too bold— but I had opportunity to discuss the details of the dowry with the Shins at length this afternoon. They are in a position to waive any dowry requirements from you. In addition, they are prepared to compensate you even more generously than set forth in the terms agreed upon by your husband prior to his death. Final details shouldn't be too difficult to negotiate. . ." He ran his finger around the inside of his shirt collar. "As you can see, all of the principal parties are assembled in this room—including the minister."

From his unassuming position, he raised his head and his eyebrows spiked as he posed his question. "Might I suggest that we perform the ceremony now?"

Heat rushed to Shiren's cheeks, and her heart pounded in her chest. She could be Dewan's bride within a matter of minutes! In her wildest imagination, she could have never conceived of a more emotion-packed day than this. She sent another timid glance Dewan's way, then quickly lowered her gaze again.

At the sight of her everyday clothes, her heart sank just a bit. She knew, in comparison to the significance of the joyous occasion or the gravity of the day's events, her apparel should be the least of her concerns, but she hated the idea of being wed in her wrinkled and well-traveled clothes.

Her expression must have revealed her thoughts, for Dewan's mother reached across Chinchuan and tapped Shiren on the knee with her fan. "You are beautiful, Dear, regardless of your clothes. My son is blessed to have found such a wonderful Christian girl for his bride. Don't worry. We'll give you time to change."

Shiren cast a bewildered look at her future mother-in-law.

Yiching looked at the package in Chinchuan's lap and nudged Shiren's mother lightly with her elbow. "Has she not seen the betrothal gift yet?"

Chinchuan simply shook her head and glanced at Shiren. The mother and daughter exchanged an unspoken vow to never reveal the reason as to why the package remained wrapped.

"You need not have waited until now to open it," Yiching exclaimed. "But never mind. Go ahead. See what it contains."

With one quick motion, Shiren's mother ripped the red wrapper away from the package to reveal a garment made of exquisite crimson silk brocade, woven with a detailed pastoral scene. Chinchuan rose and shook out the folds of the gown, then motioned for Shiren to stand. When she held the dress across Shiren's shoulders, a collection of oohs and aahs rang out.

Dewan stood and bowed deeply to Shiren. Chinchuan stepped aside, leaving her daughter to clutch the dress against her everyday clothes with one arm. He took the crimson brocade gown from her and passed it to Chinchuan. Then he held Shiren's hands in his and caressed them with utmost tenderness, sending shivers racing through her.

"This evening, we have broken with tradition and convention on several fronts. I'm wondering if you would allow me the privilege of performing a custom I learned while in America." Dewan moved forward and closed the distance between him and his betrothed. He stood so close, his sweet, warm breath brushed her lips. She felt certain her cheeks must match the crimson brocade.

"I have heard your mother grant her permission for you to marry me—" His dark eyes shimmered with an emotion Shiren had never fathomed before, and he fell silent as they shared this moment of supreme joy. "But I propose to hear from you. Before God, and in the presence of these witnesses, would you agree to be my wife?"

In a voice so soft that Dewan alone could hear, Shiren whispered, "Yes, I do."

Epilogue

Dewan and Shiren entered married life surrounded by the staggering horrors of war. Yet, while battles raged around them, the newlyweds' love grew and peace reigned within the walls of their mission home.

The outbreak of the global war prevented the Williamses from ever returning to serve in China again. Dewan, Shiren, and Chinchuan found themselves strategically placed in their village to provide safe haven for the steady stream of refugees fleeing from the city to the countryside.

Eleven years later, as the Red Army marched across China, Dewan and Shiren found themselves forced to flee their village home with their nine-year-old son, Shin Zhenmu, in order to escape the relentless persecution brought on by their public ministry. Chang Chinchuan stayed behind to quietly carry on God's work among the village people from her humble tailor shop. She followed the Lord faithfully for the rest of her days.

By way of Taiwan, the Shin family journeyed to America, where Dewan accepted the pastorate of the

Northern California Chinese Christian Fellowship. No matter where they went. . .both in China and abroad. . . people remarked of their deep devotion to one another and their service to the Lord. Like a rich, brocaded tapestry, God wove His love in and through the lives and hearts of Dewan and Shiren.

SUSAN DOWNS

Susan resides in Canton, Ohio, with her minister husband, David, and two teenage daughters, who are of Korean descent. She also has three grown sons and two delightful daughters-in-law. The Downses spent five of their twenty-six years in the ministry as missionaries to Korea, where Susan developed a love for all things Asian. She works as a freelance copyeditor and snatches every spare minute to write stories of her own.

Bindings of
the Heart

by Jennifer Peterson

Dedication

Dee, Nora, and Joshua.
Without your help,
I would not be who I am,
and this story would not be what it is.

Chapter 1

Beijing, present day

"Lisa. . .Lisa. . . It's time to get up! You don't want to be late for the meeting!" Through sleep-blurred eyes, Amy's face came into focus. "I'm going to head down to the lobby with Peter, but I'll tell Clint to come get you in an hour, okay?"

"Alright." Lisa yawned and rolled from her side to her back.

"Just be on time. Our tour guide doesn't look like the type to be kept waiting." Amy flipped on the lights before quietly leaving the room.

The soft, luxurious bed engulfed her, and Lisa pulled the thick, burgundy comforter up to her chin. *This must be what a toasted marshmallow feels like,* she mused. Her body, warm and relaxed, seemed to melt into the lush mattress. Lisa closed her eyes once more and breathed a thankful prayer. "Father, thank You for this bed and for a good night's rest. Thank You for this vacation. Amen."

A quick glance at the clock radio revealed it was 6:30 A.M. "How does Amy do it?" At least they wouldn't have to share the bathroom. "And there's just enough time for a shower. . . ." She groaned at the thought of leaving her little piece of heaven.

Throwing back the covers, she shivered slightly and reconsidered the task at hand. "Oh, come on, you big baby. Let's get moving!" The pep talk provided enough energy to swing her legs over the side of the bed and hop down onto the plush carpet. Grateful that she had set up her toiletries the night before, Lisa stepped into the steaming shower and prepared herself for the day.

After toweling her hair, she applied sunscreen and a light coat of foundation to her face. Deciding less was more today, she left her makeup at that and shaped her short bobbed hair with a round brush. "Now, what to wear? Hmm. . .Clint should be by any minute. I'd better hurry!" Ever since she was a small child, Lisa had made a habit of talking to herself when she was alone. People thought she had an imaginary friend. For some reason, that seemed more acceptable than self-dialoguing.

Opting for a black, broomstick skirt and a red, sleeveless blouse, Lisa scanned her five-foot frame. She neatly tucked her black hair behind her ears. A closer look in the mirror assured her that despite the long flight from the day before, her brown, almond-shaped eyes were bright with anticipation. *Today is going to be so much fun!*

She surveyed her room, as if for the first time. In a sense, it was true, given her state of exhaustion last night. The hotel room was lavishly furnished: a small couch in a bold floral print of burgundy, purple, and green; a writing table; a television; two dressers, and—of course—two fabulous queen-sized beds. The room had soft lighting, and the heavy brocade drapes blocked any outside illumination. Longing for natural sunlight, Lisa pulled back the curtains.

With a sharp gasp, Lisa looked down from her third-story room through a haze of smog, courtesy of the industrial scene combined with the domestic presence. She had read that the people used coal or nuclear power to provide energy for their homes, and there were no regulations about the effect on the environment. Bicycles and garbage cluttered the filthy streets. With cracked windows and rotting bricks covered with flaking stucco, the building directly across the way looked like a slum.

"China." The one word seemed to explain it all. Shaking her head, Lisa marveled at her posh hotel room—a Holiday Inn, no less. It appeared no different than an American Holiday Inn. She hadn't truly forgotten where she was, but in a sense, she had. Her group arrived late the night before, and the lights of the city seemed to be no different than those of a major U.S. metropolis. In the dark, everything looked magical and whole. However, the light of day revealed a stark contrast.

A knock at her door caused her to jump. "Clint? Is that you?" Quickly crossing the room, she peered through the peephole. Finding the smiling face of her blond boyfriend, she opened the door. "Clint, did you look outside? Did you see what these people live like?" In her enthusiasm, she practically dragged him to the window.

"Look!" she squealed. "Isn't is awful?"

"No kidding! I was so shocked when I opened our curtains this morning, I dragged Peter out of bed to see it. I had no idea it would be like this. None at all." Clint's gaze never left the world outside. Finally, he turned his eyes to Lisa. "Well, we need to get downstairs. Our guide is supposed to be meeting us there in ten minutes."

"Okay, let me put on my boots. I want as much between me and those streets as possible!"

A handsome Asian man with a softly angled face stood at the head of the hotel lobby. The small group of college-aged students huddled around him, dressed casually and coolly. Lisa and Clint pressed in beside Amy, who smiled brightly at their arrival.

"He's just getting ready to explain today's itinerary," she whispered. She swept her dishwater blond hair up with a large clip, and her green eyes danced with anticipation. "Isn't this fascinating?" She tapped a pen against her notepad. "I'm glad you wore that." She drew an imaginary line from Lisa's feet to her shoulders with the pen. "I didn't know what anyone else would be wearing. I don't mind being a trendsetter, of course, but. . ."

Lisa giggled softly.

The man held up his arms, signaling for silence. Lisa watched as the entire lobby seemed to respond—maids paused in midhustle, desk clerks strained to listen, and patrons lingered.

"Welcome to Beijing. I've met several of you before, but I also see some fresh faces. I am delighted to have you all along for this tour. I know you'll find China to be as mysterious and enchanting as Western cinema suggests. My name is John Li. My parents led tours between the United States and China long before I came along. I was born in Anchorage, Alaska, but I've spent most of my twenty-six years traveling between the two countries."

Lisa watched the man with interest. She felt acutely aware of her own Asian heritage. The frequent stares and giggles that Clint drew from the hotel staff made her uncomfortable. They seemed to be obsessed with his blue eyes and light hair. However, she didn't receive a second glance until she opened her mouth. She and Clint had discussed how easy it would be for her to blend in, given her ethnicity and her linguistic gift. She would graduate in less than six months with a major in Linguistics and a minor in Mandarin/Putonghua Chinese, the official dialect of the country. Now that she was actually here, her abilities would be put to the test.

For several minutes, John animatedly described the plans for the day. Lisa furrowed her brow. He said nothing about their evangelism work. Perhaps this had been addressed at the pretrip meeting last week—the one she had missed due to a conflict with her work schedule. She leaned in close to Clint and whispered, "Why doesn't he mention the missions part?"

John's stare fixed on her. "And you, Miss. . .what is your name?"

"I'm Lisa Perdue."

"Well, Lisa Perdue, I would appreciate it greatly if you would refrain from talking while I am addressing the group." John's voice dripped with sarcasm, yet Lisa could sense an underlying urgency.

"Oh, Mr. Li, I'm so sorry. I'm just really excited. I didn't mean to interrupt."

John smiled. "I can understand your enthusiasm. I have a great deal to go over, but please know that I would be happy to address any of your additional questions later on."

As John continued to describe their activities for the day, his brown eyes danced with excitement. John's love for his work shone through his entire being. Though she knew she had made a poor first impression, she felt sure their group was in capable hands.

Clint squeezed her arm reassuringly. Lisa merely shrugged. She knew their work was supposed to be covert, but weren't they safe here in the hotel? Surely, John was making their plight more clandestine than necessary. Obviously, he had a dramatic flair. She recalled previous warnings during the preparatory meetings that they weren't to mention their religious agenda, but she couldn't believe the lobby qualified as a dangerous scene.

"A final note, before we head out to our first stop—Tiananmen Square and the Forbidden City. Please collect any personal effects you might need while we are away. This would include reading material for the transit time and any items you will want for note-taking." His gaze swept over the small group. "I see that most of you have brought backpacks with you. Good. However, if you feel you may have forgotten something, I urge you to go quickly to retrieve it." As he spoke, he rolled the sleeves of his light violet oxford into thick cuffs, just below his elbows. He picked up a clipboard and held it against his khaki-clad hip. With his other arm, he pointed to the hotel lobby clock. "Be out front and ready to leave in ten minutes."

Amy slung her brown leather satchel over her shoulder. "Did you bring all of your. . .stuff?" She winked conspiratorially at the final word.

"I have my money. I didn't figure I would need anything else. What sort of stuff are you referring to?"

"Why don't you accompany Miss Perdue up to her room and show her the items she'll be needing today." Lisa whirled around to find John wearing a look of contempt.

"Sure, Mr. Li. We'll be down in a minute. Come on, Lisa." Amy paused midstep and turned back. "Clint, you should find Peter. You know, in case you're missing anything for today."

Lisa fell in behind Amy as they moved toward the elevator. "Wonder what his problem is," she muttered. "I don't think he likes me much at all."

"Well, you wouldn't be so out of sync if you had been able to come to the last meeting. I'm sure he's under a lot of pressure, trying to make sure we get to see everything and learn about all the points of interest." Amy suddenly embraced her and murmured in her ear. "See, we aren't supposed to say certain things here, especially in public. You have to be careful, or you'll get us all in trouble."

Lisa and Amy pushed open the double doors of the hotel and choked on the thick air. The combination of humidity and pollution created a wall, causing Lisa to feel as though she were breathing underwater. Swarming people packed the sidewalks. Thick dust coated everything. "Do you think we'll ever get used to this?"

Amy shook her head violently. "I don't see how. This is unbelievable."

A rickety bus pulled alongside the curb. "Everybody ready?" John called from inside.

"Well, at least we don't have to walk through this muck." Lisa hoisted her backpack off the pristinely kept steps of the hotel and stood in line to board.

After everyone found a seat, the driver pulled into the traffic. John stood in the aisle and clapped twice to capture the passengers' attention. "Okay, listen up! I plan to discuss this more, later today, but it appears that I need to re-emphasize a couple of points. You are safe to discuss the nature of our trip on this bus. It belongs to the missions group, and we go over it for bugs and spying devices before every trip. However, you are not free to discuss anything associated with Christianity or evangelism outside of this bus or at our park meetings, unless I tell you otherwise. Some of you seem to have forgotten the serious nature of what we are doing. I am here to remind you, in no uncertain terms, your ignorance and oversight to the sensitive nature of evangelism in a country such as this will get you and your companions killed. Don't be fooled by the presence of state-run churches—their beliefs and practices are far removed from true Christianity."

Lisa elbowed Amy. "So, we're kind of like spies, right? We need to come up with a code, don't you think? Maybe there is already a code, like pig latin or something."

"We should ask John."

Lisa snickered but said, "No, I don't think John would find this amusing at all. He's such a serious guy. I just want to tap him on the shoulder and say, 'Don't you remember the Bible saying something about the joy of the Lord?'"

"Oh, I know! Who's going to want to become a Christian with Mr. Stodgy-Pants raining on everybody's parade? It's not a very winsome tactic, in my opinion." Amy crossed her legs and settled against the cracked vinyl of the seat.

John promptly claimed the seat opposite the women. "Ladies, I couldn't help but overhear your comments."

Lisa sputtered and choked, while Amy's face flooded *red. Oh, no,* Lisa moaned inwardly. *Why can't I keep my big mouth shut?*

John continued between clenched teeth, "I assure you my sense of humor is most keen in situations that merit it. Sharing Christ with the people of China, however, is not one of them. I am confident you understand the gravity of the matter, given the preparatory classes you were required to attend prior to this trip. I also understand that China has a tendency to overwhelm first-time visitors, so perhaps the time change, combined with the culture shock, has made you a bit more lackadaisical than normal. I want this trip to be fun and exciting for you, but I refuse to jeopardize lives because of foolishness. There are more than enough legitimate ways to put oneself in the line of fire in our work. Please, just be careful to think before you speak." As quickly as he had arrived, he departed to the back of the bus.

Dumbfounded, Lisa and Amy exchanged looks of remorse and embarrassment. Lisa felt conviction wash over her in waves. "Wow. I was way out of line. I don't know why I resort to humor and sarcasm when I'm uncomfortable, but here and now, that has to stop."

"I know what you mean! I feel so stupid! He's right, of course. Those classes made it more than apparent that we are treading on dangerous ground here." Amy sighed. "You remember when we were little kids and the warnings always seemed so much bigger than the actual danger? It's so odd—the older we get, the more the pendulum seems to swing to the opposite extreme. There's no way in the world they could ever give you a warning big enough to be proportional to the severity of the situation here."

Lisa stared out the window and watched the poverty-stricken people of Beijing milling in crowded streets. Some just lay dejectedly against the walls of the alleys, covered in oily-looking rags. Vendors stood on street corners, selling unidentifiable meats—meats swarming with flies and gnats. Farther down the street, several young girls busily prepared bowls of soups for the eager patrons of a soup stand. Small shops sold trinkets and clothing to tourists. Shuddering, Lisa could bear to look no longer. China was definitely beyond her wildest imaginings.

"And to think," she said to no one in particular, "John has chosen to immerse himself in this world." Closing her eyes, she prayed silently, *Lord, please don't let my discomfort cause grief or anxiety to anyone else. I ask You to bless this work and that it would be to Your glory. Please bless the people of China; soften their hearts to Your Word and let Your Spirit move mightily in them. And though I know he doesn't like me very much—and not that he should after the way I've acted—I ask for a special blessing upon John, Father. Keep us safe, and keep me in line. Amen.*

Chapter 2

Lisa gazed in wonder at her surroundings. The ancientness of the Forbidden City amazed her. She had never seen anything older than the Liberty Bell in Philadelphia. To think she was standing within the same walls as emperors from the fifteenth century made her light-headed.

She waited for a moment on a marble bridge just inside the Meridian Gate and watched the stream beneath her. Most of the group had already ascended the stairs of Tai He Men—the Gate of Supreme Harmony. Clint was taking Amy's picture as she stood beside one of the huge, bronze lions guarding the entrance. Peter frantically scribbled in a notebook, pausing only every once and again to nod thoughtfully in John's direction. Lisa knew John would be supplying the history behind the elaborate and intricate structures, yet somehow she felt the need to distance herself from the group.

Reluctantly, she traversed the bridge and caught up with the tour as they entered the Hall of Supreme Harmony. Incense burners flanked the sides of the stairs leading up to the main floor. Lisa strained and stretched her imagination, trying to conjure what this place would've looked like in the midst of pomp and circumstance. Finding the mental picture beyond her reach, she settled instead on studying the carved dragons that adorned the central pillars of the hall.

"So much detail," she sighed. "So much beauty." Yet, somewhere a bleak thought gnawed at her consciousness. *Where are You, God?*

The artwork was glorious, to be sure, but she couldn't overlook the blatant paganism that made up the design. She felt out of place.

"So, what do you think?" Clint whispered

Lisa shook her head numbly. "I. . .I don't feel God here."

"Yeah, I know what you mean. It's like when we would take trips to the museum in Denver and see the dinosaur bones and whatnot. It doesn't feel real."

"No, it's more than that. It's not because it feels fake or contrived. This is very real. I just. . ." Her voice trailed off. How could she put words to the emptiness she felt inside? This sensation was so new and foreign. Never in her whole life had she experienced the absence of the Lord. She had always known Him to be around and near.

"You just what?" The curiosity in his voice confirmed Lisa's suspicion that he didn't understand.

Father, please show Yourself. I feel as though You've left me. "It's hard to explain, Clint. I've never felt like this before, so I don't exactly know how to say it. It's like I left God back in Colorado. Somehow I forgot to pack Him or something. Does that make any sense?" She frowned, answering her own question. "No, of course it doesn't. I don't know what I'm trying to say."

"It's okay, Lisa. Do you want to get out of here? We can go back out to the square and wait for the rest of the group." Clint's concern was evident.

"No, it isn't just in here. It's everywhere. It's China." She'd been in the country less than twenty-four hours, and already she felt ill at ease. "I shouldn't have said anything. Someone could've been eavesdropping." She sighed heavily as the gravity of the situation dawned on her. "It's so weird not to be able to just speak my mind."

Clint laced his arm through hers. "Perhaps, then, we should take this one step at a time, and enjoy culture. Let's not worry about anything today." He urged her to walk by his side. "Come on. John and the group are just up here. We might as well learn something today, right?"

Forcing a weak smile, she agreed and allowed him to lead her into the Zhong He Dian—the Hall of Perfect Harmony. But as John explained how the emperor would finalize any preparations for the ceremonies that would take place in the previous hall, Lisa mused that harmony was as far from her reach as the Rocky Mountains.

Amy emerged from the bathroom with an avocado mask and a towel turban.

"Aren't you the consummate beauty queen?" Lisa teased.

"Laugh all you like, Miss Perdue, but with this much dust and humidity, my tender skin will stage a frightful revolt."

"Okay, I'll admit you're right. Have you got any extra?"

"Oh, now you want some of it? Mock me and then request my help. I see how you are." Amy huffed, hands on hips. Despite her irritated facade, she couldn't seem to stifle the giggle that erupted from her throat. She disappeared behind the wall separating the bedroom from the vanity. "Here you go."

Lisa read the label. "Avocados and walnuts, eh? Ever thought of putting some on a bagel?"

Amy rolled her eyes. "Uh, no. It was bad enough on toast."

"I imagine. Now, my apricot peel is another story entirely. English muffins are totally the way to go there."

Another fit of laughter sent the girls in search of refreshment. "Check the minifridge. Aren't we supposed to get sodas in there?" Lisa asked, as she smoothed the gritty paste over the bridge of her nose.

"Nope, there's nothing in here. Do you want to call downstairs and see if someone can bring a few up?"

"Nah. I just really wanted some root beer. Doesn't that sound good?" With a few last strokes, she evened out the mask and stood up. "Eww. This stuff feels nasty when it starts to dry."

"You won't even be thinking about that when you feel how soft your face is," Amy assured her.

As Lisa walked to the vanity sink, a knock sounded at the door. "Just a minute!" she called. "It's probably Clint and Peter. I'll get it as soon as I wash my hands."

"Don't forget to warn them about our green faces!" Amy called.

"Oh, it'll be so much more fun to surprise them, don't you think?" Lisa snickered and wiped her damp hands on her plaid flannel pajama bottoms.

"How come you guys are still up—" Lisa opened the door to find a Chinese man in a maroon and black uniform holding a six-pack of root beer and a bucket of ice. "Th–thank you," she stammered. "We didn't order this, though."

"It's complimentary," he replied with a strong accent. "It comes with the room. You wanted soda, right?" He seemed to be an equal mix of panicked and confused.

"Yes, well, we did. But how did you know?" Lisa asked, unbelieving.

"Here—your root beer. Your ice." The man thrust the items into her arms and hurried off.

Lisa heard him mutter something about "Green-faced Americans," in Chinese, so she called after him in Mandarin, "Thank you, kind sir. My green-faced companion and I will enjoy the drinks."

A smug smile tugged at her lips as she watched the man turn, his eyebrows drawn so far back in surprise, they threatened to blend with his hairline. He opened his mouth, as if to reply, but then shook his head as if he thought better of it and hurried away.

Amy frowned. "Where did that come from?"

"One of the hotel staff was at the door with this."

"You don't suppose. . ." Amy's gaze swept over the room.

Lisa set the ice and soda down on the desk. She raised one finger to her lips but nodded solemnly. "Don't say anything more," she mouthed. "It's bugged."

Amy's eyes grew wide.

※

"So, there he was." Clint crossed his tanned arms and appeared to ponder Lisa's words as they sat on the bus the next day.

"Yeah. Soda and—"

"Not just any soda," Amy interrupted Lisa. "Root beer. Just like Lisa had said in the room." She whistled through her teeth. "Can you believe it?"

The skin on Lisa's arms prickled as a chill shot down her spine. "There is something so completely unnerving about the whole thing. . .people listening to every word you say, regardless of its content. . .something as mundane as avocado masks and root beer. I can't imagine what would happen if we talked about missionary work, or evangelism, or anything."

"You'd be arrested," John supplied, popping in from out of nowhere.

How does he keep doing that? Lisa wondered in frustration. He always managed to appear right as she made herself sound hopelessly ignorant or indomitably calloused.

"You aren't serious?" Clint questioned incredulously.

"I am dead serious." John claimed the seat in front of them. "I know you find this hard to believe, given the life of unquestioned comfort you have led. I can respect that, but only to a point. Your inability to comprehend the way things are here will provide little relief for you when you're being held in a filthy cell, awaiting judgment."

"How can God allow His people to suffer like that? He wouldn't let that happen to us, would He?" Amy's features fell, causing her to appear frightened and childlike.

John drew in a deep breath. "The Christians here face horrible persecution. Christians all over the world are enduring torture and punishment we cannot begin to fathom. It's something you don't have to deal with in America. Be grateful. These people take up the cross of Christ every day in a very real way. Their commitment to God isn't based on fuzzy feelings or heat-of-the-moment altar calls. It is founded in the undeniable truths of who Jesus Christ is and what He has promised us."

Lisa's heart began to race. She perceived his words as an attack on her and her faith. "And you're saying my walk with God is based on those things? What gives you the right to judge where I stand with the Lord?"

"Miss Perdue, I make no pretense of being able to label your walk. I do know that you don't have to concern yourself with your family being shot before your eyes, their lives taken one by one, as you refuse to denounce your belief in the Triune God. You needn't worry about attending a church service. You don't have to weigh the value of spiritual nourishment and fellowship against your own life." His brown eyes blazed with a fierce intensity that precariously balanced between passion and fury. "Those are things I do know, Miss Perdue."

"So, because I don't risk life and limb every Sunday in Colorado Springs, I'm somehow less of a Christian? Has your mission work served to fast-forward your sanctification process, Mr. Li? If you've found the inside track to spiritual perfection, I do hope you'll share it with us lowly American students." Lisa struggled to quiet the nagging voice admonishing her to rein in her emotions and hear him out. It was too late now.

John remained oddly silent for a tense moment. As the bus pulled up in front of a crowded shopping district, he exhaled slowly. "I don't mean to seem more holy than any of you. I know where you're coming from. I know that your concerns are just as real and just as valid in your personal lives. But, understand, I've been doing this for many, many years. I know what to look for when assessing who will see this through, and who is merely here to put a notch in their evangelical belt. These are real people, Lisa, with real terrors facing them. I can respect where you're coming from. Now, please, do the same for me and for the people of China." He stood up and smoothed his charcoal gray slacks. He leveled his gaze at Lisa—a look that penetrated her very soul. "After all, they are your people, are they not?"

Chapter 3

Lisa's fury abated somewhat by the time their shopping excursion came to an end. As the afternoon was winding down, John suggested they meet in a nearby park to quietly discuss some "serious matters." While she didn't relish the thought of giving him her undivided attention, she tried to keep her focus on the reason for her trip—her desire to see others come to Christ.

Clint strode over to where Lisa stood, arms akimbo. "Hey, how are you doing?" He playfully ruffled her short, black hair. "You going to make it?"

"Of course I'm going to make it. I just don't like. . . him." She jabbed her forefinger in the direction of John.

"Well, honestly, I'm having a hard time with the whole thing—the secrecy, the danger, the crowds. I don't know when we'll start witnessing to these people, but I am looking forward to it less and less. I don't want to die, Lisa." Clint's eyes were sad and frightened.

"I feel the same way, Clint. It's like I was trying to explain when we were at the Forbidden City—I don't feel God here. I don't know how I'm supposed to share His gospel when He seems thousands of miles away from me."

"Maybe John will address that tonight. We can't be the first ones who feel this way, right?" Clint put his arm around her shoulders.

Lisa leaned into the embrace. "This could almost be romantic," she sighed.

Clint chuckled. "If you're into that sort of thing, I suppose it might be," he teased.

Lisa giggled. She had to admit that his gesture made him seem more like a brother than a sweetheart. The thought didn't anger her, though. It felt comfortable and right. Together, they walked over to the area John had designated for their talk.

Amy patted the blanket beside her. "Come sit over here, you guys! I didn't want you to feel like outcasts, so you can hang out with me. I know that none of the others would have you," she joked.

Clint frowned. "Now that's not entirely true! Peter wouldn't shun us, would you?" He patted the dark-haired man on the back.

"Of course not, Clint. Why, that wouldn't be very Christlike of me, would it? I do my best to love everyone, even when they're wrong," Peter said with a gracious smile.

"Peter, you always have had quite a gift for back-handed compliments."

"Thank you, Amy." Peter gave a short bow.

Lisa held up her hands. "Now wait just a minute. Am

I correct in assuming you're referring to the incident on the bus? Why would I be rejected by anyone because of his pompous actions?"

Amy hesitated slightly. "Lisa, you and John have done nothing but clash since you met up with each other. Obviously, there's some tension running between you. I was only trying to lighten the mood by implying that no one would want to sit by you because you and John always end up in an altercation."

"Is it my fault he hates me?"

"It's not that, Lisa. Look, the issue is, none of us are really happy here. It's not at all what I thought it was going to be." Clint and Peter nodded in agreement. "Just try to get along with him. If he wants to pick on you, then let him. It's childish and ridiculous, so why do you feel the need to counter it? Don't make this trip worse by being at odds with the guide. I don't know why he's so short-tempered when it comes to you, but perhaps you would do well to ask him for a private talk. Clear the air. Then start fresh. We still have five weeks to go, you know."

Lisa's mouth dropped in shock. "I'm supposed to make amends with—with him? I didn't do anything!"

"You were a bit disrespectful," Amy offered timidly.

"And argumentative," Clint supplied.

"I was standing up for myself!" she cried indignantly.

"What's going on over there? Miss Perdue, are you at it again?" John's strong, deep voice assaulted her ears.

It might almost be an alluring voice, if he wasn't so awful, she thought.

"Here's your chance to start," Amy whispered. "Just

appease him. Let it go."

"Fine," Lisa huffed. She didn't understand why she had to present the olive branch when she had been guilty of no crime, but she trusted Amy's judgment. She didn't have to be happy about it, though.

"No, Mr. Li. I get carried away when I'm passionate about my topic. I apologize." Lisa winced at the sharp elbow in her side. "For everything," she added through tightly gritted teeth.

John's features softened. She briefly allowed herself to believe him to be handsome. "Thank you, Miss Perdue. I appreciate your humility."

"You're welcome. And, please, call me Lisa."

John pressed his lips together and nodded thoughtfully. "Alright, Lisa." For a moment, he appeared dazed. When he came around again, he said to the group, "And you can all call me John."

As he turned and found a seat at the head of the small circle they had made, Amy leaned over. "See? You caught him off guard. He doesn't know what to say. Good job!" Amy cheered softly.

"We'll just have to wait and see." Somehow Lisa was not convinced.

⚉

"So, how do you like China?" John asked the group. He knew one or two would absolutely adore the land and the surroundings. That was usually the way it worked out. About half of the group would be indifferent, and the remaining one or two would despise China and all it had to offer.

"I think it's beautiful," a woman gushed. "I just love the history and the activity."

"I'm sorry, I've forgotten your name." John hated how horrible he was with names, but with so many tour groups, year after year, he felt like a sponge that had long ago become saturated.

"I'm Courtney Meyer." Courtney had long hair the color of polished copper. Freckles dotted her fair skin.

"That's right. Thank you, Courtney. So, what has impacted you the most, thus far?"

"I think the most startling things were the Protestant churches. I just assumed that Christianity was unknown here. Now, I see that at least some acknowledge our faith but merely for the benefit of the visitors. It seems odd to me that the Chinese people are not allowed to attend the ones designated for the Westerners. The Chinese Christian churches are merely facades of our faith, laden with politics and falsehoods."

"Great observation. What sort of assumptions does that lead you to make?" He liked to encourage his "tour groups" to bend their minds—to try to think like the Chinese people, be they government or common folk.

Courtney played with the long skirt of her white dress as she thought. "Perhaps the Chinese government has associated the Christian church with the evils of Western ways. They frown upon capitalism and free enterprise and demand that the people do likewise. Maybe they have lumped it all into one."

"That's an interesting theory. There's probably some validity to it. But what about the fascination the people have with Westerners? You have experienced that for yourselves. What do you make of the way in which they will melt away from a retail counter to let you purchase your items first? Or the interest they take in the items you have chosen? What about the attention you draw with your red hair, Courtney? Or the gawking you received, Clint, because of your blue eyes? If they are so intrigued with American Caucasians, wouldn't you assume that your belief system would draw them too?"

"Not necessarily," Courtney replied.

He could tell she knew what he was getting at, and he was delighted to see her play along. So often, the students did not want to contradict or "show up" the teacher. However, in this case, John felt it was far more important to allow them to reach their own conclusions and understandings.

"Go on," he encouraged.

⁂

Lisa marveled at Courtney's genuine interest in the country and the motivations of its people. She listened in rapt attention as the passionate redhead continued.

"Well, I think it's one thing to be fascinated with the color of someone's hair, skin, or eyes; but the Chinese culture is ancient, as are their belief systems. If they associate Christianity with Western culture, and equate Western culture with Americans, we as American Christians are hardly to be taken seriously then, given the fact that our country is only a little over two hundred years old."

"Excellent." John smiled.

Lisa found herself drawn to the way he facilitated the

conversation and made his points by asking pertinent questions. She admired his knowledge. Caught up in the exchange, she was forced to ask herself why she had come here. *That's silly,* she admonished herself. *I came to evangelize to the people of China. I came because it's the right thing to do—to spread the Word and save the lost.* However, the justification sounded hollow in her mind. *Perhaps,* she wondered hesitantly, *my motives aren't as focused as I'd like to believe.*

John looked over the group. "Clint. . .I'm sorry. I've forgotten your last name."

Clint cleared his throat. "Clint Vies. But 'Clint' is just fine."

"Ah, thank you. So, Clint, what do you think of China?"

Lisa frowned at John's baited inquiry. She knew it was more than obvious that Clint couldn't stand the country or the experience. She hoped he had the courage to say how he really felt.

"Well, I am still trying to adjust. I get stared at a lot. It's been nice to have Lisa's linguistic ability, so she can tell me what the people are saying about me!"

The group chuckled and Lisa felt her cheeks grow hot.

"That's right. Lisa, you speak fluent Mandarin, correct?"

"Yes, I do. I've almost finished my Linguistics degree, and I focused mainly on Mandarin Chinese. I plan to work as an interpreter for a corporation that has its eye on targeting Asian businesses. I know the language almost as well as I know English," she admitted, hoping she didn't sound too prideful. Strangely, though, she found herself desiring John's approval.

"Wonderful. I do, as well. Perhaps that will come in helpful when we start to visit with some of the families in the area." He turned his attention back to Clint. "So, are you looking forward to meeting our Chinese-Christian contacts?"

"Uh, yes and no. I don't relish the thought that my beliefs could get me imprisoned or killed, and I know I'm a whole lot safer being a tourist than I am spending time with the Christians in the area."

"That is true. You are a lot safer. You're also quite ineffective. When we allow our fears and anxieties to keep us from action, we are letting Satan have his way. The Bible states God has not given us a spirit of fear, but a spirit of love and of power and of a sound mind. God has given us a job to do. We are to make disciples as we go, remember? It doesn't say a whole lot about being comfortable as we minister. In fact, it says quite the opposite."

John paused to take in the expressions on their faces. Clint paled considerably, as did Amy and Lisa. Courtney displayed a solemn peace. Peter's eyes gleamed in a way that John had not perceived before. Perhaps he was another who would stick with the call. The others appeared sufficiently interested.

"I'd like for us to meet together like this for a type of Bible study. Obviously, we won't be using Bibles out here in the open; but later, on your own, I'd like for you reread the verses that we will go over. Tonight, we are going to begin in Matthew 10. Jesus is explaining the costs of being a disciple. He isn't candy-coating any aspect of the walk. I want you to read this chapter tonight and pray through it. I want to discuss it the next time we meet. I'm not yet sure when we'll do that, but I am hoping it will be soon. Until then, make this passage your focus. If your Bible has cross-references, please use them as you search the Scriptures."

John continued to share his thoughts for a few more minutes then dismissed the students back to the bus. He hoped the Spirit would work in their hearts so they would learn the harsh reality of sharing God's Word, as well as the joy and contentment to be found in doing the will of the Father.

He stopped midstep as Lisa Perdue caught his attention. She was laughing at one of her companion's antics. She was so beautiful, yet so ignorant of the things in which John found passion and fulfillment. *And there's Clint,* he reminded himself. Yet, as he watched them together, the relationship seemed more fraternal, or like they were very good friends. John chided himself for even analyzing it as far as he had. *This is ridiculous.* He began to pray. *Lord, I pray Your will here will be done. I pray these students will be effective witnesses for Your kingdom. And, most of all, I pray for You to protect me. I don't think I could stand another heartbreak. Amen.*

Chapter 4

I hate this place!" Amy dejectedly threw herself across her bed in their hotel room.

Lisa knew she was homesick and exhausted. She felt the same way. Yet, somehow, she couldn't bring herself to say she hated the exotic country. "Amy, you're only making it worse for yourself," she soothed, stroking her roommate's hair.

"I want to go home," she declared miserably.

"I know, I know. We'll be home in less than a month. You can do anything for a month, right?"

"I used to think so."

Lisa's heart broke for her friend. "You can, Amy. You can."

Standing, Lisa checked her watch. A quarter of five. She had decided she needed some time alone. John's continued verbal jabs and sarcasm had lessened, but it was still quite evident that he held a great distaste for her. She wanted some time to pray and regroup, away from the added stress of despondent friends and insulting tour guides.

"Why don't you go see if Clint is in his room?" Lisa

suggested. Clint was every bit as miserable as Amy, and Lisa figured it did them good to comfort each other. Her mind was torn in too many directions to offer the consolation they needed.

Amy sniffed and wiped her eyes. "Okay. Where are you going?"

"I need some time to be alone," she stated matter-of-factly. She placed her Bible and her journal into her backpack, in case the hotel authorities decided to "clean" the room in her absence.

"Can't you come spend some time with Clint and me?" Amy pleaded.

"I suppose I could. Do you want to go get some tea or some coffee?" Lisa was still amazed that their hotel contained everything they could possibly need, from barbershops to general stores.

"Sure."

"Good. Let's go get Clint, then."

A few minutes later, the women arrived at the door of Peter and Clint's room. Amy knocked and called out to him. Clint greeted them, his expression haggard and tired.

"He's gone again." His voice sounded strained.

"Who?" Lisa asked.

"Peter, of course! He has taken quite a liking to Courtney. They're out exploring the wonders of China."

"Well, why don't we go and explore the wonders of coffee and conversation?" Lisa suggested. Clint nodded and grabbed his briefcase.

"Could we go somewhere where we can talk?" Clint asked. "I mean, really talk? I hate all of this covert, spy stuff. I don't want to keep looking over my shoulder to see who's listening. I want to just talk."

Lisa looked at her watch again. So much for a quiet time before dark. But perhaps this would do her more good than she thought. And if it turned out to be another opportunity for Amy and Clint to verbalize their misery, she could always excuse herself to wander around the city.

After purchasing their beverages, they walked a half mile or so to a small park. The trees were large and full. The overcast sky offered a bit of relief from the stifling heat. The humidity felt less oppressive somehow with the absence of the sun.

"I don't know how anyone can function under this kind of stress. They're searching our rooms, listening in on our conversations, watching our every move. . . I just want to go home." Clint sipped his coffee.

Fat drops of rain began to fall on them, as if on cue.

"See?" Amy cried. "I hate this place, and it hates me!"

"Now, don't be ridiculous." Lisa smiled. "We are coming right up on their rainy season. Just be glad it isn't July or August. As I understand it, they typically get over sixteen inches within those two months."

Amy shook her head. "Does it look like I care? I don't plan to be thinking about China in July and August, let alone contemplating their rainy season."

Lisa frowned at her friend's enthusiastic response.

"Oh, I'm sorry, Lisa. That was so mean of me. I'm just so. . ."

"Yes, I know. You're unhappy here. And Clint is

unhappy here. We're all unhappy here." Lisa raised her arms in a gesture of defeat.

"I just feel abandoned," Clint complained. "Peter was supposed to be my traveling buddy."

"But you never wanted to travel," Lisa countered.

"So he should've been my stay-in-the-hotel buddy. But, no. He becomes Courtney's travel buddy."

"What happened to Courtney's travel buddy?" Amy inquired.

"Bill was fine with the switch. He wanted to have more quiet prayer time. At least, that's what he said to me." Clint shrugged.

"What about you, Lisa? Are you miserable here too?" Amy asked.

Lisa looked at her roommate. "Yes, I am. I don't understand why I'm here, but I believe there has to be some reason for it. After all, we don't believe in chance, right?"

Amy shook her head. "No, but I'm pretty sure the reason God brought me here was to show me how good I have it and to quit complaining about the life He has given me."

"Amen," Clint agreed. "I am just praying that God will sustain me long enough to get home and back into the normal routine. I can definitely tell you I am not called to the mission field."

"Me, neither," Amy stated emphatically. "No way, nohow."

"Well, since you guys seem to be doing alright now, I'm going to go wander around for a bit. I need some time away from everything."

"Okay, Lisa, but be careful. We don't want to have to come search for you." The expression on Amy's face matched the concern in her voice.

"I'll just be looking through the little shops along the main street. I won't venture far."

"Good," Amy said, obviously reassured. "We'll see you later, then."

Lisa left her two friends under the tree in the park. She walked out into the warm rain and began to pray. *Lord, I don't know what's going on. I don't know how to deal with Amy and Clint's misery. I don't know how to deal with John and his ardent dislike for me. I want to do Your will, but I really don't like it here. I—*

She fell against the chest of a male pedestrian. "Excuse me," she apologized in Chinese. She cast her gaze to the ground in embarrassment.

"It's alright," the deep voice replied. "Lisa?"

Lisa looked up and found John regarding her with an expression of confusion. "Yes, it's me."

Evidently amused, he teased, "Has your short attention span gotten the best of you? Looking for some way to entertain yourself for the rest of the night?" Lisa winced. Given her state of mind—that she was already beginning to explore her true motives for the trip—each word may as well have been a barb.

"No, as a matter of fact, I was praying. I needed some quiet time."

John crossed his arms. "Oh, really."

"Yes. And what's more, I needed to talk to you anyway.

You may not like me very much, John, but as your sister in Christ and as a fellow human being, I feel like you're being completely out of line. There is no reason for you to treat me as you do. I have done nothing to offend you. I may not know as much as you, and I may not be persecuted, but I am no less deserving of respect and politeness."

Lisa stomped a small foot for punctuation. *There,* she thought, satisfied. *That ought to put him in his place.*

"I would respect you if you had some depth."

John's response nearly spun her around. "What?" she asked, her voice thick with disbelief.

"You heard me. You only care about yourself, your world. It's as if you live in a snow dome." His tanned face was set in a stern expression. "I would expect that this trip would mean more to you than to any of the others. You have a blood link to this country. . .to these people. Where is your sense of loyalty and kinship?"

Her shock gave way to anger. "You mean this is all about my ancestry? I have news for you, John. I'm an American. This is not my world. I am not obligated to reach out to them because of my genetics. My parents raised me like they would've raised their own flesh and blood. Besides," she added arrogantly, "I worship the Lord, not the ghosts of my ancestors."

"So you have studied a bit about your culture. Well, hurrah for you, Lisa. If you're finished with your pious, self-righteous statements, I'll tell you something: I don't believe in ancestor worship, either. Neither do any of the Chinese Christians you will meet during your time here. But there is something to be said for expressing even the slightest bit of interest in where you come from. You are in the position to serve and reach out to these people in a way that your friends could not. You know the Chinese language. You share their appearance. You would put them at ease. The only barrier standing between you would be one of culture. . .and it's a boundary you aren't even trying to tear down." John stopped to inhale sharply. "You get to leave all of the filth and fear behind, but these people will go on with it forever. I have been called to be a light in the midst of their darkness. God allowed me to recognize the blessing of my heritage. I, too, have an advantage that many missionaries to China have not had."

Lisa stood in shocked silence. She looked to her right and saw her reflection in the dirty glass window of a shop. Her almond eyes, dark skin, and black hair jumped out at her. She had always known she was Chinese. Her parents never tried to keep her ethnicity a secret, but they hadn't capitalized on it, either. They desired as normal a life as possible for their adopted Asian daughter, and Lisa was thankful for that. However, she now questioned whether she could use her ethnicity for furthering the kingdom of God.

John reached out and gripped her shoulders. "Lisa, I will continue to pray that the Lord will open your eyes and your heart. I know you would be a wonderful asset to our ministry here. I pray the harsh reality of life here will strip you of your pride and your selfishness and leave you bare before our almighty God. I hope that someday you will come to a place where your relationship with Him will outweigh your own sense of self. Perhaps spending time with those who have already come to that place will help you arrive, yourself."

Lisa stared deep into his brown eyes. When he touched her, her body flooded with tingling. Her involuntary reaction to his touch, coupled with the lingering sting of his harsh words and challenges, left her head reeling. *Lord, what is this?*

For a moment, John's features clouded with an unidentifiable emotion. He released her suddenly and closed his eyes. "Go," he said softly. "I will continue to pray for you."

Confused, Lisa turned around and pushed her way down the crowded street. Unbidden tears came to her eyes. *Why do I even care what he thinks?* The memory of his touch caused her to shudder. This feeling was so new, so unexplored—something she had never felt with Clint. She wracked her brain to identify it. Suddenly, she knew.

It was desire.

❧

John watched her as she fled from his presence. She floated through the crowd like an apparition, with such fluid grace.

He didn't regret the words he shared with her, but he knew his attitude could have been improved. *If only she could see what she is capable of,* he thought in frustration. Her friends' apathy wouldn't be of any help to her. He knew they were miserable, and Lisa was apt to identify with their plight more readily than she would see the light of his reasoning.

The longer he pondered her potential transformation, the more he hoped it would not come to pass. If it did, he couldn't possibly keep himself from falling in love with her.

Chapter 5

With each step along the dusty sidewalk teeming with bodies, Lisa's anger and resentment gave way to sorrow and remorse. John's words left her feeling naked and ashamed. She tried to stay mad at him—tried to script out the nasty, witty things she would say to him the next time they met—but she couldn't. It was as if God had doused the fire within her and gently called her to truthful self-examination.

Could it be true? Am I really as self-centered and blind as he asserted? Lisa looked around her, and, for the first time, she saw individuals. She was reminded of the blind man healed by Jesus in Mark: "I see people; they look like trees walking around." She knew her eyes had been opened, her blindness healed, when she accepted Christ as her Lord and Savior. She saw herself as cleansed by His blood and redeemed before a holy Lord, but she could not see others. Perhaps, just as with the blind man, God had used John to touch her eyes a second time so she, too, could see everything clearly.

She looked into the eyes of the passersby. In some, a

light shone brightly, as if Christ's radiance had found only one outlet and therefore poured through them with great intensity. Others looked like the walking dead. The emptiness of their gaze belied the farce of their movement. They did not know the Lord. Lisa allowed herself to ache for these lost souls.

This pain is unbearable, she decided. *How can anyone feel so much for so many and survive? Father, I can't go on like this. I just can't.*

A calming voice spoke to her heart, *I will not give you more than you can bear.* They were the words of a Father. Her Father.

"I know," she whispered into the oncoming evening. "I believe You."

She continued to wander through the shopping district when a small, secondhand clothing store claimed her attention. Entering quietly, she greeted the merchant, *"Nin hao."* She desired anonymity tonight and figured an English "hello" would not afford her such luxury.

A delicate pair of black silk slippers with pointed toes and intricate embroidery drew her. They were only about five inches long. Lisa fingered the satiny fabric. "How striking," she murmured.

Setting the slippers down on the wooden counter, she began to fish currency from her bag.

"Ah, a lovely choice," the decrepit woman commented.

"Thank you," Lisa replied, pleased that her eye for quality had not failed her.

"Do you know what these are?"

Lisa shook her head. "I assumed they belonged to a child."

The small-framed Chinese woman laughed. The infectious mirth caused Lisa to smile. "No, no, dear one! Let me tell you what these are. Perhaps they will have special meaning to you." After finalizing the transaction, she motioned Lisa to sit at a simple wooden table. Her eyes danced with a bright light, and Lisa felt confident that the gray-haired woman knew Jesus. This warmed her as she listened to the woman's quavering voice.

"Long ago, the practice of foot-binding became popular and desirable for young girls. It was believed that, the smaller her foot, the greater her beauty. Are you familiar with this?"

Lisa nodded apprehensively and added, "I have heard of the small feet of Chinese women, and perhaps even the term of foot-binding, but I don't know much beyond that."

"Ah, I see. Perhaps I should explain how it was done for you."

The woman's dialect was melodious and smooth, and Lisa found she understood with little effort.

"They would usually begin when she was still a small child and the bones were moldable. They would take a long strip of cloth and tightly wind it around her tiny foot. Then they would bind the other foot. As the girl continued to grow, so would her feet. However, the cloth caused the bones to deform and twist, and the foot would remain small. Some girls were not so lucky. When the feet of older girls were bound, it was a most horrible thing. Their bones had to be crushed and broken in order to achieve this noble look."

Lisa could not contain her disgust. "That's awful. I'm glad that practice is antiquated."

"Not so antiquated as you might think," the woman countered as she wagged a gnarled finger. "Though it was outlawed at the turn of the twentieth century, women continued to mutilate their daughters' bodies with this practice through the 1920s."

Lisa was speechless, having convinced herself that something so inhumane belonged in the past, far removed from her. To know that a generation of elderly women perhaps still lived, having endured this travesty of "beauty," turned her stomach.

"They could not walk so well, as you can imagine," the old woman continued. "Only little steps. They tired easily and usually had to be carried beyond a short distance." She reached out her bony arm and lovingly touched the slippers that lay in front of Lisa. "But they certainly had beautiful shoes, didn't they?"

The question was rhetorical, and Lisa remained silent.

"It is amazing how easily the bones deformed. Just a piece of cloth. It did not take wood or steel or stone. Just soft, pliable cloth."

Curiosity drove Lisa to find her voice. "I mean no disrespect," she began. "I was just wondering. . .if you, or rather your feet were—"

"See for yourself," the woman lifted a slender leg so Lisa could see. Her cotton shoes were no longer than the silken slippers Lisa had just purchased.

"You poor thing," Lisa gasped.

"Ahh, it was not so bad for me. My mother bound my feet when I was quite small. It could've been much worse. I grew into my deformity gradually. Others suffered far more."

Lisa pushed down the queasy feeling in her stomach. She couldn't even imagine the pain this woman had endured or how hard it must be for her to do her job. "How is it you work, then?"

"I just do what I can. I have to rest, but I keep going. You will find that often it is not the length of the stride that matters as much the dedication to the completion of the journey." She inhaled deeply, then exhaled. It was a peaceful sigh. "Poor decisions were made on my behalf. I cannot change what was done to me. They didn't know any better and did the best for me that they knew how. I am responsible for how I live now. I can spend time frozen in anger, but why? What would that accomplish? Nothing, of course! Instead, I let them serve as a reminder to me about how easily strong things can be corrupted by soft things. It is better to not become entangled at all, wouldn't you agree?"

"Yes, Ma'am. Your wisdom has opened not only my eyes but also my heart. Thank you for your time and your words." Lisa's eyes misted with tears again. She fumbled to open her bag, causing her Bible to slip out onto the table as she roughly cleared a flat space for her slippers. Lisa looked up to find the old woman's eyes grow wide.

Quickly, Lisa recovered it and zipped the bag closed. For a moment, neither spoke. Despite her initial feelings of this woman's salvation, Lisa feared the worst—arrest, imprisonment, torture. The woman reached out and grasped Lisa's wrist. Lisa began to shake uncontrollably and tears streamed freely down her face. "Please," she whispered.

The woman said nothing but turned Lisa's hand upright. Slowly, deliberately, the woman's twisted forefinger traced a "t" upon her open palm. When Lisa shook her head, the merchant seemed to see that Lisa didn't understand. Lisa sought the depths of the old woman's eyes as she retraced the figure in Lisa's hand. As she smiled, Lisa's eyes grew wide with comprehension. A cross! This woman was a believer!

Instead of abating, Lisa's tears continued. "You are—"

"Shhh. . ." The woman placed her finger to her lips as she released Lisa's arm.

Lisa nodded and sniffed. Securing her bag over her shoulder, she walked to the entrance of the shop.

"Thank you for your words," Lisa said finally. "The slippers are far more valuable to me now that I know what they are."

"I suspected that would be the case." The woman laughed. "You strike me as the sort of woman who finds meaning in the details."

Lisa smiled. "You know, I wouldn't have said that was so even twenty-four hours ago, but today, I would say with absolute confidence that is exactly who I am."

The lobby's soft lighting beckoned Lisa to rest and reflect. The hour ensured foot traffic would be at a minimum, and

Lisa felt safe to journal her thoughts. Carefully, she removed the slippers and placed them before her. She closed her eyes for a brief moment and prayed for God to soften her heart and allow the lesson He had for her to take hold.

With clear and well-formed script, Lisa began to capture her swirling and frantic feelings.

> *Sin is the soft cloth that we allow to bind and deform our hearts. It seems unassuming and harmless as it encircles our deepest desires and emotions, yet as we grow, leaving the sin in its place, it begins to thwart and mutilate our heart's growth. When God lavishes His perfect love upon us, the binding is removed and the healing can begin. However, the results—the consequences—of our sin leave a lasting impression. We are reduced to tiny, childlike steps toward our goal. The goal, of course, is becoming like Him—like our Savior, Jesus. The more we try, the longer we endeavor to be like Him and to do as He commands, the easier our walk becomes. The power to continue comes only from our faith in who Jesus is: the Son of the living God, the Anointed One, appointed to save us through His death and resurrection. Jesus has set us free for freedom's sake, Galatians 5:1 states. We should never again take upon us the yoke of slavery. We should never allow sin to bind us again. Our hearts are free to be healed and whole.*

Lisa read and reread her words, feeling their truth take hold of her crippled heart. *Oh, Lord,* she wrote her prayer. *Please forgive me for allowing the sins of pride and apathy to bind my heart. Please cut away the cloth and let my heart begin to heal. Help me to make steps, however small, toward You and Your will for my life. I thank You and praise You for the freedom You secured for me in Your Son's death. I pray that I would never again allow my heart to be bound by the things of this world. Thank You for John and for his honesty. Please allow me the opportunity to make things right. Amen.*

"Oh, Lisa!"

Lisa fumbled toward consciousness to find Amy and Clint's panic-stricken faces.

"We were worried sick! Have you been here all night? Come up to the room. It's nearly midnight!"

Lisa could not shake her exhaustion. In a daze, she grabbed the silk slippers and held them close to her.

"Clint, grab her bag, please. I'll help her upstairs." Amy gingerly took hold of her arm and led her toward the elevator. In a matter of minutes, they arrived at the door of the girls' room.

"Here's her stuff," Clint said, handing the bag over to Amy. "I'm going to bed."

"Thanks for your help, Clint," Amy whispered.

"Yes, thank you," Lisa managed. She hadn't felt this tired in a long time. All she wanted was to fall into the lush bed and return to her dreams.

As soon as she slipped off her shoes, she did just that. She was surprised to find John, smiling and more handsome than ever, awaiting her in her slumbering imaginings.

Chapter 6

"Amy, have you seen my journal?" Lisa checked the zippered compartments of her backpack.

"Yeah, you had it last night, when Clint and I had to send out a search party for you." Amy cried in exasperation, "I can't believe you passed out on the lobby couch!"

"I was so exhausted after everything that happened." Lisa shrugged. "I was being dealt with severely last night."

Amy cocked an eyebrow suspiciously. "Oh, really? Anything you'd care to share?"

"Not here!" Lisa laughed, her arm sweeping over the expanse of their not-so-private hotel room.

"Enough said," Amy conceded. "You are so right."

※

"This bus is beginning to feel like an old friend," Peter joked.

"Sure, an old friend with a bad muffler and killer vinyl," Clint added.

Amy frowned. "I don't think of this bus as a friend. A mortal enemy, maybe. Friend, never."

"Hear, hear!" Clint smiled.

Lisa watched the exchange with little emotion. Clint had been spending more and more time with Amy. Lisa knew it was due to her own suggestions. She knew Amy and Clint shared the same feelings of homesickness and isolation. They were able to comfort one another. As she'd watched them grow closer in the past weeks, she wondered why a sense of jealously had not surfaced, as she might have expected. After much prayerful consideration, she realized that as Clint and Amy grew closer together, the relationship she and Clint shared remained fairly constant. He was the same good friend. He offered the same brotherly consolation. Amy, too, treated her no differently. The conclusion she arrived at was simply that she and Clint had never truly been a couple. They were the best of friends, and everyone thought they should date. So they dated. She never felt any passion with Clint, and she never resented that fact, either.

Despite this truth, though, she knew it would be wrong to entertain any further thoughts about John until the matter had been cleared between her and Clint. She hoped she would have an opportunity to address both men with her newfound revelations.

"Earth to Lisa, come in, Lisa!" Amy poked her shoulder.

"Sorry, I was just thinking."

"Well, don't let your mind wander like that when we're at the Great Wall," Amy advised. "You're likely to fall right off."

One by one, the students filed into the small shack of a

Christian family. The furnishings were sparse, but laughter and love filled the room.

John signaled for silence and introduced the host family. "This is Chang Xiaoping and his wife Men. They are gracious enough to let us use their home for a night of fellowship and prayer." He introduced a few Chinese students, then invited everyone to sit and relax.

Softly, they began to sing hymns, with verses both in Chinese and English. The mood was reverent and the natives exuded an almost tangible peace. Lisa felt it too, and it surprised her. She realized that meetings of this sort were dangerous and forbidden, yet the object of their affections seemed to remove any anxiety.

Lisa looked over to Amy and Clint. Their eyes were wide with fear, and they continued to look over their shoulders to the front door. Lisa prayed for their burdens to be eased and tried not to let their restive spirits deter her worship.

"I hope you all were able to read John 15 over the last few days," John began. "As I'm sure you've noticed, the theme of our studies is the cost of being a disciple for Jesus Christ. Would anyone care to share a verse or two that has been particularly precious?" He shifted his gaze over the group, and Lisa noticed his glance remained upon her for a moment longer. She felt a rush of delight course through her veins as he smiled ever so slightly at her before breaking their eye contact. She hoped he perceived the change in her spirit—that he could recognize how God had freed her heart.

"Peter," he said, motioning to the dark-haired man.

"What stuck out to you as important? What spoke to you in this passage?"

"Well, I found verse eighteen to be a great comfort: 'If the world hates you, keep in mind that it hated Me first.'"

John stroked his chin. "Interesting. Tell me why those words comforted you. I would think they'd exasperate and possibly discourage, yet you have found it brings you reassurance."

Lisa found she enjoyed John's approach to study, seeing that his questions were rooted in the honest feelings few Christians cared to voice.

"Initially, the verse struck me the same way. Kind of like, 'Well, that's good to know, God, but how is that going to make it better for me? I don't want to be hated by anyone.' But then, I meditated on it, as well as verses fourteen and fifteen where Jesus calls us His friends, rather than His servants. It occurred to me that what He was saying was, 'Look, no matter what happens or how you are perceived, so long as you are keeping My commands and being My friend, you can know it's not you the world is rejecting. It's My Spirit in you that irks them.'"

"Mmm. . .that's good. Did anyone else feel like this?"

Timidly, Lisa raised her hand. John acknowledged her with a nod. "Go on."

"Well, it hit me the same way at first too. But God has really been working to reveal my own selfishness to me." She noticed a twinge of a smile played at his lips. "I have desired comfort and acceptance my whole life.

When I read on in verse nineteen, about how Jesus has chosen me out of the world, and that is the reason the world will hate me—because of Him working in me, I understood what a privilege it is to be despised by the world. I'm not supposed to fit in if I belong to Him. The only way to have the world love you is to belong to it rather than to God. Now, I can honestly say I don't want the world's acceptance anymore."

John pushed his hand through his hair. Lisa found herself lost in the simple movement. As her love and longing for God intensified, she found her preoccupation with John also increased. It was odd. She felt a pang of conviction as she heard Clint clear his throat to her left. *Lord, please be in the midst of this. . .of us.*

"It's good to hear, Lisa. Did anyone else—"

Suddenly, the door burst open and numerous soldiers filed in, each carrying a large club. "Stand up!" the leader shouted in Chinese, and then again in English.

Amy screamed, and Lisa looked over to find Clint had taken her into a protective embrace. That set her mind somewhat at ease. *They have each other. What a blessing!*

Fear shot through her like bolts of lightning. As she tried to process all that was happening, she caught a glimpse of the host couple. Their faces were calm and untroubled. Hand in hand, they looked upon the armed men without any outward sense of trepidation. Lisa prayed God would bless her with that tranquility too.

The guard spoke in English through clenched teeth. "We found this. We know it belongs to someone in your group. We have many eyes in this city. You are foolish and disrespectful, and you shall be punished."

Lisa felt all the blood drain away from her face as the man in charge held up a single item: her journal.

"Everyone keep quiet!" John commanded. Lisa felt the heat in the room rise as the bodies flooded through the door. The smell of sweat was pungent.

"So, you know something!" the leader snorted. "If you know what's best for you, you'll tell me who this belongs to." He thwacked John's chest with the broad side of the journal. Lisa cringed as John drew his lips into a tight line. "Have you nothing to say? Are you responsible for this group?"

John remained silent. The guard raised the journal a second time, only now it prepared to meet with the side of John's head.

Lisa's mind raced. The thought of John suffering for her stupidity sickened her. *Oh, Lord, what have I done?* Lisa had revealed them by losing her journal. A simple, hardback book. Why hadn't she been more cautious? This morning, she'd realized it was missing but had thought little of it, assuming she had misplaced it. She berated herself for her oversight and prayed God would spare her friends and give her the courage to do what was necessary.

"I want to know to whom this belongs. Now!" Anger contorted the man's face. He threw the journal into the midst of the circle.

She focused her mind on a single name: *Jesus.* Taking a deep breath, she broke from her place in the circle and claimed the journal, now covered with dirt from the floor.

"It is mine."

She heard Amy sob loudly, and Clint calling out to her, his voice breaking with emotion, "Lisa, what's going on?"

She tried to communicate that everything would be all right, but her mouth became chalky and dry. She couldn't form the words to comfort him, so she prayed God's peace might enfold him. Tears glistened in his blue eyes, and Lisa's heart broke. *Lord, protect him. Speak peace into his heart.*

Instantly, the soldiers began pushing around the occupants of the room and lined them up against the walls. Though the Chinese Christians maintained their composure, the members of Lisa's "tour group" were frantic. Lisa remained in the center of the room, calmly repeating the name of Jesus in her mind.

Without further contemplation, she marched over to the man who had produced and cast aside her journal. "I said the journal is mine, Sir. That's my writing. Don't punish everyone else for something I've done."

The guard eyed her, his face stern and cold. "And exactly what is it you have done?"

Lisa broke away from the man's intense gaze and looked to John. His lean face was peaceful. His arms rested at his sides. Almost imperceptibly, he nodded. Lisa felt his support for the actions she knew must follow.

The noise and chaos of the room faded to a dull roar as Lisa steeled her resolve. Locking her stare with the ruthless guard, she stated evenly, "I am a Christian. I believe in God the Father, Christ Jesus the Son, and in the Holy Spirit. I wrote those words last night, as God has been dealing with my heart."

"Lisa, shut up! Don't say anything! Don't talk to him!" Clint's voice wavered with emotion and terror. In response, a guard shoved him to the ground. Amy wept loudly, sobbing Lisa's name as another man yanked her to his side. Lisa could see the individual beads of perspiration roll down Clint's face as he grimaced at her, whimpering.

The guard sneered and pulled a small pistol from his side holster. "I didn't quite hear you, young lady," he said sinisterly. "Would you be so quick to make that proclamation with your life on the line?" He held the barrel firmly at Lisa's temple.

In a flash, everything became muted. Lisa felt an inexplicable peace wash over her. She closed her eyes briefly and prayed. *Father. You're here with me, aren't You? You won't leave me. You won't forsake me. You are worth dying for. I love You, Lord. Please give me the words.*

After what felt like an eternity, she opened her eyes and stared deeply into the face of the soldier. As she spoke, his smug smile faded into a frustrated frown.

"Yes, and may God forgive you for what you are about to do."

Chapter 7

John teetered between admiration and disbelief. Had she just said what he thought she said? Had she really said yes with the barrel of a gun pressed against her head? Had she truly interceded for the vile guard, realizing that forgiveness was within reach for even a persecutor of Christ's church?

He watched her for what seemed like an eternity. The skirt of her navy dress stirred slightly in the breeze let in by the splintered door. She clasped her hands in front of her, suggesting prayer. Her journal was held fast within the crook of her arm, secure against her side. Her features stayed relaxed, as though this man had asked her for the time, rather than for her life.

She was, in a word, breathtaking.

You've really done it, haven't You, Father? You've touched her heart. You've softened her and strengthened her by Your grace. She knows her faith has not been misplaced with You and that You are truly faithful. She has laid down her life for her friends, on Your behalf. Lord, thank You for her example—for her resolve. Thank You for her peace. Amen.

Within his chest, he could feel his heart swelling with love. It threatened to burst out and fly away. *Looks like I was right,* he admitted ruefully, remembering the night she confronted him. *There's no way in the world I can't love this woman. What do I do now, Father?*

The seconds that passed felt like days. John knew what he must do. He had to end it.

"That's enough!" All heads, save Lisa's, turned to gawk at John in wide-eyed wonder.

"Excuse me?" the head guard asked. The pistol never left Lisa's temple. Lisa never opened her eyes.

"It's over, Enlai. Thank you for your time." John pivoted and extended his hands to the host couple. "I apologize for frightening you. We will replace your door immediately."

Enlai retracted the gun from Lisa's head. John knew it to be a highly detailed water gun, but it served its purpose well. Lisa did not move. She did not whimper, nor did she show any sign of relief. She remained stoic—unmoving.

Slowly, he walked over and trailed his forefinger lightly down the length of her bare arm. She was so soft and warm. "Lisa." The name formed easily on his lips.

"Yes?"

"Lisa, open your eyes. It's over. It wasn't real."

At this, her eyes fluttered open, her dark lashes reminding him of black hummingbird wings. "It wasn't real?" she asked weakly.

"No. But," John raised his voice to address the group, "the lesson was very real. This was one of the calmer scenarios. Sometimes, the guards aren't so keen on conversation." He noticed Enlai's embarrassed smile but continued.

"Someone tell me why this 'raid' occurred."

Before he could call upon a volunteer to summarize Lisa's foolish neglect, Clint's words exploded. "Because this is a horrible place! Because it's full of inhumane bullies who could torture an innocent girl!" His cry was laden with emotion.

John felt sorry for him, yet he knew that Clint's perception of the event was highly self-centered and immature.

John prayed the Spirit would give him the words to admonish Clint to review the situation from a more objective vantage point, yet he still wanted comfort for him in the midst of his weakness.

Amy lifted her tear-streaked face. She stared directly into John's eyes. He could sense her anger even before her words came. "I. . .want. . .to go home. Now." And, just as quickly, she collapsed back into Clint's arms and sobbed against his chest.

John chewed his lip thoughtfully. He hadn't expected anyone to demand to return to the States. Of course, he couldn't keep them here. He would never force anyone to stay, though he had hoped they would stick it out. Perhaps he had gone too far. *Oh, Lord. . .if I've acted outside Your will, please don't let this have been in vain. Please be glorified, even in the midst of my selfish motives.*

Several of the others sank to the floor, notably relieved. Peter and Courtney fell to their knees and pressed their foreheads to the floor. Their muffled yet discernable words of praise began to fill the room. Xiaoping and Men did likewise, offering thanksgiving to the Lord in Chinese.

Enlai and his men nodded toward John expectantly. "Yes," he replied and motioned toward the door. "By all means, gentlemen, go. Thank you again for your performance. May Jehovah bless you and keep you."

"You also, Brother." They disappeared soundlessly into the darkness.

John closed his eyes and prayed for wisdom. He felt a small hand upon his forearm.

"Lisa."

"John, I understand now. I know what you were so desperately trying to tell me. I am sorry I was so stubborn. I am so sorry it had to come to this." He watched the tears trail down her blazing cheeks. She seemed so frail. So helpless. *No,* he rejoiced. She was anything but!

Her stare remained fixed upon him. As he searched the depths of her eyes, he felt as though a veil had been lifted. He knew her heart was bare and vulnerable before the Lord and also before him. She seemed to understand that his heart was in a similar position before her. Her gently upturned lips suggested a shared secret—an intimacy. She cocked her head to one side and squinted, as if trying to see him more clearly.

"John," she said finally, "we need to talk."

"I think you're right."

John and Lisa lagged behind the group as they made their way back to the hotel. The night was still, and the pathways were unusually clear. John was glad for the solitude.

In a hushed voice, he said, "Lisa, I just wanted you to know how much I admire you for what you did tonight."

She smiled, replying, "It was all God. I can't tell you what happened back there. I remember being so scared. I was completely unsure of how to proceed. Then, I just kept repeating Jesus' name and praying for peace and strength, and wow! Did He ever deliver!" She cast her gaze heavenward, her smile never leaving her lips. It looked as though she was sharing a private joke with the Lord.

"I'm the one who found your journal," he confessed.

"Did you read it? Is that how you knew it belonged to me?" She paused, then added, "I'm just curious. I'm not upset or anything. I prayed that God would reveal my internal change to you somehow."

John wrestled with his chagrin. He knew it was not the right thing to do, to read Lisa's private thoughts and feelings, yet he'd been drawn to the cloth-covered book. "Yes, I read what you wrote. I can't tell you how much your words blessed me. The Spirit has really gifted you with the revelation about binding cloths and sin. I hope you'll share it one day. It will minister to people; that I know for certain."

"Thank you," she said softly. "I just can't believe how much God has changed me. It's been only a short while, but I feel like a completely different person. I feel freer. I feel happier."

"What about Clint and Amy? The whole ordeal really shook them up." John stuffed the anxiety that Lisa would come to not only blame but also to hate him for the early departure of her companions.

She shrugged. "It's not a life they are comfortable with. I know they love God. They love Him the best way they know how, and they are convinced it is enough. You've shown me that cannot be the case where I am concerned. I can't fault them for their reaction any more than they can come down on me for mine. If they truly feel the need to go home early, then God will meet them exactly where they are. I am confident of that now."

"I'm glad you see His hand in this." His voice sounded husky and full of emotion in his own ears. *Lord, help me to guard my heart. . . .*

"John, it's so strange. So much has changed in me in the past few days. I can't believe how much my heart has changed in such a very short time."

John reached out and grasped her arm. The group had already retreated into the hotel lobby, and he and Lisa stood several hundred feet beyond its entrance. He felt himself grow bold in the privacy of darkness.

"Lisa," he murmured, pulling her near. He nuzzled her ear and heard her give a sharp gasp as he did. "So much has changed in a short time. So much."

"John. . ."

"Shhh. . . ," he insisted. "Don't speak. There will be plenty of time to analyze this later. Let's be caught up in the moment, just for tonight." Holding her fast with his right arm, he tilted her chin up with the forefinger of his left hand. Deliberately, his mouth descended upon hers in a passionate kiss.

Tenderly, he drew back and ushered her into the hotel lobby. She said nothing. As the moments wore on, John's mind became flooded with the reality of the situation. Lisa would be here for only a short while. This was not her world, no matter how much God transformed her heart. Soon, she would leave—not only China, but him. This truth brought an onslaught of unwelcome memories. Memories of another tour group. Another girl, not unlike Lisa. And what had become of her? John gritted his teeth against the pain he felt inside. Perhaps it was best to remain alone.

Lisa crept into her room, hoping Amy had gone to sleep. *Lord, how will I ever explain this? I am sorry. It was inappropriate and wrong. But, Father, I love him! I've never felt this way about a man in all my life. I don't know what to do.*

When her roommate didn't stir, she sighed. After changing into her pajamas, Lisa brushed her teeth absentmindedly, then crawled into bed. She stared at the ceiling, pondering John's actions. He'd kissed her! It was romantic and passionate and perfect.

Why, then, had he pushed her away? Why did he leave without so much as a word? Had she done something wrong?

Perhaps this was God's way of giving her time to sort out the details of her relationship with Clint. John was being noble. He knew that she and Clint had arrived as a couple; though he, no doubt, had seen Clint and Amy's budding affections, just as she had. Surely he realized that she and Clint had never truly loved each other in that way—in the way she loved John. Didn't that count for something? Why must he torture her with his waxing and waning emotions?

Her confusion over John coupled with the events of

the evening. Tears stung her eyes, and she let them fall unchallenged.

"I know I don't have to understand what's going on, Lord, but if You could give me a hint, I'd really appreciate it."

She fell into a fitful sleep, where she once again found John awaiting her arrival.

Chapter 8

"So you're really serious about this, Amy? You're leaving?" Lisa frowned as her roommate threw items into a suitcase with intensity. She turned on the television to be loud background noise, in order to keep their words private.

"I can't believe you can stay! Lisa, this is crazy. This place is crazy. What John does is amazing, and may God bless him tremendously. It is not for me." Amy shook her head emphatically. "I can't say I'm not still slightly perturbed by his staged raid, but a man's got to do what a man's got to do." She zipped her suitcase and placed it on the floor by her sandaled feet. "That's why I suspect he'll understand that I've got to do what I've got to do."

Lisa nervously tucked a stray strand of hair behind her ear. "I'll miss you," she said finally. It would be so strange now with Amy and Clint gone. She knew she had much to keep her occupied here, not the least of which was John, but she loved her friends and enjoyed their company.

"I'll miss you too, but you'll be home in a few weeks.

Then it'll be like old times. No more of these clandestine operations and secret, violence-inducing Bible studies. Just good, old-fashioned First Amendment rights." Amy smiled. "You take care, alright? I don't want to hear any more stories about you with a gun to your head. Got it?"

Lisa smiled and wiped away a tear. "Got it."

Amy sat down next to Lisa. "I wanted to tell you how truly awesome I think you are. Last night just opened my eyes in a way I can't fully comprehend."

"It was the Spirit. Remember those verses in Matthew 10?" She opened her Bible and read along with the text. " 'But when they arrest you, do not worry about what to say or how to say it. At that time you will be given what to say, for it will not be you speaking, but the Spirit of your Father speaking through you.' I prayed that God would make those words true in my life. He was faithful, and I wasn't afraid."

"I hope I can be that strong someday." Amy sighed. Her doubt was evident.

"No, no! I don't think anyone can plan for those sorts of things. You won't know until you're there. That's how you know it is God. If you could somehow prepare or psych yourself up, then the temptation to take credit for it would be too great."

"Well, then, God used you mightily, Miss Perdue. I am honored to be your friend."

Lisa hugged Amy close. "Thank you. Have a safe trip home. Take care of Clint."

Amy grinned. "Can do. Have you talked to him yet?"

"Nope. I'm headed his way now. Pray that it goes well."

"I think it will. Just be honest. He's a good guy. He'll do okay."

Sighing, Lisa stood up and flipped the television off. "I know you're right."

"Well, get to it. Nothing to gain by putting it off." She followed Lisa to the door and set her suitcase down.

"I'll see you later," Lisa said and closed the door behind her. As she walked down the hallway, she prayed Amy and Clint's flight home would be uneventful and safe. When she arrived outside Clint's door, she took a deep breath and beseeched God for clarity.

She rapped lightly, and Clint answered within seconds. "Oh, hey, Lisa. How are you?"

"I'm good, Clint. Do you have some time to talk? I think we have some things we need to discuss." She hoped her words sounded friendly and gentle. She didn't want to hurt him or make him angry. Maybe Clint had already perceived the very things she would bring to light, and the conversation could be quick and painless.

Clint grabbed his briefcase and wallet. "You bet. I had a feeling we were going to do this. I was trying to decide if I should come get you or wait for you to come find me. Looks like it worked itself out." He gave her a winning smile and held the door for her. "To the park?" he questioned.

"To the park."

They arrived fifteen minutes later and found a secluded bench. Lisa reached out for his hand. "Clint, this isn't going to come as much of a surprise, is it?"

"No, not if what I think is happening is happening."

He sighed. With a sad smile, he added softly, "Lisa, I've always known we were different in a lot of ways, but I also know that you could search the whole world and not find two people who are as close as we are. You're my best friend, Lisa. I don't want our friendship to change."

"Me, neither! You are very important to me," Lisa exclaimed.

"And you wouldn't want someone with as much information on you as I have, running around unchecked, right?" he teased.

Lisa laughed. Even in the midst of a breakup, he was still playing the clown. "You are so right." Lisa fidgeted on the bench. "Clint, I have to say this. God has revealed to me a great many things about my heart. I've been shallow and unresponsive to His leading. I've sought my own comfort and lived a very safe life."

"Up until last night. Lisa, I don't think I could've done what you did, and that scares me. I remembered the verses in Matthew about denying Christ before men and how He would do the same before His Father. I don't want Him to deny me, but I can't seem to get beyond myself." His eyes filled with tears. Lisa had never seen him this full of emotion.

"I think that is part of why we need to end our romantic relationship, Clint. I want you to feel confident in your faith. I want God to do for you what He has done for me. You need to spend your time focusing on Him, developing your relationship with Him. I don't think that you can do that with me."

Clint leaned his head back against the bench and

stretched his legs out. "I know what you say is true. I do need to grow spiritually, but I don't know how. It's easier for women. You are encouraged to share your emotions and to let them come out. Serving God—the way you did last night—is born out of a passion I've been taught my whole life to stifle. Guys aren't supposed to be ruled by feelings and such. We're supposed to be courageous for the sake of courage, you know? The kind of soul-searching you are implying would mean a complete overhaul in my life. Where do you start?" Desperation edged his tone.

"I can't tell you that, Clint. But I'm sure you knew that when you asked." She reached out and placed her hand on his arm. "But start in the Word. Maybe ask Peter about becoming your accountability partner. Pray. Clint, I'm not suggesting this is an easy road. Or a safe one. But it is the right one. Don't chalk it up to being a female thing or a male thing. It's a God thing."

Clint remained silent for a few moments. Lisa hoped he was beginning to process her words. She wanted so much for him to yield to God and let Him have His way in his life. "I hope you don't think I'm trying to say that I'm better than you or I've 'arrived' spiritually. I haven't. I'm still learning and growing myself. And it's hard. I never imagined I could feel as much as I do. I've never looked at people in terms of their souls before. I've never felt anguish for the lost or rejoiced in the knowledge of the saved. And these people," she said, motioning to the passersby. "God has really laid them on my heart. My heritage is wrapped up in them, and that has become really important to me."

"I can't help you there," he admitted. "For so long, it's never even crossed my mind. Your ethnicity, I mean. It never seemed to matter to you." Lisa discerned an element of defensiveness.

"Clint, you're right. I didn't care. I didn't worry about learning about my background. But I know that it's something I need to do. I need to be more involved in sharing the gospel with them. The things they endure. . . they humble me."

"I can't understand it. I admire you, and I know if anyone can do it, you can. But I can't. Not yet."

"I know."

"I'll miss having you around," he said finally.

"And I'll miss you. But I hope you won't be absent from my life. I don't want you to be angry with me."

Clint turned to face her. His features conveyed more emotion than his words ever could. "Lisa, I could never be angry with you—especially when you're heeding the Lord's call upon your life. If anything, I'm jealous. I'm in awe of how quickly He's worked this change in your life. You're so different than when we first arrived. I can see that. I know I'm not what you need, and I'm sorry."

"Don't be sorry. I'm not. I've enjoyed you. You are so much a part of who I am now. You'll always be in my heart."

They watched a group of children being led through the park. Their laughter filled the air, and their animated chatter made Lisa smile.

"Can I ask you something?" Clint sounded hesitant, and Lisa knew what he would say.

"John," she whispered.

"Yes." More silence. "Will you pursue a relationship with him?"

"I honestly don't know, Clint. I won't lie—I have feelings for him, and I know he has feelings for me. But my desire is to grow in God. I want His leading in my life. I'm praying about it."

"Well, I just want you to know that, whatever should happen between you two, it's okay. I know you don't need my permission, but you have my blessing. I know that you and I have come to this place because of who we are, and not because of John."

A tear slipped down her cheek. "Thank you. That means a lot to me. You're a good man, Clint. God will do great things with you, and I'm so glad He put you in my life."

"Likewise." He lifted her hand to his lips and lightly brushed a kiss across the back. "Good-bye, Lisa."

John sat with his back to the elevator. Lisa quietly walked over and sat next to him on the lobby sofa.

"Can we talk?" she asked softly.

"Sure." He seemed gruff and indifferent. "Let's take a walk."

"Yes, I think that would be wise." They made their way out onto the street. "Amy and Clint left a little while ago," Lisa stated matter-of-factly.

"I know."

"Clint and I had a discussion before they went. He and I talked about how we had grown apart romantically.

He is going to try to develop his relationship with God into something real and stable. He's frightened about how to do it, because he feels the emotion involved will somehow compromise his masculinity, but he knows I'm not what he needs right now. . .and he isn't what I need."

John's pace slowed a little, but his gaze remained fixed on something off in the distance. "And what is it you do need, Lisa?"

"I need God. I need His direction. I need whomever He sends into my life to love me and lead me."

"So you broke up with Clint in order to make room for this. . .someone."

"No. Yes. I don't know. I felt like it was the right thing to do, in terms of our lives. It wasn't even about anyone else so much as it was about where God has taken me and where He wants to take Clint."

"That sounds very noble."

He seemed so disinterested. Lisa's confusion gave way to exasperation. "John, what do you want from me? Do you want me to say it?" She clenched her fists. *Lord, You know my heart. Please let him know the relationship I had with Clint has nothing to do with him. Please let him know. . .*

"Lisa, I don't want anything from you. There's nothing you need to say to me or clarify for me. You've said good-bye to Clint, and I'm glad."

The bold statement took her aback.

"Does that shock you? What do you want from me, Lisa? What is it you want me to say?" John halted in the middle of the sidewalk.

"I've prayed about this a lot." Her words were all but drowned out by the noises of Beijing.

"Prayed about what, Lisa? Us? You and me? What is it that you want?" His voice was filled with pain and desperation, despite the harsh nature of his words.

She squared her shoulders and looked deep into his eyes. "I want you to love me, John. I want you to love me as I love you."

The rigid muscles in John's face softened. His eyes seemed to plead for understanding. "Lisa, I. . .there's so much I want to say to you, explain to you. I—I don't know what I want to say. I'm sorry. I'm so sorry." As he turned and walked away, his powerful strides carrying him farther and farther away from her, Lisa realized she had no more tears left to cry.

Chapter 9

T his has got to stop," Lisa announced to the empty room. "I don't have time to let his games work themselves out. Regardless of the outcome, I have to know. I have to know the truth." In the past fourteen days, she'd seen all the sights China had to offer. The Great Wall, the only ancient man-made structure visible from space, served as a harsh picture of the wall that John had put up to keep her out. More than the traditional attractions, though, Lisa's heart had had been captured by the faces of the children. She found herself wondering who would tell them the wonderful news about Jesus and teach them. She had grown attached to the few families she'd met, and she couldn't deny the desire she felt to keep in contact with them. But how could she, when the man in charge would hardly speak three words to her?

She donned a wide-brimmed straw hat encircled with a cream ribbon to match her sundress. The afternoon sun continued to blaze outside her window, and she knew rain was not likely today. It was just as well. She didn't need any distractions.

As she passed by the desk clerk, he waved to her. "Do you speak Chinese?" he asked.

"Yes," she replied. "How can I help you, Sir?"

The man was visibly relieved. "I just wanted to make sure that you and your group are still checking out tomorrow. You can stay longer, if you like. Would you like to extend your stay?"

She shook her head at his eager request. "No, no. We won't be extending our stay, but thank you very much for your kind offer. We have enjoyed our tour immensely. Your country is very beautiful."

"Yes, it is! Thank you." He tapped away at the keyboard of the hotel computer. "Checkout is at 10 A.M. tomorrow. You can leave your keys in the room."

"I'll let my tour guide know so he can notify the group," she promised, then mentally added, *As soon as I cover a few issues of my own.*

✦

"I've been looking all over for you."

John shrugged. "I just finished praying with Enlai and the guys."

"Oh, you mean 'the guards'?" Lisa remembered Enlai quite well. "How are they?"

"They're doing alright. They are hungry for more frequent fellowship meetings, but there isn't a whole lot anyone can do about that. If we met with any sort of regularity, we'd surely be discovered."

"It must be difficult for them." Her heart broke for the new Christians. John had explained that they had only been believers for a few months. Their zeal for the Lord was amazing, and they were starving for more of God's Word and His presence. She prayed their passion would survive, despite the long periods of spiritual droughts.

John and Lisa walked in silence through the alleyways. Lisa pretended to be absorbed with her surroundings while she deliberated over her course of action. As they neared the hotel, Lisa decided it was now or never. She had no intention of dragging out the inevitable. "John, I leave tomorrow afternoon."

"I know," he said heavily.

"Well, I can't leave it like this. I hate how distant you've been for the past two weeks. I can live with it if you no longer care about me, but I can't live with this silence. . .this sense of alienation."

When John didn't comment, she continued. "Even as we worked side by side with these new believers for the past weeks, I knew your mind and your heart were a million miles away. I'm so thankful God gave me the grace to keep my eyes fixed on Him, rather than on your aloofness." Knowing she may never again have the chance, she allowed all of her defenses to crumble away. "God has really matured me in this time. If it's obvious to me, I'm sure you have noticed it, as well." She waited for some indication that he agreed, but none came. His face was passionless and void of interest, as if he were sleeping with his eyes opened.

"Whatever you have to say, John, I can take it. If you're interested in a relationship with me, I'm willing to pursue it; and if you're not, I'm fine with that too. Just don't leave me abandoned here in the middle of the road. Either take me with you, or let me go home. I deserve at least that much."

John closed his eyes and said quietly, "Lisa, you deserve much more than that. I have been so wrapped up in my own emotions, I haven't been fair to you. Come have dinner with me tonight. I'll explain everything then. I need some time to compose my thoughts."

"I'll be in my room when you're ready." She brushed past him and left him alone with his thoughts.

When she had returned to her room, she laid the black slippers in front of her and pulled her journal out from her backpack. She was delighted by the inspiration they continued to bring, and she captured her feelings on page after page. When the room became dim, she flipped on the lights to battle the oncoming twilight. Hours had passed like minutes. She relished her quiet time now, whereas before, her life had been a nonstop search for more innovative distractions.

Lisa set down her pen and reached out for the slippers. She ran her finger over the delicately embroidered lotus flower designs. The bright red and purple threads stood out in bright contrast to the glossy black background. Lisa remembered the old woman who had revealed to her the nature of her purchase. It seemed so incomprehensible that human beings could mutilate one another, not in the throes of a war, but rather in the pursuit of beauty. These stunning shoes were meant to disguise the hideous deformity within. How often had she been guilty of disguising her distorted heart within the confines of a "good" life? The thought was as precious to her now as it had been when it first surfaced.

A knock sounded at her door, pulling her back into the present.

She knew it had to be John. Offering up a quick prayer, she checked her reflection before answering. She hadn't bothered to change into something different. The gesture, she hoped, would show him that she worried more about his regard for her than for her wardrobe.

She combed through her hair with her fingers, then opened the door.

"Were you ready?" he asked shyly. Lisa had not known John to ever be uncertain of himself, but it was obvious his nerves had gotten the best of him. He looked past her, and his eyes grew wide. "Are those the slippers? I haven't gotten to see them yet."

"Oh, let me grab them. I was going to take them with me, anyway. I try not to leave anything important behind, you know." She smiled.

"No, of course not. You are a wise woman," he confirmed with mock graveness.

Playfully, she pushed his shoulder. "That's for a fake compliment," she scolded. She hurried to pack away the slippers in her bag and locked the door behind them. "So where are you taking me for dinner?"

"It's a little place about a mile down toward Tiananmen Square. You'll like it, I think. Plus, it's quiet and private. As I'm sure you've noticed, that's a rare treat here."

"Treat, indeed! I can hardly wait."

Conversation was nonexistent as they traversed the heart of Beijing by means of back alleys and less-traveled side streets. Lisa knew she had said all that she could. The ball was in John's court as far as she was concerned. She would patiently wait out his words.

They shared a dinner of steamed carp in egg custard. Lisa, to her surprise, quite enjoyed the flavor combination. As they neared the end of the main course, John put in for an order of deep-fried watermelon.

"That sounds interesting," Lisa said slowly.

"Oh, you'll love it. But, before dessert, a tradition must be observed. Here you are." John nonchalantly placed two small, round items on the rim of her plate.

"What are they?" she asked, fearing the answer.

"Oh, they're a great delicacy. It's a real honor to receive them."

"John, what are they?"

"Carp eyeballs."

Lisa pretended to gag. "Uh, no, thank you."

John's lips turned down in a frown. "What? You won't eat them? Lisa, I should be quite offended."

Lisa waved her hand in effort to dismiss his mockery. "You'll get over it. You're far too strong to be insulted by my refusal of your fish eyes." The mood was so light, she had almost forgotten the serious matter pending. John had yet to broach the subject.

Once the dinner bowls had been cleared away and the couple nibbled on their dessert, John cleared his throat in a telling way.

"Lisa, I owe you an explanation. I hate myself for the way I've acted with you, but there are reasons. I know that doesn't always help—after all, who wants to hear some-

340

one's excuses?"

Lisa nodded but remained silent, hoping he would go on.

"I do have feelings for you. That's pretty obvious, I guess. But, I am. . .well, afraid. This has happened before. The situation was similar. A small tour group. A woman with a heart for God and for the Chinese people. I thought I had found someone to stand beside me for all time—a partner with whom I could share my passion for ministry. We were even engaged."

"What happened?" Lisa asked softly. "Why did it end?"

"The poverty and the stress of life here wore her down. She ended up leaving China in a manner very similar to Clint and Amy. In the process, I got left behind too. She broke the engagement and my heart." He filled his teacup and sipped. "That was five years ago, and I vowed never to fall in love again. I was pretty successful, if I do say so myself. Until now. Until you."

"Is that why you keep pushing me away? Are you afraid I will do the same thing to you? Break your heart and leave you here to minister alone?"

"I suppose it is. I think it's a legitimate fear," John replied matter-of-factly.

"I think you're wrong." Lisa almost enjoyed the look of disbelief spreading across his features. His brow furrowed, and his eyes narrowed.

"And what would you know about it, Lisa? Has that ever happened to you?"

"No, and I hardly think that is the issue. My point is, your fear is not justified in this case, because I am not her.

If you were pursuing a relationship with her again, then I would agree wholeheartedly. You should proceed with due caution. As far as you and I are concerned, you do well to guard your heart. But don't punish me because she wasn't the one. Perhaps God saved you from something you would later regret. Perhaps He saved you for me."

Lisa was shocked by her own boldness, but she knew that she had prayed over the matter and begged God for the words John needed to hear. She would just have to trust Him to come through.

"You're leaving tomorrow."

"I have to. You know that. You'll be leaving soon too. I don't intend to give up my American citizenship, if that's what you're implying. Then again, you haven't done that either, so I don't see why it's an issue for me." Lisa reached out and grasped John's hands. "I have no intention of forsaking the people of China, John. I want to continue my mission work. I want to learn more about how to reach them and minister to them where they are. And," she continued, "I want to be with you, but I am in no position to play games. I cannot let the pursuit of you compete with the pursuit of my God. He revealed to me how my heart was bound by sin—deformed from years of its subtle restrictions. He has set me free from fear and from my desire for self-preservation. I pray He will do the same for you."

Lisa released her hold on him and slid away from the table. "When you figure out what you want for the future, John, you come find me—if I have a place in your plans."

After paying the bill, John walked along the streets with

no particular destination in mind. Lisa's words seared his brain. He recalled her words—her illustration of the bound feet.

Oh, Lord! he prayed. *I ask You to touch my heart. I am bound by fear. My heart is crippled. Please heal me. I know You long to touch the broken places and make me whole. I see now that I have hidden from the richness of Your blessings by hiding within my work. Please forgive me. I praise You for remaining faithful. Help me to know what to do.*

Chapter 10

The candles gave the dining room a warm glow. Lisa put the finishing touches on the shrimp salad base while Amy added the chilled garlic-butter shrimp.

"I can hardly wait!" Amy squealed. "This is going to be so good."

"Mmm," Lisa agreed. "It was a great idea. I'm so glad I have a roommate who can cook as well as I can."

Amy swatted her with a nearby spatula. "We need to work on your humility, Miss Perdue."

The doorbell sounded, and Amy hurried to the door. "Hi, Clint!" Lisa could hear her enthusiastic greeting from the entryway, and it made her smile.

"Okay, it's just about ready!" she called. It was to be a simple, yet elegant, evening at home. It was the first time in over a month that they had all been together. When Lisa had arrived in the States two weeks ago, she had thrown herself into raising awareness for the people of China, as well as raising financial support. Though she lived with Amy, their schedules seemed so radically different during

344

the summers, they felt like strangers, and Clint had not contacted Lisa at all.

She anticipated this night with great joy.

"That looks great, Lisa," Clint breathed. "I'm starved."

"Well, before you give her all the credit, I did sauté the shrimp," Amy pouted.

"Enough, already. Let's just eat!" Lisa poured ice water for everyone while Amy sliced the French bread.

"Can I help at all?" Clint asked. "I feel pretty useless."

"We can't have that!" Amy cried and pointed to the kitchen. "Please lay out silverware. We won't be able to get by without it, and we'll be forever in your debt." She drawled the last line, doing her best impression of a Southern belle.

"Fear not, Fair Maiden!" He dashed into the kitchen and returned with the flatware.

After several more minutes of mirth and antics, the threesome sat down to their meal.

"Clint, would you bless it?" Lisa asked.

"Definitely. Lord God, I thank You for this food and for the hands that prepared it. I thank You for the call You have placed upon each life here and for our friendship. I would ask You to bless us and enable us to further Your kingdom in ways that are bigger than we can imagine. In Jesus' name, amen."

They wordlessly devoured the salad. It wasn't until just before dessert that anyone spoke a full sentence.

"So, you two. . .what's going on?" Lisa asked congenially. Amy and Clint had specifically asked to speak with her.

"Well, Clint and I want your blessing," Amy supplied

timidly. "We've spent a lot of time together, and we'd like to see one another exclusively."

"We wanted to know that you were okay with it first," Clint added. "We won't do it if it upsets you."

Lisa threw back her head with laughter. "No! I'm not upset! I think this is great. I'm so happy for you both. This is awesome. . .my two best friends. How perfect." She sipped her water, then reached out to take their hands. "Clint, we've discussed this before—we've always been friends, but we were never much of a couple. And, Amy, you are such a wonderful woman, and I know you'll be a wonderful blessing to Clint."

Amy and Clint exchanged looks of elation and relief. Lisa truly was happy for them, but she couldn't deny the dull ache in her own heart. It had nothing to do with either of the people at her table. She longed for the love of her life—she desired John. While she could deal with his silence and the lack of contact for over two weeks, she hated it. She prayed that God would take away the pain if he was not the one, but the hurt refused to dissipate.

Still, she couldn't allow her emotions to rob Amy and Clint of their happiness. They spent the rest of the evening in animated conversation and much laughter. Lisa enjoyed the familiar feelings of the good old days.

"Oh, no! When did it get so late?" Clint yawned. "I've got to get out of here, ladies. But thank you for a wonderful evening."

"Thanks for coming, Clint! You really saved the day with that whole flatware rescue," Lisa teased.

"Aww—" Clint prepared a retort as the doorbell rang.

"Who could that be?" Amy asked incredulously. "It's almost midnight."

Lisa motioned for them to stay relaxed. "I'll get it."

"Hello. . ." Her voice trailed off. "John."

The muscular frame filled the doorway. He said nothing, but his quirky grin let her know this visit was pleasure, not business.

"Please, come in." Lisa led him into the living room, just as Amy and Clint walked hand in hand to the door. "I really am happy for you two," she said as they passed.

The surprise on John's face was evident, but he said nothing.

"I'm going to sit on the steps with Clint for a bit," Amy called over her shoulder. "I'll be back in awhile."

"Hmm. . ." Lisa's mind was elsewhere as the couple closed the door behind themselves. She could only stand, helplessly confused and utterly delighted.

John hesitated only a moment before drawing her into his arms. She melted against his chest and breathed in his masculine scent. "I'm here because you were right. God brought you to me for an important reason. I was bound up in my fears. I wasn't heeding God's full call for my life, yet I condemned and stretched you. Can you forgive me?"

"Oh, John," she whispered. "You opened my eyes to see my bondage. I am forever grateful for your boldness and your honesty."

He hugged her close. "God has given me a vision for educating stateside Christians about the Christians in China—about their plight, their struggles, and their passion. I am burdened with the desire that this should be a ministry for everyone, not just the few who actually want to experience the culture and the land firsthand. I was so prideful and consumed with my own rigid demands for what I believed constituted 'ministry,' but when I released the burden and yoke of my fear to the Lord, I was amazed to find that this idea had been there all along, in the back of my mind. I just never had the time to develop it because I was so focused on maintaining my walls."

Lisa closed her eyes. She still harbored the fear she had no place in his life. "John. . .what about me? About us? I'm not sure how I fit into this."

John released her and tilted her chin up so that her eyes met his. "Lisa Perdue, I love you. I want you to be a part of my life for as long as God grants me breath. I know we don't know each other as well as we could, and I want you to give me a chance to prove my love to you. I can, you know." He smiled playfully and kissed the tip of her nose.

"Oh, I have no doubts about that, Mr. Li. See, the thing is, I've already fallen in love with you, so once again," she drew out sarcastically, "I'm waiting for you to catch up." She stretched up to lightly kiss his full lips. "But you are right. We need some time to grow in our relationship without the pressures of an alien culture vying for my attention."

"I promise to be open to our love—unique and ordained by God—and to His direction in our lives, Lisa. I want our hearts to be bound, not by sin and fear, but by love and faithfulness to each other and to God." John claimed her mouth in a slow, tender kiss. Lisa felt surges of passion course through her.

"That, my dear Mr. Li, is a binding I think I can stand."

JENNIFER PETERSON

Jennifer lives in Montana. She has always loved to write, and she desires to be Spirit-led and Christ-filled in all areas of her life. She hopes that the influence of our Father is evident in her work and longs to be salt and light in a dark and decaying world. She relies daily on the promises of Isaiah 41:10. She has two novels to her credit.

A Letter to Our Readers

Dear Readers:

In order that we might better contribute to your reading enjoyment, we would appreciate you taking a few minutes to respond to the following questions. When completed, please return to the following: Fiction Editor, Barbour Publishing, Inc., P.O. Box 719, Uhrichsville, OH 44683.

1. Did you enjoy reading *China Tapestry?*
   - ❑ Very much. I would like to see more books like this.
   - ❑ Moderately. I would have enjoyed it more if _____
   _____
   _____

2. What influenced your decision to purchase this book?
   (Check those that apply.)
   - ❑ Cover   ❑ Back cover copy   ❑ Title   ❑ Price
   - ❑ Friends   ❑ Publicity   ❑ Other

3. Which story was your favorite?
   - ❑ *A Length of Silk*   ❑ *The Crimson Brocade*
   - ❑ *The Golden Cord*   ❑ *Bindings of the Heart*

4. Please check your age range:
   - ❑ Under 18   ❑ 18–24   ❑ 25–34
   - ❑ 35–45   ❑ 46–55   ❑ Over 55

5. How many hours per week do you read? _____

Name _____

Occupation _____

Address _____

City _____ State _____ Zip _____

_H_EARTSONG ♥ PRESENTS

Love Stories
Are Rated G!

That's for godly, gratifying, and of course, great! If you love a thrilling love story but don't appreciate the sordidness of some popular paperback romances, **Heartsong Presents** is for you. In fact, **Heartsong Presents** is the only inspirational romance book club featuring love stories where Christian faith is the primary ingredient in a marriage relationship.

Sign up today to receive your first set of four, never-before-published Christian romances. Send no money now; you will receive a bill with the first shipment. You may cancel at any time without obligation, and if you aren't completely satisfied with any selection, you may return the books for an immediate refund!

Imagine. . .four new romances every four weeks—two historical, two contemporary—with men and women like you who long to meet the one God has chosen as the love of their lives. . .all for the low price of $9.97 postpaid.

To join, simply complete the coupon below and mail to the address provided. **Heartsong Presents** romances are rated G for another reason: They'll arrive Godspeed!

YES! Sign me up for Hearts♥ng!

NEW MEMBERSHIPS WILL BE SHIPPED IMMEDIATELY!
Send no money now. We'll bill you only $9.97 postpaid with your first shipment of four books. Or for faster action, call toll free 1-800-847-8270.

NAME _____

ADDRESS _____

CITY _____ STATE _____ ZIP _____

MAIL TO: HEARTSONG PRESENTS, P.O. Box 719, Uhrichsville, Ohio 44683